Dead

on the

Vine

Dead

on the

Vine

A FINN FAMILY FARM
MYSTERY

Elle Brooke White

CROOKED
LANE

NEW YORK

Published in the United States by Crooked Lane Books, an imprint of The Quick Brown Fox & Company LLC.

Crooked Lane Books and its logo are trademarks of The Quick Brown Fox & Company LLC.

Library of Congress Catalog-in-Publication data available upon request.

ISBN (hardcover): 978-1-64385-296-6
ISBN (ebook): 978-1-64385-317-8

Cover design by Hiro Kimura

Printed in the United States.

www.crookedlanebooks.com

Crooked Lane Books
34 West 27th St., 10th Floor
New York, NY 10001

First Edition: April 2020

10 9 8 7 6 5 4 3 2 1

To the beauty all around us.

Chapter One

Charlotte was flying off to a life that couldn't be farther from her fast-track advertising career in Chicago. Like a modern-day character from *Green Acres,* she was going from penthouse to produce farm. The skills that had ignited her meteoric rise with two unforgettable ad campaigns would be of no use to her there. She'd learned the hard way how fickle fate is when her peers had dismissed her after one bad ad. Yes, she could still sell a bowl of hot chili to beachgoers in a heat wave, but that was not going to help her run a small menagerie of livestock and fields of strawberries and tomatoes, clear over on the West Coast of the country.

Charlotte landed in Los Angeles and relaxed a bit as she moved through the hustle and bustle of a major airport. She could still feel the energy of a big city, but this was not her final destination. The gentleman who had sold her a car over the internet met her outside the baggage claim area. That in itself was a cosmic departure from Charlotte's signature mode—carefully considered decisions.

He led her outside the terminal and handed her the car keys. There, parked at the curb, was her classic Buick Estate Wagon.

Charlotte had been advised that if she was going to purchase a vintage automobile—this one from 1996—to do it in a region that has warm weather year-round to limit the amount of rust. She always wrestled with new and modern versus classic and timeworn, more often tipping the scales to the latter. Charlotte was both surprised and heartened that it looked as though this vehicle was going to meet her expectations. The exterior was painted bright white and had wood grain paneling along the sides. It also had the rare three rows of seating, with the back tapering off to the hatchback rear door. A light beige leather interior and vista roof completed the package. This would be perfect for trips to the garden supply store, for hauling pallets of berries to the farmers market, and for accommodating visiting and new friends on local road trips—in other words, for farm life.

* * *

As she exited the airport and found the freeway that would take her north, the Buick Roadmaster purred to life, making the drive on open road both pleasing and exhilarating. She rolled down the windows and breathed in the fresh air, to taste the freedom. She tested the radio and found an oldies station that just happened to be playing the Beach Boys. Perfect segue into her new life. She left the dial on this station and let the nostalgic, simple songs of love and fun and innocence permeate her soul.

The catalyst for this move had come when Charlotte learned that she had been named as the sole beneficiary of her great-uncle Tobias Finn's farm in Little Acorn, California. In many ways this was the answer to her prayers. She had a reason to leave her shame behind in Chicago, pay off her debts, and start over. Memories were starting to creep back into her mind from the one magical summer she'd spent on the farm as a kid. Getting back to nature seemed like a fitting fork in the road to take. The inheritance included a fifty-acre produce farm that both confounded and excited her. *I've been to a farmers market, so how hard can this be?*

As an added bonus, Charlotte's best childhood friends, the sister and brother team of Diane and Beau Mason, lived just a two-hour drive from the farm in Santa Monica. The plan was to meet up in the quaint town that Charlotte would soon call home and then head up to the farm together for a weekend reunion.

Charlotte let the sights of the scenic drive inform her arrival. Unlike the overbearing summer heat in Chicago, the sun was shining but the air was cool and comfortable. She hadn't been on a trip like this to the country since her parents had taken her, Diane, and Beau to a small cabin by the lake outside Chicago for her fifth birthday. She remembered how much she'd loved spending her days outside with nature and falling asleep to the sound of crickets. She'd drifted so far away from all that when she moved to the city and got an office job . . . *This is going to be a great return to the outdoors!*

She smiled as she let her thoughts travel back to the time when she'd happened on a doe and her fawn in the woods and to the nights of capturing lightning bugs in a jar. Coincidently, she spotted a ladybug sitting outside on the driver's side windshield. She'd seen her when she first got into the car but couldn't imagine that the bug was still hanging on after forty minutes at sixty miles per hour.

You're a tough little lady.

Charlotte put on her turn signal, slowed, and veered off to the side of the road. She shut the engine and leaned her head out the driver's side window.

"If you want to safely get off the windshield and go exploring, this is your chance, my polka-dotted friend."

The bug didn't budge.

"No? Here. Climb onto my hand, and I'll make it easier for you."

Charlotte extended her fingers and pressed them on the glass directly next to the ladybug. From inside the car, she watched the bug lift her antennaed head in the direction of her fingers as if she was considering the offer. Suddenly, she hopped onto her thumb, and Charlotte slowly brought her arm back into the car. She noticed that there was one yellow spot among the black spots on the bug's red body.

"So, do I take it from your actions that you wish to continue on to my great-uncle's farm with me? Why don't you sit up here where it's sunny and warm?"

Charlotte rested her hand on the dash behind the steering wheel, and the ladybug walked off and took up residence a little to the left and in full view of Charlotte, who started the car up again and merged back onto the highway. She'd left her window open and undid her ponytail so that her long, curly red hair could fly free.

"I've always heard that ladybugs bring good luck, so I am very grateful to make your acquaintance."

Further north she noticed that the towns became very agricultural. Charlotte passed flat acres of strawberries, followed by fields of broccoli, and then what looked to her like avocado trees.

A knot formed in her stomach as she worried about how unsuited she was for this kind of work.

Uncle Tobias was never a quitter.

She summoned up the determination not to let him down.

It was the top of the hour, and the oldies station took a break for the local news and weather. Charlotte listened intently as she realized that both were about to become an integral part of running a farm.

The Santa Barbara agricultural commissions office released their annual crop report today, and as was the case last year and the year prior, strawberries led the top ten commodities, followed by broccoli and wine grapes.

Good! She'd be growing the number-one crop.

About twenty minutes later, she took her exit onto a narrower road that wove up and through the Santa Ynez Valley. She turned off, as her phone's navigation instructed, and saw a quaint sign mounted on upright logs that read:

"Welcome to Little Acorn, Home of the White Strawberry"

Across and up ahead on the cobblestone main street, she spotted her friends and got a warm, comfortable feeling inside. She parked in the first spot she saw, excited to reconnect. Still sitting in the car, she took a moment to get acclimated to her surroundings. This was no sleepy hitching post. Little Acorn was abuzz with activity from its local people, who carried on their business with an air that was downright jovial. Charlotte let out a sigh of relief. This was the America of old movies, where people took pride in what they do and in themselves. She was far away from the second-guessing and paranoia of her life in Chicago. People weren't trying to fit in or be somebody that they weren't. They were answering to a higher power: nature.

Charlotte watched a farmer selling baskets of strawberries from an old wooden pushcart with large wagon wheels. He couldn't have been more than sixteen, and this was probably a little crop he tended on his parents' farm to sell for spending money. He already had the muscles of the man he would become, but his curly chestnut hair, poking out in all directions from under his backward cap, was all boy. He'd sold about half of the cartful, and true to Little Acorn's advertising, he had a handful of baskets filled with white strawberries.

Fascinating.

Charlotte heard laughter and saw that her friends had disembarked from their car and were giggling with excitement.

"You wait here, ladybug—we haven't yet reached our final destination. I have a feeling that we are both going to love it!"

Charlotte struggled a bit on the cobblestone walk, in her heels, and realized that she needed to let go of the last vestige of her city ways—her wardrobe.

"You're here!" Charlotte clapped as she approached her friends.

"What a cute town!" Diane remarked and opened her arms wide to Charlotte. "God, I've missed you. And you've gotten even prettier. I hate you."

They both laughed and hugged again.

"You are so tan—it must be all that beach time and endless summer." Charlotte had stepped back to get a better look at her friend. In truth, Diane looked thin and tired. The dark circles dimmed her trademark eyes—large and expressive. They'd made a point of speaking or texting at least every other day, but Diane clearly had been dealing with some issues that she had chosen not to share.

Charlotte had followed the reviews of the immensely popular restaurant where Diane worked as a sous chef, and hoped that she could coerce her friend into making a delicious meal for them. When they were teenagers, Diane had always used Charlotte as a guinea pig to taste her epicurean creations. Once she'd had Charlotte dress like a princess from the island of Monaco, and served her a five-course meal. The grand finale was a delectable Charlotte Russe made with ladyfingers, Bavarian cream, and fruit. Charlotte spoke with a French accent during the entire meal, and Beau joined the meal partway through, dressed as the king.

Mostly Charlotte longed to curl up on a sofa with Diane, chat, and resume being best friends.

"I've never seen an open air market like this in Los Angeles," Diane cooed. "Are those watermelon radishes? I'm going to need to get a big bunch because I've got the perfect snack in mind. You clean the radishes but leave the stems intact, then melt some yummy sweet butter, dip the bottoms in, and set them aside for the butter to harden. Then I'll serve them with some fine sea salt, and I promise you'll think that you've died and gone to heaven!"

"Yum-mee!" Charlotte noticed that Diane's face was already glowing from her brighter mood.

Dear Diane, it's time for some of my special brand of Charlotte nurturing.

Beau had been observing their reunion. "Are you two going to leave me out in the cold?" he asked, moving in for a sandwich hug.

"Come give me a kiss, my Beau-bro. You are definitely my brother in spirit." Charlotte pulled Beau close.

As an event planner, Beau was a master of transformation, as evidenced by his launch party for a new chain of plant-based burger stands. At the flagship location, Beau had turned the parking lot into a rodeo where riders on horseback chased people dressed as vegetables. Spectators sat in the stands, where they were given free burger samples. He liked to describe himself as an "extravaganza maker" and even had that title on his business cards.

Charlotte thought back to the antics they used to pull in the Chicago suburb where they had been raised, and giggled. Beau would create all sorts of fantasy worlds when the three of them were growing up, in part to fill the alone time because mama and papa Mason both worked. Now thirty, Beau never had shed his Peter Pan persona. He'd always approached life as a smorgasbord of delicious options, often taking the road less traveled. You might never make the same choices as Beau, but you couldn't help but share his delight in finding them.

"Are you wearing heels?" he asked, noticing their height difference. "If the cobblestones don't get them first, you're going to need me to help you move all this city attire to the back of your closet. You're a country girl now. Look around you; it's denim, red and white checks, and sundresses, my dear."

"This really is another world," Diane remarked, interrupting their banter.

A relaxed environment. Everyone seems so friendly and welcoming.

She'd forgotten the warm custom of greeting and smiling at strangers. She promised herself that she would smile at everyone.

A man in work clothes approached.

My first chance.

As the farmer walked past, he flicked his cigarette, eyed Charlotte and her friends, and spat. If Beau hadn't jumped back quickly, the spittle would have landed directly on his shoes.

"Oh dear." Diane stood, her mouth agape.

Charlotte was stunned at first but then reminded herself that farming was all about nature and natural things. Perhaps this was nothing. She studied the man as he joined another farmer outside the general store, and they both stared back at her. It looked like they were talking about her and her friends. The one who had spat looked to be in his early thirties. He had stringy blond hair that hung limp from his green bucket hat—as though it hadn't seen a comb in months. He had a beard to match that also was left to grow willy-nilly.

He's not unpleasant looking, but he looks like he hasn't been happy in a very long time.

Seeing this, Charlotte started to feel sorry for him, and she reminded herself that you never really know what someone else is dealing with in life, so it's best to be kind. The man next to him was a bit younger and, by his looks, could be his brother. He was clean-shaven and carried some extra weight. His manner was subservient compared to the other farmer's. The younger farmer hunched over to make himself look smaller, and he listened to the angry man talk, but never made eye contact. The expression on his face was born of either apathy or total passivity. In either case, she wasn't going to let one or two possible bad apples ruin an otherwise quaint, perfect place.

"Okay guys, feel free to wander about and check out the local shops, but don't get yourselves arrested," Charlotte joked, trying to lighten the mood. "I'm meeting the lawyer at the title office, and then I'm off to my late uncle's bank."

"Ta-ta—we'll procure some biscuits, cider, and cheese for the afternoon." Diane giggled.

"Let's go exploring," Charlotte heard Beau say as he and Diane linked arms and trotted off in the opposite direction.

Charlotte walked along the old brick sidewalk and admired the country shops. She hesitated in front of a bakery and coffee shop from which emanated the most enticing aromas, but instead of going in, made a promise to herself to pick up a basket of goodies on her way out of town.

She reached the title office and admired its antique, tin-tiled white façade and hunter-green shingles.

I feel like I've been transported back to the 1940s.

A tinkling bell rang as she opened the door. She found the waiting area, took a seat, and dialed the estate attorney's number.

The lawyer was running late, he told her over the phone— something about a herd of cows crossing the highway. Charlotte wasn't sure that she was ready for this rural lifestyle, but she had a prime seat in the waiting area of the title office that overlooked the entire main street through town. This gave her another chance to assess her new surroundings and the people that lived here.

So this is what Main Street, USA, looks like. How simply wonderful.

* * *

Charlotte, reeling from her meeting with the lawyer, decided to return to her car rather than continuing to explore the town of Little Acorn. She just wanted to get up to the farm. When she plopped down behind the wheel, she saw that the ladybug was just where she'd left her. Her spirits lifted, Charlotte rolled down the window and closed her eyes for a moment. This had been quite a day so far.

"Well, that was a little awkward," she heard Beau say from outside the car.

It's about to get more than awkward. Wait until they hear my news.

"Just ignore those two. They're clearly the exception rather than the rule, and as I've told you a million times, not everyone can appreciate the wonder that is Beau."

That was Diane—always diffusing a bad situation.

"Success?" Beau asked Diane.

"Are you kidding? Every second store offers delectable, home-made, savory and sweet foods. I don't even want to tell you how much sweet butter I have in my bag. While you were perusing the five-cent candy jars at that quaint general store, I popped into a shop and got a good variety of baked goods and infused honey. Since we don't know what we are about to face with the farm, I figured that we couldn't go wrong with the cornucopia of fresh items I'm carrying. And wait until you see the size of the artichokes! I see an aioli in our future while we sit back and admire the back forty."

"And how about you, dear Charlotte—are you now in possession of your fabulous farm?" Beau asked.

Charlotte slowly shook her head, and Diane leaned into the window, appearing to study Charlotte's face.

"The bank account that is now in my name contains a revolving amount consisting of direct deposits made by the produce distributor and then debits for payroll and bills. Each time this cycle happens, my account goes down to almost zero. In other words, my inheritance is a money pit."

"Oh no! But there must be a way to make the farm work—give me a minute to think," Beau said, peering into the car next to Diane.

"Perhaps you should think seriously about selling the farm as soon as possible?" Diane said. "You can move in with me in L.A. and take some time to plan your next move. Hey, we could go into business together!"

"Doing what? I make a mean soft-boiled egg, but that is where my culinary skills end." Charlotte dropped her chin down to her chest in a despondent sulk. That was when she noticed that the ladybug had cocked her head and was looking directly at her from the dashboard.

"The farm, thankfully, is paid in full, and I've begun the title transfer process. And great BFFs think alike. In fact, I've arranged for a realtor to drop by for an assessment in the morning. We've got no time to waste," she said, starting the car. "That farm has got to be in tip-top shape for a sale. You've got the address; I'll meet you up there."

Chapter Two

The drive wound through beautiful countryside, and twice Charlotte pulled to the side of the road to take in the view. The mountains dictated how the crops should be planted, their sides giving the impression of an undulating flow of lush green and brown tones. The fields were alive and gliding across the hills. At one side she spotted a grove of coral trees, each with a thick trunk that supported a virtual ecosystem of extraordinary networks of flowers with bright orange petals. Mountain lilac shrubs grew wild around a vineyard, and yellow ginkgo trees dotted the horizon. She surprised herself with how much she remembered from her one trip to the farm as a kid. Her great-uncle had made all parts of nature seem magical, and his tutelage must have stuck.

Simon and Garfunkel came on the radio, softly singing one of Charlotte's favorites.

"It takes your breath away, doesn't it?" Charlotte said to the ladybug studying her expressive face. "You need a name . . . Mrs. Robinson seems just about right for a beautiful girl like yourself," Charlotte added, and then wondered if she had in fact lost her mind.

She had never said much more than "shoo" and "go away" to an insect before in her life. Yet the red and black polka-dotted bug with one yellow spot seemed to have understood exactly what she'd said, and Charlotte imagined that she was smiling—although she'd need a magnifying glass to see it.

As Charlotte continued the drive, she wrestled with encroaching guilt for entertaining the thought about unloading her great-uncle's beloved farm to the highest bidder. She knew that people in California talked about karma and mojo, and while she never thought of herself as being the least bit superstitious, she still was not comfortable tempting fate.

But what can I do?

Finally, Charlotte turned off the road and arrived at a plateau carved into the hills. She parked under a big shade tree, stepped out of the car, and was lured by the old stone wall that surrounded the property. It seemed so safe up here. In the background were verdant, rolling hills in all directions. Their protective arms made everything inside them feel serene and private.

Uncle Tobias, you sure made a beautiful farm.

The property extended in steppes down the sides of the plateau, on two levels. At the second tier were the fields brimming with awakening fruits and vegetables. At the very back stood an orchard of apple and pine trees. Also on that level, Charlotte noted an animal stable, a barn, and an outside paddock. Tractors and other farm equipment sat idle, some seeming to be in mid-repair. The next level down held a modest house with front and backyards and a side vegetable garden. There was also a series of glass hothouses that ran alongside the garden.

The main house had the feel of an old rancho hacienda, but with two stories. In fact, given the shape it was in, it probably was the original house. It sprawled in a "T" shape across the property, surrounded by a painted brick exterior veranda supported by wooden posts. Rustic-looking swings were suspended from the roof's beams, and rockers provided relief from the sun while still affording the opportunity to be outdoors. French doors every five feet or so gave many options for entering the house. Charlotte wondered if the interior was in the same shape. The roof was made of clay tiles, more than a few of which were broken or missing. Several ducks and their fluffy offspring roamed freely around, pecking at seeds and grains and the occasional snail. To the very far side, Charlotte spotted a swimming lake that was almost drained and a broken-down boat dock.

I wonder how big a deal it would be to at least fill it? Everyone loves looking at water, and that could help push a quick sale . . . I bet the ducks would become my best friends.

Charlotte could hear voices and followed the sound. She'd called ahead to let the caretaker know when she would be arriving, and he'd promised to be there to greet her. At the side of the farmhouse, she spotted a woman unloading groceries and supplies from a flatbed truck.

"Here, let me help you with that," a man said, grabbing a box of groceries. "They should be here any minute, and we want the place to look as good as it can."

Charlotte saw Diane and Beau pull in, and waved to them. While Beau began unloading the car, Diane got out and did a twirl and then skipped her way toward Charlotte.

"I wish we'd had more notice," Charlotte heard the woman reply. "Oh, I saw Wade Avery and his hooligan brother when I was in town. He made a snide comment about seeing the new owner and how she won't last five minutes here. He said that he'll be running the place in no time."

"When pigs fly, Alice. I know that he can be intimidating, but just ignore him."

"Wow, this farm," Diane whispered as she arrived beside Charlotte. "Just 'wow.'"

There goes Diane, falling in love. She does it so easily.

Beau joined the girls. "It's a good thing we're not going to need to learn how to operate all those things," he said, eyeing the farm equipment.

"We probably won't . . . if we sell the farm," Charlotte pointed out.

Although it would be a fun challenge.

"Oh, come on, I think it would be great fun!" Diane swung a fist into the air and grinned.

She looks like she could finish plowing the back forty by dinner. Diane either loves things or hates them.

All of a sudden, they saw a skein of geese burst out from the orchard. Something had spooked them. She could see rustling in the far end of the field and wondered if they had any problems with coyotes or, worse, poachers.

"One of you must be Charlotte," said the man she'd seen helping with the groceries. He looked from Diane to Charlotte for confirmation.

"Guilty as charged," Charlotte replied, and introduced Diane and Beau. "And you are Mr. Joe Wong, correct?"

He nodded. Joe looked to be in his early forties, not particularly tall, but muscular like the boy selling strawberries that she'd seen in town. When he smiled, he dipped his head a tad and made direct eye contact with the person or persons he was interacting with at the moment. The gesture exuded a warmth and a kind of immediate intimacy.

"Pleased to meet you Charlotte, Diane, Beau. I am the caretaker here, and my wife— Alice, here—keeps us clean, fed, and happy."

Alice gave Charlotte a warm smile, but Charlotte detected a look of apprehension behind those eyes. Unlike her husband's, Alice's eyes were never still, but darted from person to place, trying to take in everything at once.

"So nice to meet you, Alice." Charlotte gently shook her hand.

"We've been living on the farm for over eight years, working for your great-uncle. Our home is just down there on the bottom level of land," Joe continued.

"We're very happy here. Your uncle was such a kind man," Alice spoke up. "I know that the place needs some work, and I'm happy to help in any way I can."

"We're going to need it—thank you, Alice. My friends will be staying the weekend to help me get settled in, and then I'll be here until—well, I'll be here to take care of things."

Alice's face had gone from a smile to a tight mouth in under ten seconds.

"I've just returned from the market. The fridge is stocked, and I can make anything you want for dinner." Alice tried to regain her congeniality. "Um, you have a bug on your shoulder Miss Charlotte." She reached in to brush it off.

"Don't," Charlotte yelled before she could stop herself. Alice recoiled.

"Alice, I'm so sorry. It's just that . . ." Charlotte realized that anything she could offer them as an explanation for her outburst would just certify her as being, well, a little crazy. She'd introduce them to Mrs. Robinson in due time.

"How about we go inside and take a gander, shall we?" Beau broke the tension.

"Of course. Let me give you a tour of your farmhouse." Joe stepped up. "I know it could use a thorough once-over, but in its heyday it was a thing of beauty and very homey. Your great-uncle Tobias would entertain the entire valley when the crops were good to us."

"Like a barnyard bacchanalia—I love that! Let's throw one, Charlotte," Beau urged her.

Joe seems kind and thoughtful, something Uncle Tobias must have appreciated.

As Charlotte entered the great room, she admired the majestic river rock fireplace, also missing some rocks but stunning all the same. Wood beams on the ceiling and Mexican pavers on the floor gave the place a rustic but cozy feel. The open floor plan afforded a view into the kitchen with its "L"-shaped, tiled countertops and dark wood cabinets. The comingling of Spanish accents and natural, "found" building materials made her appreciate the skills and care that had been put into creating the house.

Don't go getting attached, Charlotte. This place is going up for sale.

"This has a lot of potential," Diane whispered to Charlotte. "I'm starting to feel optimistic about a quick sale," she added a little too loudly.

"If you don't need me right now, I'll go to the cellar. I'm stocking up on jars of jams and fruit, and I was in the middle of labeling them before I went to town." Alice didn't wait for a response and disappeared toward the back of the entryway.

Charlotte almost went after her to once again apologize. Her emotions were getting the best of her. This had already been a long day, and she'd had her future life waft in the breeze and shape-shift at least a handful of times so far. She looked around the foyer, and a wave of memories washed over her. She'd spent one summer here when she was nine, and thinking back, she was sure that it had been the imprint year that had sparked her creativity. She'd been free to let her imagination run wild, and boy, did she. Charlotte admired the long, wooden banister that led to the second floor, and remembered sliding down it on her belly while letting out laughs that echoed throughout the cavern-ous space. She remembered Tobias applauding her athleticism; a pair of hounds or sometimes a goose or a barn cat always flanked him. As long as they behaved themselves, he had no problem let-ting certain livestock roam freely in the house. He commanded respect from his animals.

Suddenly, she saw the French doors at the back of the house push open, and in came a squealing, soft, pink baby pig. Char-lotte watched the pig pick up speed and skid across the Mexican pavers, legs akimbo, until he slammed into her, causing her to join him on the floor.

"Oh my," Charlotte said, trying to both stop the pig from lick-ing her so she could assess any physical damage from the charge.

"That damn pig," boomed a voice belonging to a tall, dark-haired, lanky man in jeans and a white T-shirt. His work boots clomped across the floor as he moved swiftly and swooped up the animal by the back of the neck. He swept back a rather long and thick tress of straight hair that fell into place and shined like polished obsidian. She was then able to notice his high forehead; aquiline nose; and warm, almond-shaped green eyes.

"Apologies for his bad manners—he's too smart for his own good. You must be the new owner," the man said, staring down at her. The pig was still trying to escape his grasp by walking in mid-air.

"This is our amazing farm expert, Samuel Brown," Joe said, introducing him. "And you are correct: this lovely lady is our new proprietress, Charlotte Finn."

Samuel nodded to her and exited with the pig the same way he had entered, leaving Charlotte on the floor where she lay.

"It appears that more than one member of the denizens here are in need of etiquette lessons. Let me help you up." Beau quickly came to the rescue.

"He's a man of few words, but your uncle Tobias never stopped appreciating his fine work," Joe explained.

Just outside the French doors, Charlotte caught a last glimpse of Farmer Brown and watched him walk away with a slight limp.

Way to make a first impression, Farmer Brown . . .

They moved to the counter around the kitchen, and Charlotte laid out her plans to Joe over coffee. Diane and Beau went upstairs to claim their bedrooms.

"I want to be straightforward with you from the beginning, Joe. I am honored that my great-uncle remembered me in his will, and it so happens that I was in the midst of changing careers anyway when I was notified. I am ready to give this the old college try, but this is all very new to me. If I can't make a go of this, then I will consider selling the farm to someone who can."

"It is in your blood, Miss Charlotte. I can tell by the way you are with the animals and by the look in your eyes when you admire the nature around you."

"You may be right, Joe, but I have so very much to learn. I know that you will help me."

"As will Samuel," Joe quickly added.

"We'll see about that. He wasn't exactly welcoming me with a brass band just now."

"That's just his way, as I explained."

"So you did. There is one other request I have for you, Joe."

"Sure."

"I need you to be entirely honest with me about the state of the farm, the challenges facing or standing in the way of success. Ways to improve our profitability. Any lingering issues with other farmers? I couldn't help overhearing the conversation you had with Alice earlier. Who is this Wade man, and why would he say that he will be running my farm?"

"As I told my wife, you have nothing to fear from those Avery brothers. They're all bark and no bite."

Two months ago I would have taken a guy like Joe at his word, but not after Chicago. That bite is going to leave a mark for a long time.

"I would prefer that we address everything at once. You'll probably want a day or so to pull together your thoughts on the state of the farm, and when you're ready, let's sit down and go through it. Feel free to include Farmer Brown if you think that it would be beneficial."

"I can be ready tomorrow." Charlotte could see that Joe was anxious to complete this task and get on with business as usual. She hoped that he wouldn't sugarcoat his report.

"Take as much time as you need. I have arranged for a realtor to come by in the morning for an assessment of the property's value, if for no other reason than to throw that into the mix of our overall evaluation of the farm."

Just as Charlotte finished, she noticed that the pig had snuck back into the house and was hiding unsuccessfully behind a small ottoman that was not wide enough to conceal his wildly wagging tail. When he popped his head out for a peek and caught her eye, he tried to quickly squeeze himself back out of sight. Charlotte tried to stifle a laugh because she didn't want the little guy to get another scolding from Farmer Brown. When she turned her attention back to Joe, she caught him deep in thought.

"Joe, while my great-uncle lived to a ripe old age, I understand that all this is still a shock to you and Alice and to the life you have enjoyed on the Finn Family Farm for almost a decade."

"As the *I Ching* tells us, change is certain. But it also reminds us that if we are sincere, we will succeed."

What a lovely man.

"If—and this is a big *if*—I determine that it is best to sell the farm to a more qualified and equitable buyer, Joe, I want you to know that I intend to impress on the buyer to keep all the current staff in place or give them at least six-months' notice. And I want to make sure that you are involved with the sales process so that they see how much of an asset you can be."

Joe responded with an appreciative smile. "Thank you."

Charlotte noticed that, beneath the counter, Joe's knee was going up and down like a jackhammer on the stool. She hadn't been quite convincing enough.

Alice returned to the kitchen and busied herself rolling out dough that had been kept cold for a pie. For a brief moment, she and Joe exchanged a look. Charlotte wondered if he was able to telegraph their future to her in those few seconds.

Charlotte's stomach sunk like a rock. She'd always been mama-bear protective of her staff at the ad agency and worked overtime to ensure that bad things didn't happen to good people. And yet that's exactly what she'd put her staff through in Chicago.

That can never happen again. I will not let these kind people down.

"Since it's clear that I am going to have to spend a few weeks getting the farm really ready for . . . for getting back on its feet, I guess I'll get settled into my great-uncle's bedroom."

Charlotte was doing exactly what she'd asked Joe not to do. She was hiding the truth from Alice.

Why am I doing this? You cannot build trust with lies.

Charlotte hoped that Uncle Tobias, an avid reader, had a copy of *I Ching* in his library. She desperately needed to use the *Book of Changes'* thousands of years of wisdom to help with her future.

"The bed is all freshly made, and the towels came out of the dryer a couple of hours ago. Please let me know if you need anything else."

"Thank you, Alice—that's so kind of you."

Diane padded into the kitchen, surveying all the beautiful produce to play with, and volunteered to create a perfect light meal for everyone. With Alice's permission, she quickly added. The two agreed to work side by side.

Charlotte took her bag and wandered out of the kitchen and across the foyer to her great-uncle's living quarters.

It had a smaller version of the river rock fireplace in the living room, a panoramic view of the hillside, a cozy sitting area, and an antique ceiling fan. It was almost unchanged from how she remembered it. On one wall still hung a wrought iron rack that held horse tackle and a couple of cowboy hats. She reached for the one that looked the most worn and brought it to her nose. She was not sure what she was expecting. She'd only spent a few weeks with her great-uncle, and that had been over twenty years ago. She certainly wouldn't know his signature smell.

Still, there is something familiar about the hat's musky scent.

"Besides the obvious painting and polishing of the wood beams and window frames, this layout makes the space seem smaller than it is," Charlotte said, thinking out loud. She mimed drawing in the palm of her hand and then spotted a legal pad on her great-uncle's desk in one corner of the room. She snatched it up along with a pencil and walked to the center of the space. It took only moments for Charlotte to lay out a new schematic, noting the pieces of furniture that should be sold or donated. When her eyes rested on a long cedar chest at the foot of the sleigh bed, Charlotte moved toward it, both excited by and a little frightened of seeing what was inside it.

The lid needed a little extra encouragement. It had probably sat shut for a number of years. Charlotte got down on her knees and applied the full force of her upper body. With the second try, it finally popped open and then locked in place with the extension of the side hinges. She'd expected it to be full of old bed linens wrapped in tissue paper and perhaps some blankets. There was some of that, but most of the space was taken up by a smaller wooden box. It was older looking, with a keyhole that was held firmly shut by an iron lock.

Someone wanted what's inside kept private.

The discovery put Charlotte a little on edge. She'd had enough surprises for one day: she put the box back and closed the chest.

The sun had almost set, so Charlotte walked around the room, turning on floor lamps. When one lit up the French doors to the outside, she spotted the pig.

This guy sure does get around.

He didn't seem to be watching her, although his head was cocked to one side, and he almost looked like he was communicating with something on the glass just above his head. Charlotte bent down for a closer look and had to blink twice to make sure that she wasn't imagining what she was seeing. There, on the inside of the glass, perched Mrs. Robinson, the ladybug, and she seemed to be looking back at the pig.

Charlotte could hear Diane and Alice chatting away in the kitchen. She caught snippets of the conversation, mostly about the beautiful produce, which Diane couldn't stop raving about.

Diane seems to be falling in love with the place, just like me.

Charlotte came across an old black and white photo of her great-uncle Tobias, framed and standing on a bookshelf. This looked to have been taken in his fifties. His auburn hair was starting to gray at the temples, but he still posed, tall and proud, for the picture. She recognized that he was standing in the paddock beside a beautiful chestnut horse, and behind him, hanging off of or sitting on the split rails, was a group of girls and boys around age eleven, watching him with admiration. This was the great-uncle that she remembered: a showman, an educator, and a lover of nature.

*   *   *

"Oh my, this is quite the spread," Beau said, bouncing into the room. As always, he was full of energy. "Those drapes look like they came off the set of *Gone With The Wind*! Frankly, my dear Charlotte, I'd ditch the damask," Beau delivered in his best Southern accent.

Charlotte laughed.

"Believe me, I've started a list," she said, holding up her laptop. "I'll keep as much as possible, for sentimental reasons I guess, but there are things in this house that, well, that I need to share with the rest of the world."

"Well put."

She figured that if she did this throughout the house, she'd soon have a truckload to take into town. Maybe that cute antique shop would be interested in some of these items.

"Do I hear thoughts of redecorating in your plans? Because you know who loves nothing more than building settings for every extravaganza. Moi!"

"I honestly don't know what I'm thinking right now, Beau. I never expected emotion to creep into the equation."

"Just relax and keep an open mind, and remember to dream big and laugh lustily. I'm off to curate some music to set the mood for a night on the farm. Let me know if you like it."

With that "the magic that is Beau" went about setting wireless speakers around the farmhouse. *God love him, he always makes me smile.*

Beau blasted a musical line-up, starting with "Bohemian Rhapsody," that interrupted Charlotte's thoughts as she browsed through design websites. She heard Diane turn on a mixer, and then . . . the lights went out. Between the three of them, they'd succeeded in tapping the electric circuits beyond their capacity.

At least that's what I think happened.

Not just in the house, but in all the surrounding farms as far as the eye could see. The dead silence didn't last long before shouts echoed up and around the hillside. On top of that, Charlotte could hear the howl of coyotes joining in the chorus.

Anyone could have caused this blackout, right?

Chapter Three

"I should be able to salvage the biscuits for breakfast, assuming that the power comes back on by then." Diane passed around a huge wooden bowl heaped with three different kinds of lettuces, tomatoes, shaved cucumber, fennel seeds, and scallions, all dressed in a strawberry mustard vinaigrette. She loved feeding people, and it showed in her big brown eyes and dimpled face.

Beau had been quick to find the candles, and set a beautiful table in back on the patio. He told everyone that he wanted to do his part to atone for his contribution toward draining the power.

Along with Joe and Alice, Farmer Brown had also joined them for dinner.

"I'm not so sure that your power usage triggered this blackout, Beau," Joe soothed. "When Tobias threw a party, we'd have all kinds of electric devices going—music, strings of lights everywhere, and sometimes he'd rent a small Ferris wheel for the kids."

Charlotte thought about that for a moment. "Joe, will you be able to find out what has caused this?"

"Will do. It could be a blown out transformer."

"So Farmer Brown, is it just you living here? What about the wife and kids?" Charlotte noticed Beau wink at Diane; he approved of his sister's prying.

"Just me. I grew up around here, so if I ever get the need for family, I got brothers and sisters and parents I can visit."

With that, the story was over. Beginning, middle, and end. *Joe wasn't exaggerating when he told me that the farmer was a man of few words.*

"Miss Charlotte has a realtor coming by in the morning, Samuel. She's hoping to get an assessment of the value of Finn Farm," Joe explained.

"Just to have in my back pocket. For planning purposes . . . strategy."

Farmer Brown stared directly into Charlotte's eyes without saying a word, so she was compelled to continue rambling.

"A starting point is all this will be. You know, from which to map out the future."

He gave no response but kept staring.

"We'll need you to conduct the tour of the fields, Samuel." Joe broke the awkward silence.

Diane carried in an impressive cheese tray that was accompanied by fresh bread that Alice had picked up at the market earlier in the day. Farmer Brown took a couple of cheddar slices and a hunk of bread and stood.

"Call when you need me in the morning, Joe."

With that, he left and headed back down to the barn.

"Under forty," Beau said to the table.

"What? His age?" Diane gave her brother a quizzical look.

"He's closer to our age," Charlotte corrected.

"No, not that. Farmer Brown said less than forty words tonight. I've been known to say more than a hundred from the time I open my eyes each morning until I sit down for breakfast."

Even Joe and Alice snickered at that.

Finally they feasted on strawberries and sliced melon marinated in cassis and doused with fresh cream.

Charlotte hadn't eaten like this, farm to table, in perhaps . . . ever. Each bite sent a wave of images and sensations to her brain. The warmth of the sun burning off the morning mist; the verdant and earthy smells of the origin of this bounty; and finally, the sense that she was feasting on love. She knew that people planted and cared for the food she was eating from tiny seeds or from nurturing goats and cows. The best part was that she was now sharing this food with the people who had created it. The diners at the table couldn't be described as either "eat to live" or "live to eat" people. They were simply paying proper respect and admiration to the pure and distinct tastes of food enjoyed in its absolute prime.

When the last morsels were consumed and the dishes had all been cleared and rinsed, awaiting a proper wash when they had hot water, Charlotte and Beau and Diane gathered on the front porch for a look at the star-packed sky.

"We should really make this an early night," Charlotte commented, mesmerized by the twinkling lights.

"Agreed. For not doing very much today, I'm suddenly totally exhausted." Diane yawned.

"It's all this country air and farm livin'," Beau chimed in. "It just makes you want to go to sleep with the chickens and wake with the roosters."

"Where did he learn phrases like that?" Charlotte looked at Diane, laughing.

"Who knows? I sometimes think that Beau has been reincarnated many times, and every so often, elements of a past life emerge. So what do you think the realtor will want to see tomorrow?"

Diane and Charlotte boarded a porch swing, and Beau claimed a wicker rocking chair.

"I have no idea, guys. I don't know what kind of demand there is for a property like this or even really how much potential this farm has, although from the look of some of the idle farmers that I saw in town, I'd have to guess that this area is in need of a source of employment for the people that make Little Acorn their home."

"There goes the Charlotte that I know and love, once again trying to save the world." Beau stood up and gave Charlotte a hug. "Stop your worrying, and get a good night's sleep. You've got the sketches that you did for renovating the master suite. That will show him how you could envision the entire farm being made over."

"You know, for a silly man, you are sometimes so wise, Beau."

Charlotte kissed him on the cheek, and the three bid each other good night.

* * *

Charlotte got ready for bed but was still too keyed up to fall asleep. She thought about taking the wooden box out of the chest again and then looking for the key, but changed her mind. Whatever was in there could keep her up all night, and that was a bad idea.

Joe had lit the fire for her in her great-uncle's comfortable bedroom, and it cast a soft yellow glow in what otherwise would be a pitch-black room. Rumor was that the power would be restored some time after five A.M.

Just as Charlotte started to doze off, she heard a knocking on the French doors, and when it didn't cease, she grabbed her phone and used its flashlight to investigate. Unable to see anything in the darkness outside, she nonetheless opened the door, and the pig scooted past her and raced into the house. Charlotte called out for the pig.

What the heck is his name?

This time she made sure that she'd shut the door to her room. She wasn't about to go rooting around and lose any more sleep, so she went back to bed. Just as she laid her head down, she heard snoring coming from inside the room. She bolted upright and reached for her phone, but it wasn't on the nightstand. She'd left it by the bedroom door. When her eyes adjusted to the dark room, she could see from the glow of the fire that the pig had settled at the foot of the bed. His eyes were closed in sweet repose, and she could swear that he had a smile on his face.

He suddenly started shaking, and Charlotte wondered if he was having a particularly active dream. She reached down to pet him, and soon after he crawled up next to her and nestled into her neck and shoulder. He nibbled playfully at Charlotte's long, curly, soft, red hair, and she noticed that his eyelashes were almost the same color.

"Do I remind you of your mama? Does she have ginger in her genes?"

He looked at her and blinked his eyes once.

Was that a "yes"?

"I hope you wiped your feet, little pig." She smiled. *He looks like a little angel.* "I'll have you know that tonight is an exception. Now go to sleep," she whispered. "You too, Mrs. Robinson," Charlotte said to the dark room, praying that the ladybug was also curled up for the night.

Charlotte fell back to sleep, listening to the soft beat of the pig's heart.

* * *

The next morning Charlotte noticed that the electricity was back on, and the pig had left.

I must have left the door ajar, and he probably didn't want to miss his morning feeding.

She dressed quickly in one of only a few outfits that she thought was somewhat appropriate for the plans of the day, a powder-blue sundress and white sneakers. At least Charlotte hoped that this attire would work. All she'd be doing was walking along the paths that run parallel to the plants. She applied ample dollops of sunscreen to her peaches-and-cream skin and was lured out of her room by the aromas of breakfast being made.

Charlotte followed the scents to the kitchen, where she found Diane scrambling some eggs.

"Good morning. Did you sleep?" Charlotte asked her BFF.

"Like a baby. I can't remember the last time that I left the world entirely behind and fell into the cottony peace of slumberland."

"Wow, those must have been some dreams," Beau said, entering the kitchen and peeking into a large basket that had been covered by a tea towel. "Praise be, the biscuits have been resurrected!"

Charlotte noticed that Beau was still in his bathrobe, a royal-blue velvet number with his initials embroidered in silver on the breast pocket. His feet were clad in leather Mexican sandals. Sunglasses completed the ensemble. Yet his wavy brown mane of hair had been combed back and held in place with product. She hoped that he'd change into more traditional daywear by the time the realtor arrived.

"Here, I'll make you a plate of biscuits and jam. Otherwise, you'll just keep picking at things and bothering me in the kitchen, Beau."

"My sister loves me." He grinned, accepting the plate from Diane. "I'm going exploring. Ta-ta!"

"Don't forget about the realtor," Charlotte shouted to him. "Have you seen Alice this morning?" she asked, turning back to Diane.

"For a split second; then she disappeared down into the cellar."

She sure spends a lot of time down there.

Charlotte heard the sounds of tires crunching on gravel and went to the front window.

"Good God, he's here and he's early. Quick—let's set a place for him at the counter so he can have a coffee and some of your wonderful baking. That should buy some time for everyone else to get ready.

"Don't worry, Char—I've got this. Go outside and greet him."

* * *

Joe had also seen the man drive up, and arrived just as Charlotte did.

"Hello again, Mr. Lurvy, and thank you for coming by." Charlotte extended her hand and then introduced Joe. "We've got coffee and fresh biscuits for you to enjoy before we tour the property."

"Oh. I suppose that I could take some nourishment—fuel for the day."

Charlotte guessed by his plump shape and round face with puffed cheeks that he'd already filled the tank at least once before coming here.

The way to a man's heart is through his stomach. Maybe I should ask Diane to make him a plate of eggs as well.

After being introduced, Diane did indeed offer a more robust meal.

"Thanks, but I've got a full day of appointments ahead of me." Mr. Lurvy downed the biscuit in two bites, leaving a good-sized deposit of butter and jam in a corner of his mouth. He slurped his coffee at about the same speed and rose from the barstool.

"Let's start with the fields, and then I'll finish up with the farmhouse."

Charlotte exchanged a look with Joe. This guy wasn't giving anything away, and she began to worry that she might not get an accurate assessment of the farm's value at the end of the tour. She also didn't like hearing about all the other people wanting him to sell their properties. *Is there that much available farm inventory in Little Acorn?*

"Alright then. Diane, I'd love for you to join us. Maybe leave a note for Beau?" Charlotte said.

"Could you leave one for Alice too? I think she's in here somewhere." Joe guided the realtor out of the house and took out his cell phone. Charlotte and Diane were right behind them.

As it had been yesterday, the weather was ideal. The sun was burning off the morning mist, spotlighting the flowing fields as if being revealed by a slowly opening curtain.

"I've texted Samuel and asked him to meet us at the paddock," Joe informed the group.

"So, what are we waiting for?" Mr. Lurvy seemed impatient or nervous or both.

"I called out for Alice but got no response." Diane eyed the realtor, and Charlotte could tell that right off she didn't like him.

Not a good sign.

"Alice knows where to find us, and we've waited long enough." Joe motioned out toward the dirt pathway, sensing Lurvy's frustration with the delay. "Let's head out to the fields this way—and watch your step. The ground can be damp and slippery in the morning."

The pig emerged seemingly out of nowhere and kept pace with Charlotte. Mr. Lurvy gave a shriek on seeing him, which Charlotte thought odd.

If this man sells farms, he really should be more comfortable around animals.

Charlotte once again admired the beauty of her surroundings as they trudged down the hill. This was true America: peaceful, normal, and humble to nature. Farmer Brown stood at the gate to the paddock's split rail fence, and the pig raced on ahead. As soon as he was granted entry, the pig made his way to an awaiting trough full of slop. In between grunts, it almost sounded as if he was humming.

Only then did Charlotte notice that Farmer Brown was talking on his cell phone.

"It's not going to change anything, Serge—how many times do I have to tell you? I run the place, and like you suggested, the extra crops we put in last fall are ready. I have produce that needs to get to market and a very short window of time. Now are you coming out for a pickup, or should I call another distributor?"

Charlotte watched him pace and kick dirt while he listened to the phone.

"He's talking to Serge Andersen—he distributes our produce to market," Joe whispered to her. They don't always get along, as you can probably tell," he added sheepishly.

When everyone had reached the paddock, Farmer Brown ended his call.

He acknowledged the group and started the fifty-cent tour, still reacting coolly to Charlotte. The realtor kept asking profitability questions, which only served to make the farmer close up tighter than a swimming duck's backside.

"What would you say is your crop yield per acre of farmable land? Both per year and per month?" Mr. Lurvy persisted, but he got no response.

Just like the day before, all of a sudden Charlotte saw the geese burst out from the orchard. Diane shrieked with delight.

"Do you raise geese for market too?" Mr. Lurvy's avarice was getting under Charlotte's nerves.

"They are beautiful," Charlotte said to Farmer Brown before the realtor could pose another question. "What makes them fly like that?"

Seemingly happy to be asked about something that he was well versed in, Farmer Brown explained. "For the benefit of you city slickers and newbies, the birds fly in a V formation for maximum efficiency. Each bird flies a bit above the bird in front of him, reducing the wind resistance. See that?" He pointed toward the tip of the V. "The birds take turns being in the front, falling back when they get tired."

Charlotte and Diane watched them do a flyover above the paddock, interrupting the pig from eating for a moment. They settled on the fence rails and barn eaves. The pig watched, and when all had landed, he gave the birds a hearty "oink, oink" greeting. They responded in kind with a chorus of honks.

The symphony was repeated, and Charlotte could tell that the orchestra was just warming up. The goat section joined in with both soprano and baritone notes of bleating. Finally, the horse in the barn produced a tenor neigh that brought the house down.

Charlotte and Diane applauded eagerly, but Mr. Lurvy maintained a look of sour annoyance, the kind of face someone might make if his or her food arrived cold.

"This is the main barn, home to the horse that you just heard and three pygmy goats that I use to help keep control of the brush that grows wild around the areas that haven't been plowed for cultivating. That's what I do with them, plus introduce them to the kids when their class comes here for a field trip. A couple days a week, a woman borrows them to teach yoga, but I've got nothing to do with that." Charlotte watched Farmer Brown's nose wrinkle at the thought.

He sure has a lot more to say when he's in his element.

Diane looked at Charlotte, and they realized that they both had the same question: Just how the heck do goats teach yoga? Before Diane could ask, Farmer Brown left from the back of the barn, expecting the group to follow.

When she exited, Charlotte saw that the farmer was waiting for them outside a small cabin.

"He really should be a U.S. ambassador in some foreign country with his charisma," Diane suggested, and she giggled. "If he weren't so cute, I might hate him."

"You think he's cute?" Charlotte immediately asked.

"In a Sam Shepherd, Daniel Day Lewis kind of way. Don't you?"

Charlotte looked at Farmer Brown again but said nothing.

"These are my quarters, nothing much to see in there—one bedroom, wood stove, bathroom with shower. We've got two flatbeds"—Famer Brown gestured toward the area where the trucks were parked—"and a couple of golf carts. They're all part of the property. The farm equipment is over by the fields, kept under a carport. We'll head there next."

When the group returned to the paddock gate, Charlotte noticed that the pig was digging into a second filled trough. "That pig's eating again," she observed. "It looks like he can put away more than that chestnut horse over there." She shook her head and smiled at the pink ball of fluff.

Joe and Diane laughed.

"I hope he's not eating up all the profits," Mr. Lurvy said, and mopped his forehead with a handkerchief. In a suit and tie, he was not at all appropriately attired for a farm audit, Charlotte thought. The clouds were gone, and it had started getting hot. With this man's pasty skin and no hat, he was sure to burn. She checked her pockets for her sunscreen, something that she rarely left the house without. She found a roll-on stick and offered it to him.

"I won't be here long enough to need it," he said, ignoring her outstretched hand.

"I wonder where Alice is," Joe said, looking at the screen of his cell phone. His furrowed brow showed that he was starting to worry.

When they reached the strawberry fields, the atmosphere changed entirely, from dry enclosures to lush green bed rows moist from the irrigation system.

"We use raised beds because we can lift the soil out of the ground and into piles. The trenches in between allow great airflow to reach the plants and stimulate growth," Farmer Brown explained.

The pig caught up and trotted along, remaining close to Charlotte's side.

"Hello, pig, are you finally sated?" Diane asked.

Charlotte looked down at him and saw a black and red speck on the top of his head that she didn't remember from being up close and personal with him last night. She leaned in for a closer inspection and grinned.

"What?" Diane asked, always up for a good joke.

"Meet Mrs. Robinson. I'll explain more later."

Diane followed the direction that Charlotte was pointing and saw the insect.

"I think that you are really 'to the farm born,' Charlotte. Have you given every creature here a christening?"

"Hardly. But trust me, this is a good story."

"What on God's green acres is that?" Mr. Lurvy howled.

Smack in the middle of the field Charlotte spotted Beau, clad in a turquoise Speedo. His blue robe was now slung over a strawberry lattice. From somewhere, he was broadcasting the soundtrack from *Oklahoma!* Beau was working alongside about a dozen day laborers who were busy picking fruit and enjoying his music. Almost every other berry went into his mouth.

"I represent quality control," he announced to the pickers, and they laughed.

"That's my brother, Beau," Diane explained. "Unlike some people, he chooses to enjoy life."

That brought a chuckle out of Farmer Brown.

"Indeed. It looks like the pig isn't the only one eating into your profits, Charlotte," the realtor snarked.

"I don't trust this guy," Diane whispered.

Beau spotted the group and, piqued by curiosity Charlotte assumed, slung his bathrobe over his shoulders in a fashion drape and turned off the music from his cell phone. He loaded up the plate he'd brought from the kitchen with strawberries and joined the tour.

"Adios, amigos. I'll be back to help soon, and I'll bring lemonade and more show tunes!"

Beau offered the plate to Mr. Lurvy, but he just waved his hand in a gesture of "shoo."

"Suit yourself, sir. I'm here if you change your mind." Beau's mood couldn't be dampened.

Charlotte shook her head in disbelief and draped her arm over Beau's shoulders as they walked.

"You must have a strawberry, Miss Charlotte. They are to die for." Beau grabbed a stem and held the berry over her mouth.

"Don't mind if I do." She bit off the fruit, warm from the sun and bursting with flavor.

It seemed that everywhere Charlotte looked, the farm was brimming with life. If the strawberries had voices, she was sure that they would be singing right now. She was also sure that if she sat down right here in the field, she'd be able to see the berries growing.

*   *   *

Farmer Brown led the group from the strawberry fields to the tomato vines, some resplendent with little yellow flower buds and others carrying plump fruits in various stages of ripening. He explained that they staggered the planting and growing so that they could sell virtually year-round.

He really seems to know what he's talking about.

"These rows of cages are heirloom tomatoes of six different varieties and sizes. We sell them in mixed baskets."

Charlotte examined the nearby plants. She saw some with fruits that were a dark, dusty pink; others that were larger, gold with red streaks; and some that must be beefsteaks, but they were a dark purple color. Across the path were varieties of cherry and pear-shaped tomatoes. She felt like she was walking through an expressionist museum with vibrantly colored works of art.

Along the way Farmer Brown stopped to examine several broken valves in the irrigation system.

"Damn," he muttered.

"Animals?" Charlotte suggested as the culprit. "I keep thinking that something is spooking those geese."

"No, this is the work of the two-legged variety. Although 'animals' is the right word."

As they moved deeper into the field, the pig became agitated and kept trying to block Charlotte's path.

"What are you doing, little man? This is important, and we need to keep going."

"I think that this heat is getting to *you* if you are talking to the livestock," Mr. Lurvy snidely remarked.

The pig stopped in his tracks. It was as if he had taken offense to the realtor's sass.

Charlotte almost tripped over him and managed to jump to one side in the nick of time. She shooed the pig away, but after another few steps, he tugged on the hem of her sundress.

"No!" Charlotte said firmly to the pig. She'd had enough, and the mood among the group had turned darker. When she looked down and saw his big eyes turn glassy, Charlotte immediately regretted shouting.

Did I just make a pig cry?

The pig dropped back and watched them continue on.

"These are Yellow Brandywine tomatoes," Farmer Brown told them as they walked. "They are beefsteak shaped and have a sweet, old-fashioned tomato taste. We sell a lot of these to grocery stores—they're great on sandwiches and in salads. Over there are Early Girls. They're an abundant producing plant, and we stagger starting them each year so that we always have crops to sell."

As Farmer Brown continued his narrative, Beau, Diane, and Charlotte huddled for a confab.

"Does that guy ever crack a smile?" Beau gestured with his chin toward Lurvy. "He acts like he was born constipated."

"Shh—he'll hear you." Diane placed her index finger over Beau's lips.

"I don't think that I can sell the farm with this guy. Uncle Tobias would say that he eats cranky flakes for breakfast every morning."

"Do you have a profit and loss statement on these Early Girls? Buyers are going to want to see that sort of thing, you know."

Farmer Brown stopped in his tracks and turned to him.

"That's the kind of thing that you're going to have to take up with Miss Charlotte and our distributor, Mr. Lurvy. I'm much more on the organic side of making the farm work. But I would suggest that right now you just focus on finding some of those buyers and worry about the rest later." Charlotte watched Farmer Brown swing around and double his pace along the cages, possibly hoping to run the portly man out of breath.

"Touché." Diane whispered.

This confirmed what Charlotte had suspected. This tall-drink-of-water farmer was more at home with land, propagation, and irrigation than capitalization.

With each moment of immersing herself further into farm life, Charlotte was becoming more conflicted. It made sense to sell the farm; she knew nothing about running one, and she'd have so many more opportunities in L.A. But she was also becoming enchanted with the prospect of a simpler life.

All of a sudden, they heard a loud, sharp oinking bark that sounded like it was coming from the belly of a hound in Hades.

"What is it, pig?" Farmer Brown asked.

The pig stood atop some stacked wooden crates.

All the commotion caused the realtor to trip and go down face first onto the field. He was quiet for a moment, probably assessing his possible injuries, but then, when he turned his head to one side, he released a hyena-like howl.

"Oh no, are you hurt?" Charlotte put her hands to her mouth in shock.

Farmer Brown quickly moved in along with Joe to spread apart the leaf-laden branches where a long wooden handle stood at attention. What was revealed justified Lurvy's wail.

Charlotte saw, lying faceup next to the realtor, a motionless young man with his eyes still open, his body held in place by a pitchfork that had pierced his neck. Blood had made the soil beneath him turn a dark, sticky red.

"Oh. Dear. God. Is he—is this real? Or is this somebody's idea of a cruel joke?" Charlotte dropped to her knees half-hoping that the young man would break into a smile, and it would all be over except for a good tongue-lashing.

Beau and Diane gently helped Charlotte stand and coaxed her to back away from the body.

"I'm afraid that this is no joke, Miss Charlotte. The poor lad is dead." Farmer Brown had checked for a pulse and now stood back up. He extended his hand to the realtor for a lift up.

The realtor didn't see his hand or else ignored the offer, and crab-walked himself upright as quickly as he could muster while shouting, "No one will be interested now—that guy has bought the farm. You'll have as much of a chance selling as you will of seeing pigs fly." Mr. Lurvy then charged off.

Upon hearing this, Charlotte saw the pig make several attempts to jump into the air from atop the crates, leaving Charlotte to wonder just how much language this little guy could understand.

"Anyone recognize this man?" Farmer Brown asked.

No one responded.

"I'll call the authorities," Joe announced.

"Let's have everyone move back, try and retrace the footsteps you took getting here. Pig, you don't come any closer—this has nothing to do with you." Farmer Brown took charge.

When Charlotte looked behind her, the pig had gotten off the crates and stood about ten feet back. He was shaking.

You may be wrong about that, Farmer Brown. The pig sure acts like he knows something.

Beau asked to no one in particular, "Just out of curiosity, what's the pig's name?"

Charlotte was in shock and reeling from the repercussions of finding a dead man in the farm's beds, but she still felt the need to answer Beau, and quickly replied, "Horse."

When Beau gave her a blank look, Charlotte replied, "Because he eats like one." Farmer Brown, Diane, and Joe nodded in unison.

Chapter Four

The gang returned to the main house to wait for the police. Farmer Brown stayed behind to keep a close eye on the spot where they'd found the body, to make sure nothing and no one disturbed it.

"It shouldn't be long," Joe told them. "The chief said that she was close by."

"Joe," Charlotte said as she approached him, "when we were walking through the fields before . . . Farmer Brown discovered a number of broken valves in the irrigation pipes. He wouldn't actually assign blame, but he gave me the impression that this had been done deliberately. Do you know who he was thinking about?"

Joe slowly nodded and closed his eyes in muted anger.

Diane and Beau gathered around him to hear his response.

"Afraid so. There's been a long-standing feud between your great-uncle and, by association, Samuel and the Avery family. There's two boys—men actually—Wade and his brother, Clark. There's an older sister as well, but she wants nothing to do with the hooligans. The guys have some hair-brained idea that they should own this farm. Only they haven't been able to offer any evidence to support it. So they pass the time trying to sabotage our crops, shutting down the water, introducing mice and rats into the fields to eat the produce—even tearing up some fresh plantings. We've never been able to catch them in the act, but that doesn't stop them from bragging about their deeds."

"That's awful!" Charlotte's new "Garden of Eden" was starting to show some cracks.

"It sounds like the town bullies need to be taught a lesson, and I know just the person to do it!" Diane hated injustice.

"I do too, you!" Beau said, saluting Diane.

Just then a Ford Explorer with police markings appeared and rolled to a stop in front of the farmhouse. Out stepped a woman in uniform, with strips of foil in her hair.

"I've come straight from the beauty shop, Joe, so there'd better be a body down there," she told him.

"Everyone, this is Chief Theresa Goodacre, this is Charlotte, the farm's new owner, and her friends Diane and Beau. I'm afraid that the realtor got so spooked that he turned tail and ran."

"More like he limped away with his tail between his legs," Diane added.

"What's his name?" Chief Goodacre asked.

"Mr. Lurvy," Charlotte offered.

"Never heard of him, and I know everybody."

"I told you." Diane elbowed Charlotte in the ribs.

Chief Goodacre had a pleasant face and naturally rosy cheeks. She was tall and sturdy and carried herself with an absolutely straight back. But Charlotte also noticed signs that she enjoyed being a lady when off the job. Her nails were manicured, and she wore a necklace of freshwater pearls, a dainty and delicate juxtaposition to her professional attire.

"Who else was present when the body was found?"

"Just Farmer Brown. He's still down there making sure that the scene is preserved." Charlotte hoped that she sounded reliable and respectful.

Chief Goodacre quickly spun her head back to Joe.

"Samuel—she means Samuel." Joe nodded to the chief.

"That is his last name . . . Brown? I never knew that." Chief Goodacre tried it out on her tongue. "Farmer Brown. That's funny."

Beau approached her and lifted one of the foils in her hair.

"Excuse me!"

"Girl—ma'am . . . Chief, your roots are done. We've got to rinse out your hair right now. I can't believe that they let you leave the salon like this."

"I didn't exactly give them a choice," Chief Goodacre replied, looking to Beau to save the day.

Beau did a quick scan of the area and spotted a garden hose next to a trough that looked like it was used in gardening.

"Quick—over here. Joe, will you get that milking stool and place it right at the edge of this basin?"

"You sure you know what you're doing, son? I'm an authority figure, after all."

"I was born ready," Beau told her while guiding her to her seat.

"Now sit down facing me. Here. You can use my robe to cushion your neck. Just lean back a bit."

Beau rolled the blue robe into a long rope and draped it under the chief's neck and around her shoulders. He then picked up the hose and nodded to Joe to turn it on.

"The water will be warm for a short bit because it's been sitting in the hose in the sun, but then, I'm afraid, it will turn cold. I'll work as fast as I can. So, you married?"

Alice appeared in the doorway of the farmhouse, mouth agape. As her eyes took in the impossible scene playing out in front of her, she looked to Joe, surely for some possible explanation for why a nearly naked man was washing the police chief's hair with a garden hose. He just shrugged his shoulders and smiled.

"I'll get some towels" was all that Alice could muster saying.

Where has she been all this time? Alice knew what time the realtor was arriving . . .

* * *

"Beau, you are a lifesaver," Chief Goodacre said to him once he'd towel dried her hair and combed it into place. His robe was now too wet to wear, but thanks to Alice, he'd wrapped a towel around his waist. If the lake had been filled, his attire would have made perfect sense.

With Chief Goodacre's looks restored almost to normal, Charlotte saw that they were close to the same age, and the chief had made it all the way to the top in her career—even if it was a relatively small pond.

"You all wait here for the medical examiner, and when he shows up, Joe, you can escort him down to us. Charlotte, since you own this place, you'd better come along with me. We haven't had a murder here in over ten years. You're here one day, and we've got a body."

Charlotte winced. *Does she think that I had anything to do with this? She should talk to Alice, who's been missing all morning.*

An age-worn pickup truck appeared on the plateau, windows rolled down, with hard rock music pouring out of the vehicle like a downpour from over-saturated rain clouds. Charlotte couldn't see the driver clearly, but there was another man riding in back in the bed. She thought that she recognized him as being the friend or brother of the spitter from town. It was confirmed when the driver leaned out and caught sight of Beau and said, "Well looky here. You sure are making yourself at home pretty fast, boy." A cigarette hung from his lips. The man in the back hopped out of the truck and walked around Beau in a circle.

"Wade, turn that damn music off immediately or I'll arrest you!" the chief said to the truck driver.

"For what, Chief?"

"For disturbing the peace and being butt ugly. And give me a minute and I'll come up with some more charges, like proof that it was you who shot out that transformer last night, making the power go down. Clark, you get back in the truck. I don't remember hearing anyone invite you to visit." She crowded Clark and made him walk backward to the truck bed, where he stepped up onto a tire to hoist himself in.

So these are the Avery brothers.

Silence was restored.

Wade slid over to the passenger seat and stuck his head out the window.

"So, what're you here for, Chief? I heard from a friend that you tore out of the beauty parlor with rollers still in your hair. Something about a dead body? Who is it?"

"You can't sneeze in this town without someone catching a cold a mile away. Don't you boys have anything better to do? Don't answer that, but stay put. I may need you to identify the body. Come on, sister"—she gestured to Charlotte—"let's go take a look. And it was foils, not rollers, Wade," the chief shouted over her shoulder as she led Charlotte away. "Go ahead and introduce yourself to the twenty-first century."

Charlotte followed her down the hill, accompanied by the pig, now named Horse. It relaxed her a bit to see that Mrs. Robinson was still riding on his head.

"Were you and Tobias close? I don't remember seeing you here before."

"Yes and no, Chief Goodacre. I spent a month here one summer when I was a kid, and we were both big fans of letter writing."

"A lost art," the chief said.

That surprised Charlotte; this lady was not conforming to the stereotype of a cop who uses force rather than words. She wondered if they could be friends. Charlotte figured that she was going to need one when Diane and Beau went back to Los Angeles.

"Those men that came by in the truck—do I need to worry about them?" Charlotte bit a corner of her lip; she always did when she was uneasy.

"Trust me I'd love nothing better than to put them behind bars. They are mean-spirited and unkind. But I suspect, otherwise harmless. Don't get me wrong. I'd happily change my mind. Hello, Samuel."

"Chief Goodacre, I'll lead you to the body. I made sure that no one came near it after that realtor tripped over it."

"That reminds me, what was his name again, Charlotte?"

"Mr. Lurvy, Max Lurvy. He overheard me talking in the bank and introduced himself. He said that he knew the farm and would help me sell it."

"Do you have his number? Did he give you a card?"

"Yes." Charlotte thought for a moment. "You know what? He showed me his card but took it back. I never did actually get his phone and address information."

"I'll have to track him down. Which real estate company does he work for?"

Charlotte stopped following Farmer Brown for a moment. "I feel like such a fool. I don't even know who he represented."

"Interesting."

"Chief, here he is." Farmer Brown stopped about ten feet away from the body and pointed.

"Okay, don't get any closer. I'm just going to get a look at his face to see if I know him, and then we'll wait for the M.E. I don't want to destroy any evidence."

Chief Goodacre peered down at where he lay.

"Don't know him. No one mentioned the pitchfork before—that's a nice touch, and it tells you a few things."

"Like what? It's so heartless." Charlotte couldn't bear to look at the victim again and had hung back with Horse and Mrs. Robinson.

"That's one way of looking at it. Rage could be another. Or the murder was unplanned, and the pitchfork was there and available. But I don't want to speculate. We need to know what caused this poor fellow's demise. I suggest that we put all preconceived notions about this way on the back burner."

Now that she was over the initial shock, Charlotte screwed up her courage to study the murder victim. He had dark hair, almost black, that served as a dramatic contrast to his very fair complexion. Almost as light as hers. He had a square jaw and high cheekbones, qualities every girl wishes that she possessed. But on him they seemed to be going through a transition from soft to chiseled. He couldn't have been older than his early twenties.

Chief Goodacre backed up as well and turned to Samuel.

"So, *Farmer* Brown—I hear that's what they call you these days."

"Not 'they'—just her."

The chief looked at Charlotte and nodded like she sensed the tension.

"Prior to discovering the body, when was the last time that you went out to this particular part of the tomato field, Samuel?"

"It would have been three days ago. I have a set rotation that I make."

"And to your knowledge, did anyone else have reason to be here since then?"

"No, but clearly at least two people were. This guy and whoever killed him."

"Tell her about the broken sprinkler valves, Farmer Brown," Charlotte requested, and noticed Horse's nodding head signifying approval.

"Oh, that. It happens every now and again, but I've never been able to catch anybody. Probably kids, vandals bored with a need for something to do."

"Joe says it's Wade and Clark."

Horse emitted a growl at hearing this.

"It sure sounds like something they'd do. You say you've never seen anyone actually in the fields tampering with your irrigation?" the chief asked.

"No." Farmer Brown had a hangdog look on his face. "And since the damage has escalated recently, Joe and I take turns doing a drive around at night.

"Too bad."

In response Horse let out a succession of squeals.

"Action from the peanut gallery. If only you could talk, little pig." The chief gave him a pat.

Charlotte looked at him and tried to read the signs.

"Ah, there's the M.E. Over here, Burt." Goodacre waved him over.

*　*　*

Chief Goodacre, Charlotte, and Farmer Brown walked back up to the house so the chief could begin questioning witnesses in an orderly fashion.

"So, let me get this straight, the group on this little tour of horror was comprised of Samuel, Charlotte, Joe, dear Beau, and Diane. And this Mr. Lurvy character, if that's his real name."

"And Horse." Diane gave the little guy a pet.

"Hah! She can't tell a pig from a horse, Clark," Wade shouted, and they both belly -laughed.

"The pig's name is Horse. Try and keep up Wade!" Chief Goodacre gave him a look of disgust. "Alice, my friend, where were you while all this was going on?" The chief's tone had done a three-sixty turn.

Aha.

"I was in the cellar. I'm making lots of jam right now and canning fruits and vegetables. I'm hoping this year to be able to sell them at the farmers market in the fall. For the farm, of course." Alice addressed this last bit directly to Charlotte.

Alice looked tired, with her thick black hair off her face in a messy braid. *This invasion of a new owner and friends must be really taking a toll on Alice. Or is it something else?*

"If you go to all this effort, Alice, you should certainly reap a percent of the profits." Charlotte knew that they had gotten off on the wrong foot because of a misunderstanding about Mrs. Robinson when Alice tried to wipe the ladybug off her shoulder. She'd promised herself to be extra nice to her in an effort to mend the fences. She was rewarded with a small smile from Alice.

They were interrupted by the noise of footsteps and squeaky wheels as Burt and his assistant returned, wheeling the gurney with the body up the hill. The pitchfork had been removed but was lying on top of the sheet-covered body.

"Please tell me that you have a good idea of the time of death within a small window?"

"I wish I could, Theresa, but until I get him on the table, the best I can say is that he died between midnight and about eight in the morning. He was a young, healthy guy, and the air was cold last night, so I have to look internally for better clues. Oh, and he had no I.D. on him—or anything for that matter. This could either be on purpose or because the killer took all the evidence with him."

"So more questions than answers. Will you lift the sheet so that these two fellas can hopefully identify him?" the chief asked Burt's assistant.

Wade and Clark had gotten out of their truck when the body was brought up.

They both took a good look and shook their heads.

"Of course not," Chief Goodacre muttered. "Burt, make this a priority please."

"Priority? This is the only murder victim I've had in years. I'll have more for you tomorrow."

"I've radioed my two deputies to come over right away to collect evidence. In the meantime, nobody go anywhere near the scene—understood?"

Charlotte and her group all nodded obediently. Horse followed suit, making Charlotte giggle.

Wade made a show of pulling out a cell phone from the bib of his overalls.

"Serge? Yeah, it's Wade. Listen, we're at Finn's; you might want to reconsider selling for a farm that also produces dead bodies. They got one here that had a pitchfork in his neck. No lie, and you know how fast news spreads around here."

"You're a real class act, Wade. Now you two buffoons get out of here—you're trespassing. And quit that filthy smoking. This is fire country." She crowded him all the way back to the truck and stood an inch away from him until he got in and turned the ignition.

Charlotte was beginning to really like Chief Theresa Goodacre.

Horse then added his two cents by letting out a displeased grunt and turning his head away from Wade.

Chapter Five

"Every time I entertain thoughts about making a go of it with this farm, something awful happens that tells me it's a bad idea."

Charlotte, Beau, and Diane had repaired to the porch swings for a much-needed calm down. They sipped Alice's homemade lemonade and just let a moment of peace wash over them.

"I have to agree Charlotte. This is not the way I pictured the day going. If I'd known, I certainly wouldn't have worn a turquoise swimsuit." Beau had changed into madras shorts and a white polo shirt for the afternoon.

Charlotte knew that, despite being all smiles, the jabbing from Clark Avery had left a mark.

"You know people have short memories. Hopefully this murder will be solved very soon, and we can get on with our lives. That Chief Goodacre seems pretty sharp, and she sure doesn't take any crap from anyone." Diane grinned. She loved women with spunk.

"Amen to her. I saved her blondness, so she's beholden to us now." Beau hoisted his glass, and they all toasted the air in front of them. They were trying to lighten the mood but couldn't quite get there.

"I like her too, but it doesn't bode well that no one has recognized that poor young man. I still can't believe someone was killed on my farm! And everyone says that the city is a dangerous place to live." Horse had his head cocked, listening to Charlotte.

"Look at it this way: you'll have time to get some of the cosmetic changes done to the farmhouse, and I'll bet in a month's time people will be lining up to make an offer on the place."

"That's sweet of you to say, Beau."

"Oh no."

They all turned to see Alice standing in the doorway. Charlotte wondered how much of their conversation she had overheard.

"What's 'oh no,' Alice?" Diane asked.

"I completely forgot that Miss Fern's third-grade class was coming today. They were scheduled to pet the animals and learn a little about farm life. I'll just have to send them away. We certainly can't have kids running around a murder scene."

They all watched a half-size yellow school bus labor its way up the hill.

"Nonsense. We can certainly think of some activities to make this a learning experience." Diane was on her feet. "Beau, come with me into the kitchen—you too, Alice. Let's get some cupcakes started and gather an array of fruits and vegetables on the long farm table."

Charlotte loved Diane's positive attitude and usually found it infectious.

"Horse, can you round up a goat or two and bring them up here to meet the children?" Charlotte asked him and then realized that she was letting her imagination get the better of her.

I've just named him, and now we're having full conversations.

Charlotte introduced herself to Miss Fern, who in turn made the introductions of her students. The eight- and nine-year-olds were wide-eyed with excitement, and Charlotte found herself wishing that her great-uncle were standing right beside her. How he would have loved entertaining this group. She remembered how magical the farm had been to her when she'd visited at their age.

"Can you show us where the dead body was found?" asked one boy, tall for his age. "My brother says that he had a stake through his heart like a vampire."

"Brad! Don't say such awful things, and you should know better by now than to believe everything that your older brother feeds you," Miss Fern admonished him, and she gave Charlotte a "sorry" shrug.

"Word certainly does spread fast in Little Acorn," Charlotte tried to offer as a way of curbing further conversation, but now the other kids were asking Brad all sorts of questions.

Just then a minivan pulled up behind the bus, and a woman with a worried look rushed up to Miss Fern.

"I'm going to take Becca home, Miss Fern—this is no longer a place for children to visit." The woman reached for her daughter's hand.

Charlotte watched as another mom pulled up to the farm. This was quickly getting out of hand.

I have to do something.

When a third car approached, Charlotte really started to panic. Some of the children started crying at the growing frenzy of the situation. Then, like the phoenix rising from the ashes, Horse trotted up to the farmhouse with several goats in tow and a handful of geese hovering above.

"Ah, the entertainment has arrived," Charlotte announced. "May I present to you the Finn Family Farm's most treasured artiste, Horse."

"But he's a pig," said Becca.

"Yes, but he eats like a horse. Miss Fern, is that a pitch pipe I see you holding?" Charlotte asked.

"Yes, we were singing on the bus."

"Could you and your class possibly give Horse and his orchestra the key of G?" Charlotte prayed that Miss Fern would comply, because at least for the moment, the moms had stopped corralling their kids.

"Ready children? Animals?" Miss Fern found the correct spot on the tuning wheel, took a deep breath into her chest and ample bosom, and belted out a perfect G. The children mimicked her.

This is the moment of truth. Please, Horse, give them a squeal, a grunt, anything . . . to get their minds off murder.

A moment later Horse joined in. The kids laughed, but their jaws soon dropped when the goats began their chorus and then the geese alit, strutting and singing some impressive tenor honks.

When Charlotte saw a couple moms videotaping the concert, she took a breath. Horse had saved the farm.

At least for now.

"Who wants to decorate cupcakes and eat fresh strawberries?" Beau said, appearing in the doorway in a cooking apron.

* * *

Two hours later the kids loaded back onto the bus and into cars, carrying bags of cupcakes with fruit-themed icing and a giant strawberry made out of red napkins and twine. The once worried parents each gave Horse a wave and went back to their cars, having had a wonderful afternoon. Horse had indeed delivered, and the little ones squealed with delight when they petted the goats and watched a mother goose lead her goslings on a recon mission around the farmhouse.

"Joe, how difficult would it be to fill that artificial lake up again?" Charlotte asked.

He walked up next to her on the porch and leaned against a support post.

"Your uncle loved looking out at the water too. He would sit for hours on a porch swing, waiting for the sun to set over the lake. It got partially drained during the fire of 2008, by the Superscooper helicopters. The water from this farm was instrumental in saving some nearby structures and crops."

"That makes me feel good." Charlotte looked back toward the large, cracked concrete basin. In places, grass and weeds had pushed through the bottom and taken up residence.

"It would seem to me that this could once again be a valuable resource in times of emergency," Diane said, joining the conversation. "Perhaps the county has some funding they could spare to restore it in exchange for access to the water when needed. This is much closer than the ocean for smaller aircraft."

"That's true, Diane. I know some people to approach. Maybe you could come with me. You make such a persuasive argument." Joe smiled at her.

"You bet!"

"I can talk to Chief Goodacre too. I have no doubt that we will be spending more time together until this murder is solved." Charlotte gave the now moribund lake one more look, and a memory flashed in her mind of jumping from the dock with kids from the neighboring farms.

While Diane and Joe wandered into the house to see about dinner, Charlotte let her thoughts continue to replay from that summer she'd spent on the farm. The watering hole had been legend around the canyon, and Tobias gave anyone who knew how to swim a day pass. More images popped in and out of her memory, like the water safety test Tobias put every new swimmer through; the canvas chairs he set out for the parents on the dock; and a fleeting sight of her uncle and a woman holding hands and watching Charlotte get in a last quick swim as the sun was setting. For the life of her she couldn't remember who that woman had been. Although he had never married, Charlotte had heard through family rumors that he was seldom lacking for female companionship. At nine years old, she hadn't thought holding hands meant much; she'd had to do it with a classmate whenever her class went off campus. But thinking back now, that younger woman with the dark hair was clearly someone who'd made Tobias happy.

"Earth to Charlotte, you look like you just drifted off to Marrakesh for a private, sunrise, hot-air balloon ride over the desert."

She hadn't seen Beau approach, and he'd startled her.

"Did you have fun with the kids? They looked like they were having a blast," she said to him.

"I did, but I'm afraid that we humans played second fiddle to Horse and his merry menagerie. Good job my little pink friend!" Beau bent down to Horse's level, and they gave each other an air Eskimo kiss.

Only Beau would train him to do that.

"Beau, do you think that I could actually make a go of this? I'm remembering more and more about the time I spent here as a kid, and it all seemed so ideal. Everyone was happy. We were outdoors from dawn until dusk, and every fruit and vegetable and living creature was magic to me."

"Of course you can. And not just make a go of running the family farm, dear Char—you could make it spectacular. You just need to return to the old "take no prisoners" girl I grew up with and stop second-guessing yourself. You've got this in your blood, sweetie. You may like to trip the light fantastic in heels and silk gowns, but deep down you're really a gingham-and-sneakers kind of girl."

"Sweet Beau." She gave him a generous hug. They both froze in place for a moment with their noses in the air. Charlotte thought she detected the aroma of a roast chicken. "Does it smell to you like a delicious dinner is ready?" she asked Beau.

"Why yes, it does, and tonight we'll be able to see what we're eating. Allow me to escort you, my dear."

Beau offered his arm, and they skipped into the house.

* * *

Tonight it was just the three of them at dinner, and that was fine. They could talk in their own childhood code, finish each other's sentences, and howl, laughing about the silliest things. Charlotte was almost able to erase the day's horrible scene from her mind. She told them the story of Mrs. Robinson, the ladybug, and all three marveled at her tenacity and loyalty.

"I've made a couple of peach pies for you. We'll have some tonight, and then you may want to share the rest with Joe and Alice. Or bring Farmer Brown a warm slice in the middle of the night," Diane teased.

"You are so bad—stop it. Besides you're the one who thinks that he's cute."

"And you, Miss Charlotte, never said what you think."

"He's cute, trust me," Beau said, adding his two cents.

"He's my employee, and I plan to keep it professional." Charlotte took the plates into the kitchen, thereby ending the discussion.

When she returned with the pie, plates, and ice cream, she sat and held her friends' hands. "I wish you could stay longer. I feel like we've only just gotten back together, and I've been too distracted to really be with you guys. Tomorrow night at this time, I'll be dealing with all these problems on my own."

"You'll be fine, and we're only a phone call or a drive away, luv. Now dig into this pie. I'm getting spoiled working with ingredients directly from the tree, ground, and stalk!" Diane laughed.

Charlotte heard the sounds of metal scraping across tile and watched a chair that had been against the back of the patio glide toward their table. It had gotten dark while they were eating, but no one had bothered to turn on some lights or get the candles out again. Beau and Diane were digging into their desserts and had closed their eyes to concentrate on letting the flavors melt in their mouths.

That explains a lot. This place is haunted.

Charlotte's eyes were open to the limits of their sockets when the chair came to a stop at the table.

Beau noticed Charlotte first. "Honey, what's wrong?"

Just then Horse sprang from his back hooves and landed on the seat in one smooth movement.

Charlotte screamed, and Diane and Beau immediately joined in. Thinking this was a game Horse added his squeal to the party.

* * *

"I really believe that he was just trying to show you that you won't be alone, Charlotte—that he'll be by your side."

"You really think so, Diane? I've been wondering if I'm going crazy thinking that Horse understands my every word."

They were in the kitchen, about to finish up for the night.

"Pigs are very intelligent—way up there in the animal kingdom. Just behind chimps, elephants, and dolphins."

"And where'd you get that tidbit? Are you still watching Saturday morning nature shows like we used to?"

"Hah! I wish that I had time—you remember how much I love them. But Saturday mornings I'm in the restaurant early, prepping for a hopefully busy night."

"Too bad. So did you just make that up, Diane?"

"Nope. Farmer Brown told me."

"Oh, and just when did you and the produce proprietor have this discussion?" Charlotte was teasing her but also curious about their encounter without her.

"I ran into him when I was picking the peaches. Are you jealous?" Charlotte laughed.

"You are!"

"She is what?" Beau appeared in the kitchen doorway, back in his bathrobe, but Charlotte was relieved to see pajamas poking out beneath it.

"I think that our sis-once-removed has got a little thing for Farmer Brown!"

"Stop it—I thought that we'd settled this." Charlotte's Irish anger was surfacing.

"Okay, good talk. Time for me to go to bed." Beau had raised his arms in a surrender pose and was backing out of the room. He'd been on the receiving end of Charlotte's wrath before, when they were growing up, when he'd pulled a few too many shenanigans.

"Me too." Diane kissed Charlotte's cheek. "You know that I was just teasing. You are right to take your job here seriously, and you're going to make a great farm owner."

"If I stay . . . thanks, Diane."

"You turning in too?"

"Shortly. I want to run this pie down to Joe and Alice, so they can enjoy it tonight or for breakfast tomorrow. You remember how I shouted at Alice when we first met? I was afraid that she was going to hurt Mrs. Robinson, and I reacted irrationally. I still feel some discomfort with her when I'm around, and I really want to settle that."

Charlotte kept to herself the idea of observing Alice in her own home, where she was likely to let her guard down if she was hiding anything she knew about the murder.

"Charlotte, it's dark out, and you barely know the roads down there."

"Don't worry. I'm not going alone."

"Oh, I'll get my jacket," Diane said.

"Not you, silly—I'll have my trusty pig with me for protection."

"Well, that's a horse of a different color." Diane cracked herself up as she left the kitchen.

* * *

The road was lit, albeit dimly as the ground lights were stretched far apart. Charlotte was carrying a pen flashlight with her that she'd found in a utility drawer in the kitchen. She could see her destination from the lamps lit in the Wong house. Plus, Horse appeared to know exactly where they were going.

Charlotte fought to block her mind from thinking about a night similar to this when someone else had been moving around the farm in the dark. Had he been trespassing? Maybe he was the one breaking off the sprinkler valves. That would mean that someone had caught him, and the obvious choice would be Farmer Brown or Joe. The farmer was a surly man, maybe carrying a chip on his shoulder, but still, murder was awfully extreme for what amounted to little more than a misdemeanor. Plus, from the brief look Charlotte had gotten of the body, Farmer Brown outweighed him by perhaps fifty pounds. He could have just knocked him out and called the police. Charlotte decided to reserve her judgment about Joe until after her visit to their home.

Because of the steep incline of the hill, the road to the bottom level ran in long "S" curves, which meant that Charlotte would be traversing it parallel to the fields on the second level. A sudden chill had picked up in the air, and Charlotte came on a narrow path that dissected directly through the strawberry fields. Taking this would cut her walk time in half, if not more. She turned her penlight along the path to ensure that it was clear as far as she could see.

"Horse, should we go this way?"

He walked a short way along the dirt with his nose pointed down to the ground. At first Charlotte thought that he was just rooting for food, but he suddenly stopped, looked back at her, and wagged his tail.

"Okay then, onward."

The fields at night were an entirely different experience. What was a lush, bountiful, happy place during the day had turned eerie and predatory in the dark. Charlotte kept hearing odd noises that made her stop mid-step and brace for a surprise attack from behind one of the thick raised rows of red berries and plentiful, camouflaging leaves.

This might not be one of my better ideas . . .

She convinced herself to put her trust in Horse and decided that if he were happily marching along, then she would do the same.

All of a sudden Horse quickened his pace, and Charlotte learned that he could really move when he set his mind to it. She broke into a run to keep up. "Horse, stop!"

He may have heard her, but he didn't obey. His grunts got louder and fiercer. Charlotte needed to catch and restrain him because she certainly didn't want to be left alone in this field. Up ahead she heard footsteps that were much heavier than the little pig's hooves, but she couldn't see who was making them. She'd put the penlight in her mouth when she'd started running, so she could use both hands to keep the pie upright. The shaky, small beam of light was no help. She tried to hold the pie tin steady in her hands as she picked up speed, trying to keep up with Horse. For all those reasons, she couldn't possibly have seen the plastic storage container that had been left in the middle of the path. Her foot and shin hit the box and although it skidded forward Charlotte thought that she might step on the pig, so she dove down shoulder first into the dirt spitting the penlight out just in time before it was driven down her throat. The pie went flying and landed with a thud about six feet away. When she slowly picked her head up, she saw that the container had come to a stop just out of reach. Instinctively, she crawled toward it but couldn't see inside in the pitch black. Charlotte felt around for the light, following a dim beam that was pointed in the opposite direction. It was at that moment that she heard the distinct cocking of a shotgun.

"Don't move," boomed a deep voice in the distance, and Charlotte flattened herself against the ground. Horse had raced back to her and, thinking that this might be a game, had started foraging around her head. That was when she heard a bullet loading into a second gun.

"Go. Run, Horse. Save yourself," Charlotte whispered to him.

Instead, he let out the same oinks that he had used to greet the geese that morning.

Charlotte started saying her prayers, and when a wide light flooded her body, she figured that it was probably the last thing that she'd see.

Footsteps approached from two directions.

"It's Charlotte," she heard a woman's voice utter.

"What the hell?" a man said.

Someone bent down low to her face, and she screwed up her courage and squinted open her eyes.

"Farmer Brown?"

"Damn it, woman, would you please call me Samuel like everybody else does?"

"Is she hurt?" Charlotte thought the woman's voice sounded familiar, but for now she couldn't place it.

"Can't tell yet. Can you sit up, Miss Charlotte?"

"I think so."

Samuel helped her roll over and bend at the waist.

"I'm going for a cart," the woman said.

"What did I trip over?" Charlotte asked.

"What were you doing out here by yourself at night?" Samuel ignored her question.

"I was bringing a peach pie down to Joe and Alice. I thought they would enjoy it fresh out of the oven."

Samuel let out a sigh and slowly shook his head.

"I thought that I made it clear that we've had some problems with a couple of people trespassing and trying to sabotage our crops. Not to mention the dead body we found not far from here. What were you thinking? I could have shot you. Luckily, I heard the pig and that warned me off firing. Do I have to remind you that there is a murderer on the loose?"

Charlotte felt her cheeks flush bright red at the scolding.

"I'm sorry. I realize now that it was foolish, but I am trying, in the middle of all this upheaval, to establish a sense of order and cooperation on the farm. I was headed to see Joe and Alice to take them a freshly baked pie. This has all come on so suddenly for them. I recognize that the farm is their home, and I wanted to reassure them that everything is going to be fine."

"Is it?" Samuel asked, surprising her. Seeing her expression, he continued. "Around here we rarely have a murder, and if we do, it is more likely to be due to a couple of drunk farmers fighting over a girl or land or both."

"Well, in Chicago we have them all the time, and we learn how to take care of ourselves." Charlotte's tone was defiant. She'd already apologized and had had just about enough of the farmer's chastising.

"May I remind you that this is not Chicago or any other big asphalt jungle? This is Little Acorn, and as long as there is a killer out there, I'll be patrolling at night with a loaded gun. Next time I might not hear the pig and might go ahead and fire."

Samuel reminded her about Horse, and she quickly looked around for him. She worried that all the shouting had scared him into hiding. She located his pink body ducked into the plastic bin.

"Horse!"

That drew Samuel's attention to what had tripped her up, and he dragged the bin over to where Charlotte was sitting.

"Aphids—I knew it," he said after shining the light into the bin. Samuel searched for the lid and got up to retrieve it.

Charlotte peered in when Samuel returned with the light.

"That's what those tiny green things are called? What's so important about them?"

"What's so important? They can ruin our entire crop because they multiply fast as lightning. If you don't control the population right away, you'll be overrun."

"We use as much natural deterrents as we can." Charlotte followed the sound of the woman's voice and saw that it came from Alice, who had pulled up in a golf cart.

"Then why was there an open bin here?"

"Good question, Miss Charlotte. Someone put it here and if you hadn't been wandering around, I might not have discovered it for at least two days. By then the damage would have been out of control." Samuel started to put the lid back on the bin.

"Wait!" She grabbed his hand and he stared at her.

"You might have hit your head harder than I thought." Alice got out of the cart and went to her.

"It's not that, it's Mrs. Robinson. She must have dropped off Horse's head when he stuck it in." Charlotte reached her hand in and let the ladybug climb onto her hand.

Samuel looked at Alice for some explanation, but she shook her head.

"Let's get you inside so we can check your injuries," Alice said, helping her up.

Samuel helped Charlotte into the back seat of the cart, and Horse hopped into the front next to Alice. All four rode off toward the lights from Alice and Joe's farmhouse.

* * *

If Charlotte thought that she couldn't look any more foolish in front of people that she depended on to help her with the farm, she was about to prove herself wrong when she was asked to explain Mrs. Robinson. The only silver lining was that Joe had overhead Charlotte tell the story to Diane earlier in the day, so at least she proved that she hadn't lost her marbles in the fall.

"That was so unnecessary for you to bring us a pie tonight, Miss Charlotte—kind, but a risk these days being out on the farm at night." Alice had made her a cup of chamomile tea for warmth and comfort.

"Samuel told me that the tampering with the farm has been escalating," Charlotte explained. "Please be straight with me, Joe. You promised not to sugar-coat anything." Charlotte welcomed the tea from Alice and, cupping it, warmed her hands.

"I'm afraid so," he replied, and looked at Samuel.

"Do you think that this is tied to the murder in some way?" Charlotte shivered at the thought.

"Could be. I told you that we've been taking turns patrolling at night," Samuel explained. "But whoever is doing this is onto our schedules and knows just when we won't be covering a certain area."

"How could that be unless they were informed by someone who is very aware of your exact activities each day? It could only mean someone who works on the farm. Anyone come to mind?" Charlotte studied all three of their faces.

"We three are the mainstays," Joe replied. "Everyone else is part-time or seasonal."

"What about people who are not directly involved with the farming but perform other services like equipment maintenance, housecleaning, water and power, animal feed delivery, and so on?"

"I'm coordinating a list of those names with Joe and Samuel," Alice told her. "At Chief Goodacre's request."

"Thank you, Alice. I'm sure it will help. And to each of you, I am sorry to have caused such a disruption tonight. I am clearly way out of my depth." Charlotte sighed.

"Well, not entirely. You saved us a lot of headaches by discovering those aphids." Samuel smiled at her for the first time.

"And your Mrs. Robinson reminded me that ladybugs are excellent natural combatants against them. Someone told me at the garden center that one ladybug can eat up to five thousand aphids in its lifetime! I'll pick up a bucket of live ones tomorrow and release them around the area where you found the aphids!"

"If I'm not imposing, I'd love to join you, Alice. The more I immerse myself, the faster I'll hopefully learn."

"I'd be delighted. Joe, will you run Miss Charlotte, Horse, and Mrs. Robinson up to the house?"

Alice has been nothing but kind tonight. Am I missing something?

"Of course. Oh, and I found out what caused the blackout: a summer lightning strike."

So Wade wasn't responsible. For that, at least. If Samuel is on patrol tonight, then Joe was out last night . . . when the murder took place.

Samuel stood. "I don't think they'll try anything else tonight, but I'm going to take one more turn around the fields. And you, Miss Charlotte, don't try to rush it. You'll get the hang of things. Remember, Roma tomatoes weren't built in a day."

Samuel nodded at her and left.

Did Farmer Brown—er, Samuel just crack a joke?

Chapter Six

"He really said that about Roma tomatoes? I might be in love," Diane announced from her place at the stove, where she was flipping another batch of blueberry pancakes.

"First, no words, and now, humorous ones—the Finn Family Farm is truly a magical place. What is the best way that we can help you today before we have to head back to L.A., Char-char?" Beau popped a blueberry into his mouth.

Having learned his lesson, this morning Beau was sporting rolled-cuff dungarees, a starched white T-shirt and a newsboy cap. Charlotte had to admire his resilience and creativity.

"I hate leaving you in the lurch like this." Diane frowned. "It's one thing if you're going through old stuff and deciding what to sell and something else entirely now that there's been a murder on the property. Maybe I should call and tell the chef that I'm taking the week off. I certainly have the time coming to me."

"Absolutely not, Diane, when you take time off, it needs to be for a real vacation, not babysitting me, a little pig, and fields of strawberries. Besides, Samuel and Joe are taking turns roaming the property at night like hungry watch dogs."

"Still, that's not the same as having an old friend by your side, someone you can talk to."

"Agreed, Diane, and I promise to holler when I really need you. I'm going to the garden center with Alice this afternoon. You and Beau can follow us into town. But perhaps for the next few hours we could go room to room through the farmhouse? You could help me take notes on the unquestionably necessary repairs that will need to be made."

"Perfect. What's your guess on whether you'll hear from slimy Lurvy again?" Diane shook her head in disgust before tucking into a maple-smothered stack of pancakes.

"I have two guesses: slim and none." Beau beat her to it.

"Agreed. Listen, I hadn't planned on signing a contract with a realtor immediately anyway. He was the one who approached me in the bank. I hadn't even seen the property yet. But there he was, and it seemed like it couldn't hurt."

"And how exactly did he know who you were and that you were interested in selling?" Diane had a naturally suspicious mind.

"He must have overhead me talking when I was signing the deed papers and such for the farm, Diane."

"You did this out in the open?"

"No, of course not. It was in the bank manager's office—I see what you're getting at!"

"Curious, isn't it?" Diane gave her a knowing nod.

Charlotte thought back to when she overheard Alice tell Joe that she'd run into the Avery brothers in town the day that she arrived. They'd bragged about the farm being theirs.

"What would be the reason for someone to pretend to be a realtor to get a tour of the farm? He could have simply said that he was interested in buying the farm, and I'd have given him a tour." Charlotte couldn't believe that they were talking about this.

"Maybe so that he could give you a lowball value, hoping that you'd sell quickly and leave town." Diane's mind sometimes could conjure up bad things.

"Do you think that was the reason why someone was murdered in my fields?" Charlotte's voice had ascended an octave in panic.

"It's way too early to make that assumption. Remember, Chief Goodacre told us all to keep an open mind. I'm just suggesting that we weigh some possibilities," Diane said soothingly, trying to calm Charlotte down.

"I've been played the fool, haven't I?"

"No, love, but it does sound like the cards were stacked against you even before you arrived. I've got to return a couple of calls, and then let's start the rooms audit, shall we?" Beau tipped his cap to the girls and left the room.

"He's right. There are things at play here that we are going to need to wrap our minds around. I'm hoping that Chief Goodacre can enlighten us."

"About what, Diane?"

"I'm not sure, but you can ask her yourself, Charlotte—she just drove up."

* * *

"Good morning, Chief. I hope you're hungry. Diane has made blueberry pancakes," Charlotte greeted her as she stepped out of her Ford Explorer.

78

"Sounds delicious and I may just take you up on it, but first we need to take care of some business. You may rescind the offer after you hear what I have to say. Is there a room we could meet in? I'll need the other usual suspects. Could you call Joe, Alice, and Farmer Brown?"

"Samuel—I call him Samuel now."

"What a difference a day makes. I'll wait in the living room."

Charlotte rushed back into the kitchen. She'd been coldly jarred back into the harsh reality that she was a murder suspect, and on paper a very good one.

"Something serious is about to go down," Charlotte half-whispered to Diane. "She's summoning all of us, and by her expression and tone, it isn't to invite us to a barbecue and barn dance."

"Oh dear, it could be another kind of grilling. I'll get Beau."

Charlotte called the others, and ten minutes later they were all settled in the sunken and wood-beamed living room. Chief Goodacre had acquiesced to a cup of coffee that had seemed to take the edge off her mood a bit.

"Thank you all for coming at such short notice. I have some news, more questions, and an announcement," the chief began.

Horse wandered into the room, wagging his tail at seeing all his friends. He took up his post beside Charlotte, who was perched on the arm of an overstuffed chair. She was too nervous to sit and kept fidgeting with a piece of twine she'd found.

"As you heard there was no identification found on the victim's person yesterday. We are proceeding with other means of ID-ing the body including fingerprints and dental records. But in the meantime, we had started circulating a photo of his face in hopes that someone in town knew him."

Alice reached for Joe's hand; they were sitting close together on one of the sofas.

Were they in on this together?

"We told you yesterday that we didn't know him. That hasn't changed," Samuel said looking from face to face in the room in case someone had had an epiphany.

"And I believe you all, for now." Chief Goodacre's tone had grown ominous. "Here's the news part: in the process of getting the photo out, with careful cropping to avoid the pitchfork marks, my officer, Maria Dodd said that she thought she'd seen him before."

"Oh wow, so he was a local boy?" Charlotte watched Diane now scan the room with a suspicious eye.

"I had Maria take her time studying the photo and then asked her to view the body."

"You sure are a 'measure twice, cut once' kind of boss, Chief Goodacre—bravo," Beau said with admiration and amity.

She showed no indication of returning his friendship at the moment.

"You're scaring me, Chief. Please just give us the bad news." Charlotte had started to shake.

"It isn't necessarily bad, but Maria remembered him from a day trip she'd taken with the kids to the Humble Petting Zoo. Along with a friend and her two kids, they were given a behind-the-scenes tour as a show of gratitude for Maria helping the owners when an animal transport vehicle broke down on the road. When we talked to the husband and wife that own the petting zoo, they confirmed that they employed an animal keeper named Marcus Cordero. He'd been working for them for about six months when he disappeared a couple of days ago. Naturally, they were shocked when they learned of his fate."

"I'm not surprised," Joe remarked. "Violence like this just doesn't happen around here. Did they say if he had any enemies, Chief?"

"Not that they could think of. He kept to himself. Did his job well and loved their animals."

"How about family? A girlfriend?" Diane asked.

"Again, none that they knew of."

"Sorry to ask, Chief, but do you think that the owners were telling you the truth?" Alice said this in a shy whisper.

"Here's the thing, Alice: like Edgar Allen Poe said, 'I believe only half of what I see and nothing that I hear until I have all the facts.'"

"But do you have any thoughts as to who did this?" Joe asked.

"At the moment, almost everyone and no one. To some degree each of you had the means and opportunity."

"Along with the rest of the farms on these hills. Including the Humble Petting Zoo." Samuel stared out into the fields.

"You are correct, Samuel, so until we find a motive I can't rule anyone out."

Knowing the poor man's name is even more gruesome. He was somebody's son. I wish that I'd never come here.

"The plot thickens." Beau looked toward the ceiling as if he was trying to remember something. "Isn't this the part in an Agatha Christie novel when Hercule Poirot tells the suspects in the parlor that nobody should leave town?"

"It is, and that's what I am telling you. If you and Diane have jobs to get back to, then I suggest that you call your employers.

I'll need you here for at least a couple of days, to give time for some more information to surface and for us to chase down leads."

Charlotte piped up. "Are you saying that we can't leave the farm, Chief?"

"You can, but just don't stray farther than Little Acorn until I give the okay."

Everyone was silent for the moment, letting the news sink in.

"Remember that I'm doing this to catch the murderer so we can all get on with our lives. I don't need to remind you that this wasn't just a simple shooting. This was a particularly grisly, angry murder. Keep your doors locked when you're home, and for heaven's sake don't go wandering out at night."

Charlotte avoided Samuel's gaze.

Chief Goodacre nodded to the group and left. All eyes went to Charlotte, including Horse's baby blues.

Charlotte gulped audibly.

*   *   *

"This is all my fault . . . and now you're missing work . . . and Samuel and Joe can't go and track down Serge, the distributor, to see why he hasn't shown up . . . and they can't collect the money that the farm is owed."

"For Pete's sake, Charlotte, this is not your fault. And the good news is that we get to spend some more time together. Which had been my plan anyway. If you could go through the rooms in the house and put a sticky note on the pieces of furniture that you want to sell, then perhaps we can borrow a truck and take it all to town tomorrow." Diane wrapped her arm around Charlotte and walked her into the foyer.

"I can do that."

"Good. From what I hear the farm has a little cash flow problem at the moment, so every little bit helps. I'm meeting Beau and Alice on the back porch, and we are going to brainstorm ways to add steady income to the farm. Along the lines of what we did for Miss Fern's classes, but to give visitors more of an 'experience,' as Beau calls it."

"I don't know what I'd do without you, Diane."

"Luckily, you don't have to find out."

Charlotte walked back to her uncle's suite, followed by trusty Horse. She grabbed a pad of sticky notes off the desk and was about to start her audit when she spotted her laptop. She walked around the desk and sat down in front of it.

"Did you know this Marcus Cordero, Horse? Did he have something to do with the farm?"

Horse stared at Charlotte for a moment, she thought allowing her words to register. He then hopped up onto her lap and stared at the computer screen.

"You think we should do some research, do you? Mrs. Robinson, do you agree?" Charlotte asked, seeing the ladybug atop Horse's head. "I need to take control of my own destiny. If I do nothing, then I'm a sitting duck, and I could possibly end up spending the rest of my life in prison."

Charlotte saw Horse's eyes widen at the word "duck," but the rest of that sentence flew right over his head. She opened a browser on her computer.

"Okay, we'll start here, but if we don't find what we want, we'll have to continue our sleuthing in my uncle's library."

Horse extended his neck closer to the computer and smiled.

* * *

An hour later, after having learned precious little about this Marcus Cordero, Charlotte, Horse, and Mrs. Robinson could be found in Uncle Tobias's library, sitting on the floor, surrounded by photo albums and journals that her uncle had kept. While the temperature outside was climbing into summer digits, the room with its Spanish pavers and decorative tiles, stone walls, and thick mahogany bookshelves remained cool. Charlotte made use of a leg blanket that she'd found draped over the back of a red leather club chair.

"For a man with very little family, my uncle sure enjoyed collecting photos of his time on this blessed farm. Look at this, Horse—it was taken during one of his famous parties that he would have to celebrate a good season. There he is, looking fine in his straw Stetson. He always seemed to have a bunch of little kids following him around, and—is that a very young Samuel?"

At hearing the name, Horse wagged his tail and squealed.

"Could be," came a voice from behind her.

"Oh, you scared me. How long have you been standing there, Samuel?"

"Less than a minute." He chuckled. "Let me take a look at that picture."

He crouched down next to her and examined the few pages of the album covering the party.

"Sure looks like me. I was one of those kids that followed Mr. Finn around and wanted to be just like him. I guess he appreciated my interest, because he would spend extra time teaching me things about the farm."

"Didn't the other kids get jealous?" Charlotte asked, and Samuel lowered himself all the way down to the floor and sat next to her.

"Not really, or I didn't notice. Except for one grumpy kid who just never seemed to be happy. Always wanted what he didn't have. Can you pick him out of this lineup?"

Samuel had pointed to a photo of a group of kids all perched on the top rail of the fence around the paddock. They were all looking at Uncle Tobias, who was standing in the center, holding a rope rein attached to a llama. Charlotte carefully scanned the faces of the girls and boys and stopped on a guy who was standing behind the fence rather than sitting, watching with a naturally downturned mouth.

"Him!"

Samuel nodded. "You recognize him?"

Charlotte looked again. "Is that Wade?"

"Yep. He couldn't have been more than eight or nine. Already, he was mad at the world."

"That's so sad." Charlotte let her focus expand to the entire photo and noticed a shadow at the entrance to one side of the barn. "Is that a person?" She pointed to the spot.

"Can't tell in this light. Let's take the album over to the window."

They did so and almost bumped their heads together while trying to get a better look.

"It looks like a woman, young and with dark hair. Did my uncle's caretaker at the time have a wife or daughter?"

"Not that I remember. The only one I ever saw was old Carlos, and he was too ornery to keep a woman around. But what did I know? I was just a kid."

"She looks a bit familiar to me, but I can't really make out her features. I do remember seeing my uncle with a lady the summer I was here. It could be the same person, but I can't be sure."

"Hey, we've got a great idea! Come join us on the back porch and we'll unveil our brilliance," Beau gleefully announced, barging in. "What were you two doing huddled together by the window?"

"Looking at some photos. I can't wait to hear what you all have cooked up," Charlotte said, and yanked Samuel's sleeve, pulling him along.

* * *

"Oh good—Beau found you," Diane said. "Like you suggested, we've been doing some brainstorming on ways for the farm to make more money."

She and Alice had set up an easel pad and had drawn schematics and lists on the extra-large pages. Alice was in the process of hanging them on the siding of the porch, using blue painter's tape. "Please sit, you two, and we will amaze you with our entrepreneurial minds and ingenuity. I'll start us off," Diane said.

Joe joined the group and handed Diane a spreadsheet.

"Thanks, Joe—not looking good, is it?" Diane started to shake her head but then turned to the pages on the wall and gave everyone a positive smile. "Alice and Joe have been giving us the rundown on the farm's monthly expenses, which are down to just the bare minimum. As you've probably guessed, Charlotte, we need an infusion of cash to get production and profitability up."

"How much cash?" Charlotte found a small pad and pencil on the table and used it to take notes. Horse trotted over to see what she was doing.

"About twice as much as the farm is currently making per month, but if you are thinking about a bank loan, I don't believe that institutions will be receptive until this murder is solved and everyone here is exonerated."

Charlotte slumped her shoulders and stared at the figure she'd written on the pad. "What about making the farm a destination for special occasions? My great-uncle loved entertaining guests." Charlotte looked to her friends for a reaction.

Beau jumped up and went to the first page hanging on the wall. "Can you say 'par-tay'? We know your uncle loved them, and now we're going to throw them for all kinds of special occasions: birthdays, graduations, anniversaries, and holidays. People can book their events with us, and we'll build a custom-themed celebration around the fields, facilities, food, and animals of the Finn Family Farm. All planned by famed extravaganza maker Beau Mason!"

Charlotte applauded; Beau seemed so pleased with the idea. But in the back of her mind she knew that the competition for party venues here and in Los Angeles was huge, and without a proper advertising budget, it would be nearly impossible to get the word out.

"Once we get some memorable parties in our portfolio, then we can market to people thinking about destination weddings!" Diane said this in almost a cheer, but Charlotte suspected that she knew the truth as well.

"Wouldn't we need to make some investments in order to properly provide this? A bigger kitchen, more appliances, and such?" Charlotte still tried to sound enthusiastic.

Alice nodded. "We talked about that. We could use the kitchen in our cottage as well to double the efforts. We'll make the dough and batters in advance and freeze them," Alice explained, looking to Diane for affirmation. "And I'll work harder at making jams and jellies that we can sell and use as gifts for people at the events."

"Great thinking, Alice! I love that idea. What about clearing out a space for a gift shop and antiques mart? I already know that I'll have lots of my uncle's furniture and knickknacks to pass along to others." Charlotte felt a bit more encouraged about this venture.

"There's an old carport a little ways around the old lake. With some wood, hammers, and nails, we could get it back into shape."

"Perfect, Samuel!"

Charlotte caught Diane grinning at this exchange and gave her a stern look.

"And since you mentioned the old lake, Diane and Joe were going to see if they could get an advance from the county in exchange for offering free access during fire emergencies. Any news on that?" Charlotte didn't like Diane's expression in response to her question.

"Joe and I did some research and made some calls," Diane explained. Unfortunately, the last disaster depleted their budget for the year. And we haven't even gotten to fire season."

"But there is one bit of good news—and this was Diane's idea." Joe grinned. "The fire department and their reserves have agreed to participate in a fundraiser by the old lake site and do safety demos. All we have to do is provide the food."

"Great thinking, all of you! What we need now is an estimate of what it will cost to get that big watering hole back to its glory. Just like it was that summer I visited my uncle. I was just nine, but he made me feel so grown up." Charlotte smiled, remembering.

"The biggest issue is the pump. The water source was an underground spring, which is necessary given how little rain we get around here." Samuel had a faraway look, and Charlotte could almost hear the thinking going on in his head. "Until that's dug up, it's hard to know what we're up against. The tremors and quakes through the years have most likely moved and cracked the pipes. But the good news is that some water is still draining into the lake, so it may be a repair rather than a redo."

"You really are a Samuel-of-all-trades," Beau said, beaming at him.

Charlotte agreed but wondered why a man with his skills would be satisfied in his current role. Surely he could run his own farm as well as anyone.

Is Samuel that unambitious?

"The PVC lining needs to be replaced in all the torn areas; the cracks need to be sealed in the concrete; and new rocks and sand need to be dumped." Samuel either was so focused that he hadn't heard Beau's compliment, or he was ignoring it. "Joe, maybe tomorrow we can borrow the Espinoza Farm's backhoe and get a look at that pump."

"I'll give them a call. It sure would be nice have a lake again. It adds so much more charm to the place." Joe looked at Alice, who nodded vigorously in agreement.

"And once that's done, we can explore the idea of promoting the farm for summer camp," Beau exclaimed.

"Not if it is going to interrupt my farming!" Samuel replied.

"Or harvesting—we have enough trouble doing that in time already." Joe shook his head.

"Harvesting? What's holding us back on that, Joe?" Charlotte grabbed her pencil and was ready to write down his response. Horse got back up on his hooves to observe.

"Man and woman power. We can only afford to pay for about a dozen or so day workers, and then only for a few days a week during peak season."

"So, this is where the bulk of the monthly cash flow needs to go? And if we don't pick the produce when it's ripe, then it rots and we lose the income, correct?" Charlotte already knew the answers and wrote something down on her paper.

Joe and Samuel nodded their heads.

"Then that is the first thing that needs to be fixed. If we can't get the ripe, fresh fruit to the markets in time, then we need to bring the people to the fruit!"

Charlotte got blank looks except from Horse, who she could swear caught on as she saw his mouth stretch up under his snout and his cheeks form rosy apples.

"We need to offer a pick-your-own program. We give people baskets and take them to the fields that we designate for this purpose and charge a discounted price per pound. This won't interfere with running the rest of the farm, and the income can be repurposed to hire more day laborers." Charlotte gave them her "impassioned close" smile from her advertising days.

"Does this mean that we don't have to pay Serge Andersen commission on those sales?" Samuel asked, standing up.

"Sure does, because he'll have nothing to do with those transactions." Diane also stood.

"Then tell me what I need to do, and let's get started right away!" Samuel exclaimed.

Charlotte had never seen Samuel so excited.

"I think the promoting can be simple and straightforward. We go into town with baskets of strawberry samples and a card that explains about the farm's pick-your-own concept, days and hours it's offered, cost, etcetera. We paint a few signs to place outside the property's perimeter, and after we work the kinks out, we can expand our messaging to neighboring areas that attract lots of tourists."

"Charlotte, I *love* it!" Beau lifted her up by the waist and twirled her in the air.

"There's one problem with this," Alice said barely above a whisper.

"What's that?" Joe didn't look happy.

Charlotte studied Alice's expression.

Does she or doesn't she want to save the farm?

"This murder. Even if we use a field that is nowhere near the spot, do you think that parents are going to want to bring their children here?" Alice's eyes grew glassy.

"She's right. No matter how much we try to bury the news with a positive, it isn't going to go away until they catch the killer. I can't sell the farm without taking a loss, and I can't raise money from it while this murder is fresh in people's minds. Case and point," Charlotte added, catching sight of a local news van snaking along the road to the farm.

Chapter Seven

Thanks to Joe's quick thinking, Chief Goodacre made it to the farm in a flash. Charlotte and the group watched from behind the drapes that hung over the front windows, as the news van was unpacked and the satellite antenna was raised. The local news anchor, Kelly Bartiromo, was getting final touch-ups to her makeup and doing audio checks. A producer kept pounding on the front door while his assistants performed recon around the farmhouse.

Meanwhile, Horse kept squealing, confused as to why they weren't letting him greet the new guests.

"Horse, quiet. We're playing something like a game of hide-and-go-seek. They're trying to find us, and we don't want them to."

Horse obediently trotted to an undetected spot behind a leather club chair.

"I don't know what I find stranger, Charlotte—you explaining your actions to a pig or that he appears to understand you."

"Don't wonder, dear sis—just go with it." Beau gave Diane a peck on the cheek.

"There is nothing to report here. I'll answer a couple of questions, and you nice people will pack up and vacate the property." Chief Goodacre's voice boomed over the bullhorn, which, frankly, was overkill, Charlotte thought.

With the news team corralled out in front, Samuel left for the fields. Alice went to the kitchen with Diane, and Joe slipped out the side. Horse was seen following Samuel, perhaps in search of a mid-morning snack.

From what Charlotte and Beau could hear, the questions from the reporter were of the standard "any suspects?" variety, for which the chief only offered the vague response "We are pursuing all leads." After several rounds of this Q&A, the news team reluctantly agreed to leave the premises.

When the coast was clear, Charlotte and Beau stepped outside.

"Thank you, Chief. I was beginning to think that we would have to hide in the cellar until dark. I was sure that you didn't want us talking to the press, and anything we told them would just be guessing. We don't have any news about the murder." Charlotte gave her a warm smile.

"Guesses are the equivalent of a canary dying in a coal mine in my business. You were correct to remain mute."

"Has anyone else ever told you that they love your mind, Chief?" It was an odd question, but it was clear that Beau meant it.

"Not until now, Beau, and I'll take that as a compliment."

"Is there anything new that we should know about, Chief?" Charlotte secretly crossed her fingers on one hand behind her back; she was desperate to start getting the farm back on its feet.

"Barely anything. This Marcus Cordero had a driver's license that was issued at the DMV in Santa Barbara, but he is no longer at the address listed on it. Nor, for that matter, is the place itself. That whole block was razed to make room for a luxury shopping center. He also seemed to pay cash for everything, because we found no credit cards issued in his name."

"What is this thing called 'cash,' Charlotte?" Beau was only half-joking.

"The license had his age listed, didn't it, Chief?"

"His birth date, Charlotte, and if my math is correct, Marcus was twenty-two when he died."

"Such a horrible shame." Beau shook his head as he teared up.

Charlotte did a little mental mathematics herself: he was ten years younger than her. Such a tragedy. He'd had his whole life ahead of him. Charlotte's thoughts were interrupted when a caravan of three cars drove up.

"Now what?" Charlotte looked at Chief Goodacre, hoping for another interception.

"That's Annabel, Serge's wife. Among other things, she fancies herself as a yoga guru. I'm afraid that you're on your own here, honey. When I see her, I break out in hives, and it's not because I don't like yoga. I'll call you if I need anything else. Meanwhile, stick close to home."

The wheels on the chief's car kicked up dirt as she sped away, hoping perhaps to convince Annabel and her group that she had a hot lead. Beau walked up and stood beside Charlotte, and they watched the spandex-clad, vinyl-mat-carrying men and women troop down the hill to the barn.

"Beau, I have a feeling that we are not going to want to miss this. Let's grab Diane and find a hole in the knotty pine barn wood that we can peep through."

Beau ran up the stairs toward the house.

Charlotte followed quickly behind him.

*　*　*

The three friends quietly approached the barn and took a stealth position by one side of the door that was open just enough to give them a sliver view of the class posing on their mats. Goats roamed about freely and saw the downward-dog position as an invitation to climb onto people's backs.

I wonder if the goats think people come to entertain them?

"Is that one peeing?" Diane asked, her mouth agape.

"Probably," said a male voice from behind them. The surprise caused a shriek from Charlotte.

"I guess we're busted." Diane hung her head in shame.

"You can go join them if you want," Samuel continued. "Now that the nanny has gone, you should be safe. Just stay away from that billy."

"How did all this come about, Samuel?" Charlotte took one more incredulous peek into the barn. She couldn't see too clearly the woman who was leading the class, but she could hear her.

She must be using a microphone and portable speakers.

"I believe that Alice met Annabel at a yoga studio in town, and they got to talking. The next thing I knew, these people were traipsing through the paddock, half naked—and not necessarily the pretty half."

"She must be a good yoga instructor for all these people to follow her here—what did you say? Twice a week?" Diane said.

Samuel gave a dry laugh. "I suspect that the goats are more the attraction, and who knows, she might not even be certified or accredited or whatever they do in yoga. She's Wade and Clark's older sister, so I don't believe anything that comes out of her mouth."

"Does Alice know who Annabel is? It seems a bit unnatural for her to be friends with the sister of Little Acorn's resident bullies, Wade and Clarke." Charlotte nodded.

"She hardly ever admits to them as relations—thinks she's above us all and is just biding her time before Serge hits it big and they move on up in society. You'll see—hey, pig!" Samuel grabbed Horse's back leg just in time. He'd used his snout to roll the barn door open enough to allow his round pink body to squeeze through, and was just about to make his entrance into the yoga class.

"He doesn't understand why the goats get to be there and he doesn't," Charlotte said, taking him from Samuel. "Horse, you have more important things to do with me."

That seemed to settle him down, and he relaxed in Charlotte's arms.

"I've seen enough here to convince me that I'll do my stretching on a tennis court." Diane headed back up to the farmhouse.

"Right behind you." Beau scampered along as well.

"I'm going to ask Alice about this arrangement. It seems awfully disruptive to you and the animals. Unless Alice is getting paid for renting out the space. You would know that, Samuel, wouldn't you? If that's the case and expenses are being covered, then I could let it go. I don't want to appear to be undermining Alice's initiative."

"Hah!" The farmer guffawed and led Charlotte away from the barn. "You clearly haven't met Serge and Annabel Andersen. 'Free' is what they expect. I'm sure that Annabel is getting paid a nice sum for her classes, but she isn't passing anything along to Alice. Alice is allowed to participate at no cost, but she's usually too busy."

"Then this needs to stop. Besides we'll need the space for our you-pick-'em business."

"You really think that's going to help Charlotte?"

"First Alice, then you, Samuel. Why are you giving up without a fight? Whether I stay or not, I'm for sure going to make this the best farm that I can. Better than I remember it, which was already pretty great."

"I understand, but—"

"Would you look at that gorgeous red hair!" shouted a woman approaching who Charlotte guessed was Annabel. "The men must just go weak at the knees every time they see you. But who needs men, right?" She was looking at Samuel when she said that last sentence.

"Samuel, wait and finish what you were saying," Charlotte said. But he ignored her and moved back to the paddock fence.

"I'm Annabel Andersen, and you, lovely one, must be Charlotte!" She said this last part as if she'd just discovered the missing link. The goats followed her out and appeared to be having a confab with Horse about the yoga session.

"Yes, I am. Pleased to meet you, Annabel. I see that your class is over. How often do you have them here?"

"It depends on the sign-ups but lately, twice a week. Everyone wants to partake in the total relaxation of goat yoga!"

This woman says everything in the form of a major announcement.

"I've heard so many lovely things about you," Annabel continued. "I'd be honored to take you to lunch in town and introduce you around a bit. I know the one place that can make a good Crab Louie salad, and they add grilled goat cheese!

Charlotte noticed that as soon as the words "goat cheese" were uttered from Annabel, the goats went crazy. They ran around the paddock, hopping and jumping in the air, and made loud noises. They then kept circling Annabel's legs.

Samuel, who had been watching from the paddock rail, laughed. "They get fed whenever they're milked to keep 'em calm. They're going to follow you around now that you said 'goat cheese,' Annabel, and they expect you to give them something to snack on. Goats are as clever as dogs, and they can learn words."

While Samuel had been talking, Charlotte was able to notice the telltales that Annabel sported to signal a more sophisticated lifestyle: manicured nails, a designer yoga bag, diamond jewelry. Serge must be doing well in the distribution business.

Where was her bedazzled water bottle?

"That's a very kind invite, Annabel, but with the murder still unsolved, I doubt that the locals are pining to meet me. Perhaps when this is all settled." Charlotte hoped her declining the invitation was gracious enough.

"Oh yes, that. I heard about the pitchfork. Someone must have really hated that boy."

Horse joined the goats and sniffed at Annabel's bag, making her recoil and scream.

"Sorry about that. He probably smells something edible in your bag. He's cute and harmless, really." Charlotte picked Horse up before he could cause any more trouble.

"My fault entirely—I overreacted. You just never know what you'll encounter out here in the fields." Annabel quickly gathered her composure.

"Didn't you grow up on a farm?" Charlotte asked, thinking again about Wade's claims on her place.

"Me? Goodness no, I'm more like a city girl. The boys worked summers on a neighbor's fields, but I stuck to reading and fashion."

This woman clearly isn't an animal lover, so what is she doing hanging around goats?

"How's this coming Thursday for lunch?" Annabel brightened and returned to the present. "I'll let them know we're coming, and I can swing by and pick you up in my Beemer! About noon?"

She doesn't take "no" for an answer.

Before Charlotte could respond, Annabel, who was indeed limber, had started speed-walking up the hill, with the goats close on her heels.

As she watched, Horse let out a low, guttural growl, something Charlotte had never heard him do before.

"Odd that she'd be spooked by a lovable little thing like you, Horse."

He smiled back at Charlotte, seemingly happy to be cradled in her arms.

* * *

100

"We're heading off to the Garden Center. Either of you want to join us?" Charlotte found her friends on the front porch, where Diane was planning menus, and Beau was using Charlotte's computer to do research for an upcoming event.

"I'm good. I have to text these thoughts to my chef, so he has them when he comes into the restaurant around five today." Diane continued scribbling.

"I'm working remotely, even if I am exploring what it takes to rent an elephant for an evening." Beau hadn't even looked up from the screen.

"Okay, but please stick around the farm until I get back," Charlotte told them. "I guess we're on our own, Alice. Do we need to take the truck?"

"Probably a good idea. I have a list from Samuel of items that he needs to check the pump for the lake."

"I met Annabel today," Charlotte said to Alice as they drove into Little Acorn.

"That's right—she had a yoga class. I never seem to be able to make those."

She sounds casual, but she won't look me in the eye.

"How did all this come about Alice?" Charlotte thought it best to hear her version of the story before she put an end to the practice.

"I'm trying to remember. I think that her husband, Serge, was at the farm, working with Samuel, and noticed the goats. He must have said that Annabel teaches yoga and insisted that she be allowed to try out one of her classes in the barn with the goats. She'd seen a story about a studio doing this in Los Angeles and was dying to try it. As is typical, after she came once she just assumed that she could make a habit of it. Joe is furious that Samuel won't put a stop to it."

Wow. Those are two extremely different stories. Samuel and Alice are pointing the finger at each other.

Charlotte wasn't sure what to do with this and decided to file that knowledge away and perhaps talk it over with Diane and Beau. Diane was the voice of reason, and sometimes Beau could be incredibly intuitive. And maybe she'd press Joe sometime when his wife wasn't within earshot.

"What is her husband, Serge, like? Since Annabel tries to deny being related to Wade and Clarke, I'm guessing Serge belongs to a very different type of family. Danish origins, right?"

Alice laughed.

"Yes on the Danish part, but not so much about his family being different. They moved away from the traditional Danish town of Solvang to seek out the American ideal of getting rich quick. Serge's family moved around to areas where they saw better financial opportunities, and with a little success, they became greedy."

"So Annabel thought that she was moving up, but in truth it was just a different side of the same coin?" Charlotte asked as they pulled into the gravel parking lot of the Little Acorn Garden Center.

"That's a good way of putting it, but you can decide for yourself. There's Serge standing at the entrance to the center."

Charlotte followed Alice's gaze to a blond man who looked to be in his early forties, dressed a bit like a used car salesman in a short-sleeved white shirt and too wide tie. A gold pinkie ring put the icing on the cake.

Alice grabbed a flatbed cart on the way in, and when they reached Serge, she introduced Charlotte.

"Such a terrible thing, having somebody killed right on your property. That kind of stigma could stamp a place for years. I expect that you're anxious to sell that farm and get back to your life in the big city, aren't you?" Serge held onto Charlotte's hand after the shake, for his entire speech. She noticed that his nails were manicured and painted with clear polish.

Ew. I wonder if he's the one who sent Mr. Lurvy?

"You know, Serge," Charlotte said, yanking her hand out from between both of his, "for someone who's known me for all of—what, six seconds?—you sure must trust your intuition."

"That's why I'm in sales. You got to be able to read a customer even before the conversation starts." Serge's voice had gotten louder as he noticed some people around them had stopped to listen in. It was clear that Serge loved an audience.

"First of all, I am not your customer. That was my uncle's arrangement, and I am reviewing all of his decisions. Second, I said that you must trust your intuition—I said nothing about whether yours about me was correct. But if you're wondering, I'd suggest that you talk to our farm's pig. He seems to know me very well in the few days that I've been here, and he can set you straight. His name's Horse."

"Because he eats like one," Alice explained to the crowd around them that seemed totally amused by the exchange.

"Does anyone shop here often enough to give me some pointers?" Charlotte asked the group at the entrance and got several volunteers.

"How kind. We've been talking about having a shaded picnic area outside a carport that we are converting into a gift shop and a mini antique mart. I think that we have the trees, but we'll need some landscaping to make the area pleasant for families to visit for a while. And ladybugs—we need lots of ladybugs!" Charlotte saw but didn't respond to Serge shaking his head in disbelief at her comments.

He's someone to keep an eye on.

Chapter Eight

With the weather having turned so warm, Diane's plan for dinner was to grill burgers outside. Samuel wasn't in his cabin, and Alice and Joe had their own plans, so the three friends and Horse sat around the large barrel grill, on Adirondack chairs, sipping homemade iced tea.

"It sounds like you really showed him," Beau said after Charlotte had filled them in on her encounter with both Andersons during the day. He was setting out coals and building a chimney of fuel to get the fire started. This brought back wonderful childhood memories of the three of them spending long weekends camping at Horseshoe Crab Lake, near where they grew up. She could almost taste the fresh-caught trout. Beau had probably perfected his fire-building skills from the man he idolized, his dad, who was known almost throughout Chicago as the "Smoke Daddy of Cook County."

They ate under the stars on a crystal-clear night and then sat back to digest their food and get lost in their thoughts.

"Do you really think that this Serge clown could have set up Mr. Lurvy?" Diane asked.

"It's possible. He's well aware that I know nothing about the area or, for that matter, farming. Perhaps Serge thought that he would swoop in and take it off my hands for a bargain-basement price. He is certainly someone who is always trying to make a buck." Charlotte was thinking aloud.

"But then a dead body was found, and now everything is in limbo," Beau said, popping the last bite of meat, cheese, and bun into his mouth.

"Maybe Serge is trying to squeeze me until the money runs out, and then he'll show up to take it off my hands for pennies on the dollar. I'll admit these first three days on the Finn Family Farm have been anything but dull." Charlotte sighed.

"True, that," Beau agreed, and got down on the grass to nestle with Horse.

"Be careful of Mrs. Robinson," Charlotte warned. "She's sleeping behind his left ear."

"Thanks for the heads up."

Charlotte got lost in thought for a moment.

"I need to take control of my life and this murder investigation. It is one thing to sell the farm for a fair price to people who will appreciate it's beauty, and quite another to practically give it away to a shifty con man. I could never forgive myself. I think it would help if we went over some of the mysteries that we need to solve. I may be new to all this, but the farm has been loved and cared for by my family for generations. I am going to save this farm, and I'm not about to let anyone try to steal it from under my nose."

Diane sat up in her chair at Charlotte's suggestion and quietly applauded.

"Great. Diane, would you mind taking dictation on your phone, and I can start?" Charlotte volunteered. "Okay, just what do we think that Wade and Clark Avery are up to? They claim that there's a will stating that they should have inherited the farm."

"Right, but they haven't shown any proof over all these years. If they had anything, don't you think that they would have produced it by now?" Beau asked.

"I wonder where they got this harebrained idea in the first place?" Charlotte stared up at the stars. "It sounds like this rumor goes back a long time, because everyone seems to have heard about it."

"So do we ignore it and hope it goes away? It hasn't so far." Diane thought for a moment. "Or should we get ahead of it and find out if there is anything plausible in the Avery's premise?"

Charlotte nodded to Diane. "We can't ignore any clue, no matter how far-fetched it seems. Chief Goodacre is dealing with the evidence her department gathered from the crime scene, but we have the inside track, and I strongly suspect that the answer to solving this murder is right here in this house or out in the fields. The farm, I believe, brought the murder victim here, and when we can establish a connection to one of the suspects, then we'll have our murderer."

"I volunteer to do some genealogy research on that clan of miscreants. I'll let you know what I come up with," Beau said while playing with Horse's ear.

"Perfect—thanks, Beau. It may help put a rumor to bed, or it might just lead to more questions. But it seems to me that we have a long list of possible killers, and any evidence that will help winnow down the number would be greatly benefi-cial." Charlotte tapped her feet on the floor a couple of times. "You know, Joe and Samuel alternate nights doing a patrol of the farm in the hopes of catching whoever is vandalizing our property."

"They really care about this farm, don't they?" Beau said, primarily to Horse, who smiled and let out a happy sigh.

"Where are you going with this, Charlotte?" Diane had low-ered her voice, sensing that this was going into a touchy area.

"The night of the murder, it was Joe's turn to patrol. It just seems to me that with all that violence, he would have heard or seen something. I hate even saying this, but the Wongs could be looking for ways to protect their home. It's true that if I sell, I can't guarantee that they will be able to stay here." Charlotte bit her bottom lip.

Diane nodded. "True, and then there's Alice. Where was she the next morning when Lurvy showed up? And what is she always doing in the root cellar?"

"Alice and Joe know this farm inside out, perhaps even more than Samuel because they keep the books and can see our dire financial situation. In a way, they're the ones who have kept the place going for this long." Charlotte took in the last vermillion shades of the sunset. "They must have been disappointed, maybe even shocked that Uncle Tobias didn't leave at least part of the property to them."

"It would be only natural, and the Wongs must know where the bodies are buried, pun intended."

"Beau!" Diane and Charlotte exclaimed.

"What? It's the truth."

"Since I spend so much time in the kitchen with Alice, how about I try to get her to share some farm experiences with me and discretely ask her about this Marcus guy?" Diane offered. "I have always thought that she knows more than she lets on." Charlotte accepted the offer with a gentle squeeze of Diane's shoulder.

"I'll have to investigate the cellar. I haven't been down there yet." Charlotte reached down and gave Horse a little pet as well. "I'll wait until I know that she is going to be away for a couple of hours. We are just starting to become friendly after that bad start, and I don't want to do anything to jeopardize it." With one more pet, Horse left Beau and climbed up onto Charlotte's lap.

"Story of my life." Beau got up and returned to a chair. "And I'd like to know more about the elusive Samuel Brown. He seems to be very accomplished at managing the crops and keeping the farm in good working order. With those skills, how can he be satisfied working for someone else?"

"He did say that the financial part of this business wasn't his thing. Maybe that has scared him off?" Charlotte looked around to make sure that he wasn't lurking in the moonlight.

"He could get someone to manage that aspect. It sounds as if Joe would be an ideal candidate. He does walk around angry about something; maybe he resents being passed over as well," Beau pointed out.

"Are you saying that Samuel thinks he should have been the one to get Uncle Tobias's farm, Beau?" Charlotte asked.

"He's never said that to me in so many words, but he sure is perpetually cranky about something!"

"This is giving me a headache." Charlotte sighed again. "Let's not forget the aphids that I tripped over in the field. If that box hadn't been found when I fell, the produce could have been in real trouble."

"Let's put Mrs. Robinson on that one. She can get all the ladybugs that will be released tomorrow to spy for her." Beau laughed and Charlotte joined in as she studied the sleeping beauty on Horse's head.

"And there's the biggest question of all, of course."

Diane and Beau looked at Charlotte for clarification.

"Who killed Marcus Cordero? And why?" Charlotte almost shouted.

"Thank goodness, the lord made us pretty," Beau said scratching his head and slumping his shoulders.

"Then I suggest that we all get our beauty sleep. We want to look our best when we catch a murderer!"

* * *

Charlotte was awakened at dawn the next morning by the sounds of heavy machinery and trucks honking.

Has the farmhouse been condemned? The dead body was found in the field, not here.

When her head finally cleared from sleep, Charlotte remembered something about borrowing a backhoe for the lake pump, and quickly got dressed.

Horse had already gone to get breakfast, she assumed. When Charlotte looked out the French doors, she could see the heat vapors bouncing off the grass. Today was going to be a hot one. She could cover her arms and shoulders with her shirt, but she really needed something to cover her head and protect her face from the sun. She glanced over at the wrought iron rack where Uncle Tobias's favorite cowboy hat hung. It was made of straw that was once white but now was dirty with wear and sweat. A lighter colored ring at the base of the straw Stetson hinted that it had originally had an outer hat band. There was a darker area at the top front of the hat with a shredded bit of straw that marked a hole. Charlotte could just picture her uncle palming that exact area to tip his hat in respect each time he encountered a lady.

It looked like it would be too large on her, but Charlotte's red curls filled in the extra room. Something about the Stetson made it tilt to one side, but Charlotte didn't have time to futz with it now. She quickly headed out to see what all the noise was about and to let them know that she was in charge: she had the hat to prove it.

Charlotte arrived just in time to watch a small yellow back-hoe being backed down a ramp from a flatbed truck. The man driving it looked to be about fifty and appeared to be the owner of the machine. He'd brought along two young helpers. When the hoe had all four wheels on the ground, Joe approached Charlotte.

"That's Javier Espinoza, he owns a farm about eight miles from here. He and your uncle were friends. I think that he even worked for Tobias for a while," Joe explained as the farmer disembarked and walked toward her, smiling. He took off his hat when they were face-to-face, and by reflex Charlotte did the same.

Charlotte looked into the man's caramel-colored face, weathered from a life spent outside. When he smiled at her, his eyes squinted and a dimple appeared on his upper right cheek. It gave him an endearing, almost puppy-dog look.

"Joe tells me that you and my uncle were friends, which automatically makes you one of my favorite people. I'm Charlotte," she said warmly, extending her hand.

"Nice hat," Joe said, nodding at the Stetson she was holding. "It's my pleasure to be able to be of assistance. That's what farm friends do around here. I can't even count the number of times Tobias, Samuel, and Joe have helped us out of a jam. But we don't keep tabs; if someone needs something, we drop what we are doing and help. That's just our way."

"Everybody should have that attitude, Javier, and you know who to call if you need anything. We're going to be having a barbecue with the fire department, to fundraise so that we can get the lake filled. All our friends and neighbors can swim on hot days like today. We'll also offer it as a resource during fire emergencies. I'll let you know when it is. Please come and bring your family for an afternoon of fun!"

"Joe told me that was the plan. We'll all sleep a little easier knowing that we have water nearby. We barely survived the last big fire."

"Thank goodness you did," Charlotte said, seeing Samuel approach. "I'll let you all get to work, and be down with lemonade and snacks in about an hour."

"You sound just like your uncle, Miss Charlotte—always throwing parties and feeding people. It is so good to have you here." Javier placed his hand on his heart.

"It is good to be here." Charlotte smiled and looked again at Samuel, who actually broke into a half grin.

"And who knows? When the lake is filled, the kids might ask their moms to take them swimming at Finn Lake and after that go into the farm shop for treats and antiques!" Charlotte said, trying out the idea with the others for the first time.

"Sounds like a plan," Javier said, replacing his hat.

*   *   *

"Does this mean that I'm going to have to really get up with the roosters each morning?" Beau asked, wandering into the kitchen in pajamas printed with images of sheep with numbers on their sides. "I know that it's hard to believe, but I need my beauty sleep. Especially after last night's intense brain challenge."

"Sorry about the noise. Farmer Espinoza has brought his backhoe and some helpers to dig up the lake pump. We need to look at a calendar and set a date for the fundraiser. I'm excited!"

"Nice hat." Beau sat down at the counter. Diane had also been woken and was quietly making coffee. Charlotte knew from their long-time friendship never to speak to Diane in the early morning until she spoke first. She'd explained the rule once as trying to preserve that half-sleep, semi-awake state for as long as possible.

After coffee was poured, Diane grabbed a seat at the kitchen counter and woke up her phone. "When I talked to the fire chief, he said that this coming weekend or the one after were good dates for them. After that, they couldn't make it until a week after the fourth."

"This weekend is impossible—it's already Monday. But the following gives us a good two weeks to prepare. I guess I should say 'me.' I can't imagine Chief Goodacre forcing you both to stay much longer." Charlotte took a deep breath; she didn't like the idea of going it alone on this.

"We'll talk about everything over the phone, and we're closed Mondays, so I can come back up in a week." Diane patted Charlotte's back.

"And you have Alice. Diane says that she's great with picnic food. Plus, she must have helped your uncle with the parties he was always throwing."

"Good thought, Beau. I should ask her about her role in planning those," Charlotte said to him.

"Are you wearing that hat at a slant on purpose? I think that's more the trend with a French beret rather than a Stetson. Unless you're Frank Sinatra miscast in a Western." Beau giggled. "I did it the cowboy way," he crooned.

Charlotte took it off and peered inside. She soon found the cause for the lopsided deportment. The hat was lined with a leather sweatband that bulged on one side. The bottom part of the leather was sewn into the straw, but the top of the band was loose. She separated it from the inside of the hat and ran her fingers along behind it. When she hit the bulge, her fingers felt something hard with some heft. She closed her thumb and index fingers around it and pulled it out. It was a small key.

"Wow—I wonder what that opens." Charlotte thought for a moment.

Diane held her hand out for a closer look. "This was your uncle's, correct?"

"Refill your coffee, and follow me into his bedroom!"

Charlotte couldn't wait and raced off to the wooden box. Horse caught up with her in the foyer, and always up for a race, he tried to gain enough purchase on the sleek Mexican tiles to pick up speed. To his chagrin, this only served to splay him out on his belly. By the time he was upright again, he was able to follow Diane and Beau into the bedroom.

"I found this the first night I stayed here. It was buried under blankets in this hope chest." She held up the wooden box that was about the size of a small dresser drawer. "I've tried the key, and it fits but it won't turn," Charlotte continued with a frown.

"It can't be a coincidence that this hidden key works with the box. We need some sort of lubricant to free up the mechanism." Beau looked around the room for a candidate.

"I saw some orange oil under the sink in the kitchen. Would that work?" Diane asked while examining the lock.

"Sounds perfect, I'll go get it and be right back!" Beau scampered out of the room.

"It is so peaceful here. I don't miss Los Angeles at all," Diane mused.

"I'm not surprised. You always were the most spiritual and organic one among us. You like it here, don't you? Despite everything." Charlotte walked up next to Diane, who was staring out the window at the fields below.

"I do—don't you?" The wistful look in Diane's eyes was unmistakable.

"A turkey baster filled with orange oil—we are in business ladies." Beau was holding the baster by the bulb and was ready for action.

"Let's do this out back so nothing drips onto the wood floors." Charlotte carried the box through the French doors.

"Shoot some oil in, Beau, and I'll try wiggling the key," Charlotte directed.

It took several attempts before the lock mechanism had some give. Finally, the key turned and the box's lid popped open.

"It looks like there's a bunch of letters and old photos in here. I wonder why they had to be kept locked away." Diane peered over Charlotte's shoulder. "Maybe we should lay everything out on your bed—unless of course you'd rather look at the contents privately."

"Are you kidding, Diane? We keep no secrets from each other." Charlotte carried the box back into the room and tried not to be concerned that Diane hadn't immediately confirmed that she'd kept nothing from Charlotte.

The first photo that Charlotte picked up was of the woman with the dark hair that she'd remembered from her summer visit to the farm. She studied it for a few minutes, hoping some other memories would emerge, but her mind was blank. She turned the print over and read the inscription in her uncle's handwriting on the back:

Hera, summer '95.

She flipped the photo back, and this time focused on the space where Hera was standing when the photo was taken. It looked like some sort of country inn. Charlotte could make out a two-story white building with black shutters and part of a metal bracket with a sign hanging from it. She could only see a couple of letters: an "O" and on the line below, a "W."

"Um, maybe we shouldn't be reading these." Beau dropped a letter back on the bed.

"I agree," said Diane. "I realize now why they were kept under lock and key."

"Why?" Charlotte picked up a handwritten note.

"They are love letters, passionate love letters from your uncle Tobias's many girlfriends over the years," Diane explained softly, to prepare Charlotte.

"Dearest Tobias," Charlotte read, *"Your love and kindness is something that I never expected to find in my life. I was content as I was until I met you, such a generous lover. Yours, Marion"*

"Oh my," Beau said, using a letter to fan the flush that had come to his cheeks.

"After some more of these, there are a bunch that are addressed to this Hera woman, but returned unopened. How sad. I wonder what happened." Charlotte sat down on the bed and picked up an envelope.

"Are they all from the same year?" Diane asked, holding up a letter.

"The bulk seemed to have been sent in 1995, according to the postmarks," Charlotte replied. "Nothing later."

"Except for this one—it was sent about seven years ago. Brace yourself—it's a doozie." Beau sat down on the bed to read to the girls.

Dear Tobias,

By now you have certainly forgotten me and are living happily with several lady friends or perhaps even a wife. Enough time has passed, and I wanted to put your mind to rest about why I left.

You see, despite the growing affection that we had for each other, we were from completely different worlds. You are such a sophisticated and educated man; you love history and the arts.

You were my mentor and I looked up to you, but there came a point when we both needed to get on with our lives. Plus there are too many years between our ages.

Which is why I had to go away.

I know that when I first left, you tried to find me, but I returned all your letters. I have a happy life now, and I want to put your mind at rest that I made the right decision for myself and for my family. I wish you all the happiness in the world on your beautiful farm.

Hera

"Is there a return address on the envelope?" Charlotte asked.

Beau picked up the envelope. "Nope. Just a San Francisco postmark."

"What about the earlier letters?"

"No again," Diane told Charlotte.

"The letters that my uncle sent that were returned unopened—who were they addressed to?" Charlotte was talking fast. A thought was beginning to form in her mind.

"To Hera, care of the Olive and White Oak Inn."

"How sad. Despite the age difference, she may have been the love of his life. I wonder what made Hera just up and leave without telling my uncle? She must have married, since she mentioned a family."

"Well, at least we know what this Hera looks like." Charlotte rubbed her temples as she felt her head pound. She picked up the photo of Hera that had been in the box. "The 'O' and the

'W'—they must be part of a sign for the Olive and White Oak Inn here in town."

"I wonder if, after all this time, someone working at the Inn would remember Hera?" Beau pondered.

"It's definitely worth a call to find out." Diane stood, grabbing her phone. "At the very least we need to learn her last name."

"Okay, but please be discrete." Charlotte tensed up. "These letters were locked away because my uncle wanted to keep them private. It would serve no purpose to make his love life public, unless—"

"Unless what?" Diane stopped in mid-dial.

"Unless this somehow ties to the murder."

Beau slumped down on the bed. "What are you thinking, Char?"

"Nothing. That's the problem, I have this hunch, lurking deep down in my brain, that is just out of reach."

"Maybe the chief can help you retrieve it. She just drove up."

Chapter Nine

"I was just a kid in '95. I could barely remember my name and address at the time. And I didn't hang around your uncle's farm," the chief said, handing the photo of Hera back to Charlotte. "What is it about this woman? You think that she's somehow tied to the case?"

"I don't know, but they were close, and then she abruptly disappeared. It just seems odd." Charlotte handed Hera's final letter to the chief to read.

"What seems odd to me is why Hera chose to reach out to your uncle, what, seven years ago? It would appear that he stopped trying to find her many years before that. Why not just let sleeping dogs lie?" The chief looked at the photo again. "This mystery may just have to remain unsolved. At the moment I have no cause to try and track down this woman."

"You're probably right." Charlotte couldn't disguise her disappointment. "Was there something you needed when you came here today, Chief?"

"Yes. I'd like to get DNA samples from everyone on the farm for comparison purposes with the evidence that we've collected.

If this gives you pause, just remember that it could also take you off the suspect list."

"I understand. Whatever I can do to help you find the killer." Charlotte tried to sound bright about this, but her stomach had done a nosedive when the chief reminded her that she was a suspect.

"I'd also like to try and get a DNA sample for your uncle before any trace is obliterated. It might shed light on whether the murder victim had ever been in contact with him. Obviously, a cheek swab would be ideal, but not possible. Do you think that you could find a toothbrush of his still lying around?" Chief Goodacre was gentler with Charlotte this time, perhaps seeing that this part of the process was sensitive.

"No old toothbrush that I've seen, but he kept lots of hats. Maybe you'll be able to find a hair sample on one of them. Follow me." Charlotte was a bit unsteady on her feet. It had already been a very long morning. When they reached the bedroom suite, Charlotte handed the chief a hat off her uncle's rack, her hand visibly shaking.

"Why don't you call me Theresa when it's just the two of us? It certainly looks like we are going to be tied together for a while, and I want you to feel comfortable confiding in me."

Charlotte smiled but wondered to herself if this was nothing more than a police tactic. She watched Theresa use tweezers to retrieve a hair from inside a ball cap and hold it up to the light coming through the French doors.

"That looks like it was his. The color's the same," Charlotte offered.

"For this test to have any validity, I need a sample with the root attached, to test the DNA," the chief explained.

"If there's a match, what does it mean for the murder case?" Charlotte asked while checking a few other hats from the stand.

"First things first, Charlotte. Let's establish that your uncle and Marcus Cordero had met. This is going to take awhile without a strong sample, so I'll have to send the hairs out to a specialized lab."

"What if it shows that they have more than just met?" Charlotte said this so softly that the chief asked her to repeat it.

"You think that this guy was your uncle's illegitimate son? That's really a stretch."

"My uncle had lots of girlfriends; it is possible that he had a child and never knew about it. I don't like the word 'illegitimate.' If he'd known, he certainly would have done the right thing." Charlotte didn't try to hide her scorn.

"I'm sure you're right, but think about the consequences if he is proven to be your uncle's son. That would move you right up to the top of the suspect list." The chief was suddenly very serious.

Charlotte crossed her arms tightly around her waist.

"I wish that I'd never come here."

"Don't say that, Charlotte. This will get resolved, and if you're proven innocent, then hopefully you can get on with farm life." The chief handed her a saliva swab kit. "Just rub the wand along the inside of your cheek, and then replace it in the tube."

Charlotte did as she was told.

"You said that Marcus had been here about six months, according to the owners of the Humble Petting Zoo. You think that he made friends with someone during that time?"

"Entirely possible and all things that I need to check out. Say, how about you meet me at the Records Office tomorrow morning around ten, and we can look into your family and find out who's related to whom. Maybe shut Wade and Clark up once and for all."

"You don't have to do that for me." Charlotte gave her a half smile.

"I'll have to do it anyway because my deputies need to be out on patrol."

"No matter what the outcome, just doing something to work toward solving this makes me feel better. Thanks, Theresa."

And I better watch what I say, since I'm on the top of her suspect list. Theresa doesn't miss a trick.

On the way out, they ran into Samuel.

"I hear that you're restoring Finn Lake, Samuel. That's a big undertaking from what I see, but all of Little Acorn will be grateful. Let me know if you need me to grease any skids."

"I appreciate that, Chief. I just might. Is this a social visit, or is there news on the murder?" Samuel asked while rinsing off his boots. He used the same hose that Beau had used to rinse the dye out of Chief Goodacre's hair a couple of days ago.

"No news yet, but lots of questions. I've left some kits to collect DNA from everyone. You don't have to provide a sample, but it would sure help me narrow down the list of suspects. You can bring along the labeled samples when I see you in the morning, Charlotte."

"How's the pump for the lake looking?" Charlotte asked Samuel as the chief drove away.

"It's got to be replaced, along with a bunch of pipe." Samuel finished cleaning his boots and walked into the sun to let them dry a bit. He sat down on a tree log and patted the spot next to him.

Charlotte remained standing. She was too shaken up for chitchat on a sunny afternoon.

Samuel squinted. He was clearly taken aback and a little embarrassed that his invitation had been declined.

Charlotte noticed a cement and stone outcropping from the side of the house, with wooden and iron-braced doors attached at about a forty-degree angle.

"Does that lead to the cellar?" she asked Samuel.

"Yes, but you're better off going down there from the door inside the house. We keep this side locked at all times. You'd be amazed how enterprising the raccoons can be. We learned the hard way when they ransacked Alice's apricot jams one summer."

"Wow, something else to learn about life on a farm."

* * *

The minute Charlotte entered the foyer, she knew that it was too hot to remain inside, even with the ceiling fans going. Horse seemed to understand and tugged on her sneaker lace, signaling her to follow his lead. He was headed to the paddock, and Charlotte followed along, just happy to have her mind occupied on something fun.

When Horse arrived at the paddock, Charlotte reached out to open the gate, but the little pig gave a squeal. He continued trotting around the far side of the rails until he reached an over-turned metal bucket. Then he looked up at her and grinned.

"You are a happy little thing, aren't you, Horse?" Charlotte bent down to scratch his ears. He dipped his head back and closed his eyes for a moment.

"Aw, you like that." Charlotte giggled.

Just then he opened his eyes and dug one hoof into the dirt and flipped the bucket over, revealing a dug-out tunnel from the inside of the paddock out.

"You sneaky creature! So this is how you used to get out at night before I gave you unlimited access to the farmhouse."

Horse made what sounded like a giggle. His long eyelashes glimmered in the sun, and his upturned nose seemed to be in constant detection mode. The light behind him made his pointed, upright ears look translucent, and coupled with the turned-up corners of his mouth, he reminded her of an impish, fluffy elf.

"So, what did you do during your late-night escapades, Horse? Can you show me?" That earned Charlotte another smile from the pig, and before they left, she replaced the bucket over the hole.

"This will be our secret," she said to him.

Charlotte had to work to keep up with Horse; his excitement had sent his short legs into overtime. They raced all the way along a path until they reached the apple orchard at the end of the farm's property line. When they got to the trees, he continued on, but at a much slower pace. To one side of the orchards was a clearing that was covered with grass, except where there was a small pond.

"Oh wow, what is this beautiful sanctuary?" Charlotte asked him.

Horse tugged her toward a wooden structure that was built low to the ground and was about the size of a small tool shed, only it wasn't more than three feet high. Charlotte carefully knelt down to one side of the open area that must serve as the entrance.

"Who's in here, Horse?"

Horse looked in and then tiptoed up the ramp and into the structure. Charlotte stood up prepared to run if whatever came out with Horse wasn't human friendly. A moment later, the pig stuck just his head out of the opening and moved it side to side, looking for Charlotte.

"Up here, Horse. I couldn't squat any longer."

Great—now I'm lying to a pig.

Horse looked back in over his shoulder and then back at Charlotte. He slowly trotted down the ramp, his head held high with pride. Behind him, marching in single file, came baby birds with yellow heads and chests and tan backs. Their feathers resembled the soft fuzz on a mohair sweater and stuck out in all directions.

Once Horse reached the ground, he continued on to a lush portion of the grassy area. Charlotte counted eight goslings before the mother goose appeared out of the shelter. When they reached Horse, they got busy eating the grass.

"My oh my, how am I going to name you all?" Charlotte lay down on the lawn and placed some grass blades in her palm. At once, at least six of them raced over to her. "And mama, you must be so proud of your brood!" Charlotte turned her attention to the goose. "I hereby christen you Mumsy."

Horse jumped with glee.

"And now, you eight." Charlotte surveyed the scrambling little balls of fluff. "What comes with eight things or parts? A spider, but I can't name you each leg. No, it needs to be something more special. Something drawn from your environment." While Charlotte thought, Horse watched on expectantly.

"I've got it! If only I can remember them all. Let's see, in V8 juice you have—Beets." she pointed to one gosling. "Celery," she continued, pointing as she named them, "Lettuce, Carrots, Parsley, Tomato, Spinach, and Watercress. I'm not even going to try and remember who's who, so I hope you all were listening."

Charlotte stood and took in a deep breath of the fresh air. She was definitely feeling better. The farm had a way of doing that to her.

"Shall we go and see what everyone else is up to, Horse?"

He squealed a farewell to the birds and started running up the hill. Charlotte was about to follow him when she noticed that one of her shoelaces was untied from Horse's tugging at it. She sat down on a log to lace up her sneaker.

Ping. She heard the sound of a stone making contact with a horseshoe propped up against a tree.

Plop. This time a stone landed about six inches from her shoe. She looked around, trying to find the thrower. The geese had gone back into their hut, and when she looked up into the trees around her, all she saw were apples.

"Over here."

Charlotte followed the sound of the male voice all the way to the barbed wire fencing that signaled the end of the Finn farm's property and the beginning of another's. She still wasn't able to spot the culprit until suddenly a man walked into the clearing past the tree. He was carrying a shotgun in his inside elbow crease, and to Charlotte's relief, the barrel was separated from the body of the weapon, which meant that it wasn't loaded. When her gaze moved up to the man's face, she recognized that it belonged to Wade Avery. Suddenly that shotgun didn't seem so harmless in his hands.

"Hey there, Miss Charlotte. I see that you've almost got this farming business down pat, what with naming the baby geese and all. I'll remember the name of the one that'll be on my table at Thanksgiving."

"You're an animal," Charlotte responded, quickly tying her shoe.

"I've been called much worse. I'm just warning you that around here we don't like trespassing, and I've been given strict orders by the man that owns this property to shoot first and ask questions later."

Charlotte eyed a stepladder that was about the height of the fence, leaning against one of the posts on Wade's side. Charlotte stood.

"That goes both ways, Wade. We know that you've been messing with our irrigation and using other ways to try and sabotage our crops."

"I'm crushed that you think I would do anything like that to you. Here I was hoping that we'd become good friends." Wade clutched his heart, feigning emotional hurt. "Oh, and those stones? I just wanted to show you what great aim I have." He loaded two shells into the barrels of his shotgun and swung it shut.

"I suggest that your time would be better spent gathering alibis rather than rocks. New evidence in the murder just came to light, and Chief Goodacre sees a big, bright neon sign pointing to you as having means, motive, and opportunity."

"Really? And I heard that you're just as good as locked up for life soon as those DNA results come back." Wade gave her an evil grin.

"The pendulum swings both ways, Wade. I bet that you're already in the chief's database, given what I've heard." Charlotte didn't wait to see what would happen next and swiftly walked off to find Horse. When she was sufficiently hidden from him by the orchard, she broke into a run.

*　*　*

Charlotte tracked down Horse in the field above the Wong's house, where Alice was methodically releasing ladybugs into the field. When Charlotte reached them, she was out of breath from racing up the hill.

"You really should try and do your exercise in the early morning, Miss Charlotte; this afternoon sun is brutal. Want me to get you some iced tea?" Alice asked.

Charlotte shook her head, but it took another moment before she could speak. During that time, Alice opened a folding chair and set it under a makeshift tent that had been strung up between field posts, using a piece of muslin cloth. She set up a second chair for herself and motioned for Charlotte to join her.

Charlotte sat and recounted her episode with Wade.

"Too bad you didn't catch him in the act of vandalizing our equipment. I'll let Joe know about this and where you saw him. Maybe he can put up some kind of surveillance or trap for the next time he comes over the fence.

Horse stood right by Charlotte's side with a concerned look on his face. She noticed that Mrs. Robinson wasn't perched on his head. Charlotte looked over the rest of his body for her.

"Looking for Mrs. Robinson, the ladybug?" Alice asked smiling.

Charlotte nodded, surprised that Alice was using her name.

"She's overseeing the newcomers. Come here and take a look—it is really quite a miracle of nature."

Sure enough, as the newly released ladybugs where getting acclimated with their new home and aphid buffet on a leaf above them, Charlotte recognized Mrs. Robinson and her one distinctive yellow spot. She was perched on wooden stake, watching the ladybugs move out of the box and into the field.

Charlotte hoped that no one who loved nature as much as Alice could be a killer. "Well done, Mrs. Robinson. I hereby appoint you Assistant Farmer, Aphid Division."

Charlotte could swear that she saw a smile on the ladybug's face.

Chapter Ten

At precisely ten the next morning, Charlotte was waiting outside the Records building in Little Acorn for Chief Goodacre. She supposed that she could have waited inside, but this gave her a chance to observe the locals, both for friends and possible suspects.

"Good morning," said a man in his early thirties, walking with twin boys that looked to be four or five. "We're looking forward to your"—he paused for a moment and looked at a piece of paper he was holding—"bodacious barbecue." He laughed. "The boys and I have never seen a dancing pig."

She watched them walk by and head into the barber shop, but not without protests from his sons.

What has Beau promised on that flyer?

Charlotte looked around for a spot where he and Diane might have left some fliers. It didn't take her long to spot a pile sitting atop the giant vinyl cone outside the Little Acorn Ice Cream Shoppe. She reached for one of the fuchsia-pink pages just as a woman in sweats did the same.

"My one morning to myself: first dance class and then a frozen yogurt," she explained, eying the flyer. "This sounds fun. I'm Margie—count my family in!" Charlotte smiled, but by the time she'd extended her hand, Margie had already gone in to get her post-exercise treat.

Charlotte retreated to the Records building, almost afraid to open the flier. When she did, she gasped.

You Wouldn't Want To Miss This Bodacious Barbecue Bonanza!!

We're grillin' up burgers, dogs, and veggies. There'll be corn, chips, and all the fixin's!

And don't forget the watermelon juice! Lip-smackin'!

The Little Acorn Firehouse will be out giving all kinds of amazing, fiery demos.

And here's a secret—but don't tell!! You'll also meet a dancing pig, goats doing ballet, and the **Finn Family Farm All-Animal Choir.**

Help us restore our lake for your swimming enjoyment and for safety during wildfires.

"Oh no."

"What now?" Charlotte heard the chief ask. She hadn't realized that she'd groaned aloud.

"Have you seen this?" Charlotte held up the flier.

"I sure have. Great piece of work—you'll have the entire town attending. Good job."

Chief Goodacre held the door for Charlotte, and they entered the Records Office.

"I just hope that Beau, with his zealous nature, didn't over-promise."

"Beau's in charge of this? Then what are you worrying about? It will be fantastic, and I bet you'll make plenty in donations to finish and reopen that lake. A lot of the people around here remember fondly your uncle's parties, even if they were kids at the time."

"Thanks, Chief, that's nice to hear."

"You may call me Theresa today." She smiled at Charlotte and walked up to the front desk. "Morning, Eleanor. You have all the files I requested set up in the conference room?"

"Sure do, Chief, and there's a thermos of fresh coffee waiting for you as well."

Eleanor smiled at Charlotte.

"You're a peach, which reminds me I owe you some of my peach cobbler. I'll bring it by this afternoon." Theresa led Charlotte down the hall and into the room, where three large boxes of files were sitting on the table.

"Wow, is all this about my family and the farm?"

"Don't be intimidated by this. I asked for everything that I could think of, so I'm sure that there's overkill here. Coffee?"

Charlotte shook her head and glanced at the tabs on some of the folders. So many had names on them that she didn't recognize.

"Do you think that you would be able to draw your family tree, Charlotte? At least on your father's side? We'd need to go back to your great-grandparents." Theresa handed her a legal pad and paper. "Start at the bottom with yourself, and work back in the Finn Family tree."

This was the easy part, as Charlotte was an only child, as was her father.

"I know that Tobias was my grandfather's brother, so he was my great-uncle. I vaguely remember hearing that there was a third sibling, but for some reason nobody ever talked about it."

"Okay, good—let's see if we can track him or her down." Theresa reached for one of the boxes and leafed through the folders. "The goal is to discover who all could have stood to inherit the farm. That's step one, next we'll need to try and find a connection to Marcus Cordero's murder. If there is one. The motive could be something entirely different."

Charlotte once again felt the weight of a huge target on her back. It was looking like this case would never be solved. Or worse yet, it would be pinned on her.

"Here, open this one and place the papers in order of oldest to youngest at this end of the table." Theresa handed Charlotte the folder and then resumed digging through the box.

"Oh, and preliminary analysis from the coroner is that Marcus Cordero was killed by the pitchfork severing both his carotid artery and his jugular vein. Someone didn't just want him out of the way but wanted to exact revenge." Theresa went back to the boxes.

Charlotte shivered on hearing this. She looked at the files and saw that she'd been given the birth certificates for Annabel, Wade, and Clark, and this list was the birth order.

"So, Annabel's the oldest. That explains a little why she thinks she's better than her brothers. But what do they have to do with me? I'd never heard of or met them before coming here."

"The Avery boys—actually, Wade—has been going around town saying that there's a will that precedes your uncle Tobias's will. If we can prove that they're somehow related to the Finns and might have been eligible to inherit even a small portion of the farm, then you look a lot less like a killer, and they look a heck of a lot more guilty."

"What would that have to do with poor Marcus?" Charlotte asked, rubbing her temples. She felt a headache coming on.

"If your theory is correct that Marcus is Tobias's biological son, then he could possibly have had a claim to the farm as well. Like I said, that points the finger strongly at you, but as you've seen, there are very few secrets in Little Acorn. If the Avery boys lied and they in fact knew Marcus, then they could have wanted him out of the picture to lay claim to the farm."

"That's a lot of 'ifs,' and I don't want to even entertain the idea of being related to Wade." Charlotte couldn't help her exasperation.

"Relax, Toots. If it's true, it still wouldn't mean that you have to spend the holidays together. If we're lucky and the pieces fall into place, the brothers Avery will be celebrating Thanksgiving with pressed turkey eaten off a tin tray."

Charlotte thought back to Wade's comment about eating goose, and her stomach turned sour.

*   *   *

An hour later they had filled in some of the blanks but still didn't have many answers. They found the marriage certificate for Wade and his siblings' parents, Thomas and Lucy Avery. Her maiden name had been Ursin. Thomas's family came from Canada, but there was no point in following that trail as he was clearly not a Finn. As for their mother, Lucy, Charlotte found it odd that the paper trail just stopped—or didn't exist. There were the birth certificates for the three Avery children that Charlotte had just sorted through, but nothing about their maternal grandparents. Charlotte pointed this out to Theresa.

"It is odd. I was just a kid, but I remember the Avery parents. They kept to themselves. Thomas never saved enough to be able to buy his own farm, and they struggled with money. When he got sick of working other people's crops, he and his wife, Lucy, moved to Vancouver, where land was affordable. He had family there, so they could start a small dairy farm.

"The kids stayed behind. Wade and Clark had steady pay-checks working other people's farms, and they still live in their childhood home. Their sister, Annabel, was set to marry Serge and he had already bought a cottage for them in anticipation. She moved in, but the engagement was suddenly called off with no explanation. Serge kept paying her room and board, and they eventually married about ten years later."

"What a sad story all the way around." Charlotte sighed. "Do the parents ever come back to Little Acorn to visit their kids?"

Theresa shook her head. "I was definitely old enough to feel the impact when word came out that they'd been killed by a drunk driver, coming home one night from seeing a movie."

"Good god, no wonder the boys are so angry," Charlotte said. Theresa's phone rang.

"I need some air," Charlotte said, and left her to her call.

* * *

She stepped outside and stood under the shade of a bottlebrush tree. All this talk about family made Charlotte feel homesick for her own parents, and she decided to give them a call. Her dad picked up, and she filled him in about the farm and casually mentioned the possibility of having family in Little Acorn. She told him about rumors of an earlier will, leaving out any mention of murder.

No need to worry them unnecessarily.

"Honey, your great-uncle Tobias left the farm specifically to you because of the wonderful summer you'd spent there with him. That should throw out any question of heirs or birthright. But I too had heard that grandpa and Tobias had a third brother, so if you'll hold a minute, I'll go into my office and dig out an ancient file folder."

"Sure, Dad." Charlotte used the time to make a mental list of all the shops she wanted to visit before returning to the farmhouse. When she zeroed in on the Wine Tasting Room, she saw two figures standing inside the door, engaged in a passionate embrace. This was no cursory "goodbye" peck. The sign on the door was turned to the "Closed" side. Charlotte assumed that they didn't open before noon. She smiled; love was in the air in Little Acorn. Her dad came back on the line and started giving her the dark side of her family history. She pulled out Beau's flier and made some notes on the back as her father spoke.

The door to the wine tasting shop opened, and the man that had been involved in that love fest stepped out. He bent in for one more peck on the lips and then turned to leave. That was when Charlotte recognized him. He was none other than Serge Andersen. Then the woman stuck her head out the door for a "goodbye" wave, and Charlotte saw that she was not his wife, Annabel. So in addition to being slimy, Serge was also a cheater.

Why am I not surprised?

"You look like you've seen a ghost," Theresa said, poking her head out.

Charlotte returned to the conference room.

"What's up?"

"Nothing scary, just interesting. I called home and asked my dad about my family. It's what I witnessed going on across the street that's the shocker." Charlotte sat down with a thump and relayed what she had just witnessed.

"Ah, Little Acorn gossip. There's plenty of that going on. Let's finish up here; I've got a staff meeting shortly."

"Okay, my great-grandparents did have a third son, named Henry," Charlotte explained, consulting her notes. "According to my dad, he was the black sheep, and his parents seldom spoke about him. My dad only met him once, at my grandparents' funeral, and from then on the story was that he'd gone away and would never return. Dad thinks that he had a daughter, but couldn't confirm her name."

"Gone where? Did your dad say?"

"He's going to do some more digging, but he found a newspaper article, tucked in a photo album, saying that Henry Finn had been convicted of murder and sentenced to life in prison. The paper was from Sacramento, so I assume he was incarcerated somewhere around there."

"Give me the year and date of the article, and I can check for confirmation and current status."

Charlotte's cell phone pinged.

"I'll text you the article—my dad just sent it to me."

Moments later, Theresa looked at her phone. "So Henry Finn was caught trying to rob a bank near San Jose. He shot the manager after he activated the alarm. The poor soul later died from his injuries. I'm forwarding this to my officer, Maria. She'll contact San Jose PD and get the skinny. It will take a lot more digging to be able to connect any Averys to your great-uncle Henry. Oh, and I see no reason to hold Diane and Beau in Little Acorn any longer; they're clearly not a flight risk. If there's a DNA match to either of them, that's another story, but it doesn't seem likely. You've got some good friends there, Charlotte."

"It looks like I'm going to need them." Charlotte sighed as she felt the constricting threats to her future livelihood and happiness grow.

*   *   *

"You sure that you don't want to wait until morning?" Charlotte watched from a porch swing as Beau loaded their bags into the car. "It will be dark in a couple of hours."

"We'll be back in L.A. by then and besides, last I checked, they make these things with lights now." Beau smiled and kicked the front tire of Diane's car.

"I've left a few things in the bedroom dresser. I know that I'll be back next weekend, if not before." Diane motioned for Charlotte to scoot over on the swing so she could sit.

"I'm being selfish. Of course you need to get back to your lives." Charlotte tried to hide her apprehension.

"Listen, it's totally understandable that you'd be rattled finding out that you had a great-uncle who was a murderer, but it's more than likely that he's gone to hell by now. Your Uncle Tobias was ninety-two when he passed. I doubt that Uncle Henry reached that milestone. I don't think that prison is conducive to living to a ripe old age." Beau gave a consoling smile to Charlotte from the porch steps.

"The chief doesn't let any grass grow under her. I'll bet she'll have the whole story before you wake up tomorrow." Diane reached for Charlotte's hand.

"I doubt that it will be much comfort, I'm already disgusted that I share even a thread of a bloodline with the Avery kids. And now I'm going to have to address Wade's claims that my great-grandfather had a will that stipulated that with his passing that the farm was to be split between his sons Tobias *and* Henry."

"First the problem, then the solution, Charlotte. The onus is on them to produce the document and then have it authenticated." Diane always seemed to know the practicalities. "And it doesn't sound like Annabel cares one ounce about farming. From what Alice says, all she talks about is moving to San Francisco for a better life in the big city. She says that Serge's distributorship is doing great."

"Oh my god, I almost forgot!" Charlotte jumped up from the swing, sending Diane into a vigorous pendulum.

"What?" Beau asked, and Horse came racing from around the back of the house.

Charlotte told them about the not-so-clandestine tryst that she had witnessed this morning between Serge and another woman.

"Theresa—I mean the chief—says that this is nothing new. Apparently that guy's made an attempt on every woman in town.

She warned me that I might be next. That was the only good news that I had all day. I'm going to go to sleep tonight dreaming about the evil ways that I'll return his advances." Charlotte picked up Horse for comfort.

"I've seen that Irish redheaded temper in action. Serge will be lucky if he comes away still being able to eat solid food," Beau said, and all three of them laughed.

"You should clue Samuel in on the latest events. He's been moping around, and he deserves to know. Especially when it concerns his future as well," said Diane.

"And I have news about Samuel that the chief told me as she walked me out of the station." Beau and Diane quickly huddled around Charlotte.

"Do tell!" Beau said, touching his fingertips of his right hand with those on the other hand.

"Wade is a couple of years older than Samuel, but they went to the same school. As did the chief. The story is that Samuel was a track star, so much so that as a freshman they let him race with the seniors. Wade was always ragging on Samuel, so the race gave him the opportunity to show up Wade in front of the entire student body."

"I love this story already," Diane interrupted.

"The race was a thousand five hundred meters, and they started out staggered. After the turn, the lanes opened, and Samuel was able to easily pass two of the runners. Wade had gotten a fast start and was way up ahead, still pushing hard. There was no way that he was going to make it to the finish first at that pace. Sure enough, Wade started slowing down, and he yelled something to Samuel as he closed in on him. Samuel got alongside of

Wade and looked over and smiled at him. Then Samuel waved goodbye to him. The chief was sitting close enough to witness the entire exchange. Wade's stare turned to rage, and suddenly Samuel was airborne and ended up landing on the side of his foot, breaking his ankle and tearing lots of ligaments."

"Oh god, Wade tripped Samuel, didn't he?" Beau had now moved both hands over his mouth.

Charlotte nodded. "That's why he walks with a limp. His ankle was never set properly because treatment was delayed while Wade basked in the glory of winning the race."

"Poor, poor Samuel. No wonder he mopes. I wish that I could stay and cheer you and Samuel up." Diane got a bit teary.

"We'll be back before you've even had a chance to miss us," Beau said, moving in for a group hug.

"Call me anytime, day or night—I mean it," Diane said getting into the car.

"Drive safe." Charlotte watched them drive off and sat back down on the porch swing.

"It's you and me now, Horse. We got this, right?"

Horse hopped down, looked at Charlotte, and let out a very manly grunt.

Charlotte smiled at him even though she was feeling more out of control and afraid than she ever had in her life.

Chapter Eleven

After breakfast the next morning, Charlotte vowed to get the farmhouse organized and then work on advertising the "you pick 'em" concept. She'd found some tags with strings in one of the kitchen all-purpose drawers and went room to room, tagging and pricing the items that she wanted moved to the carport/antique store/jams and jellies store.

She'd learned her lesson from the Stetson and made sure to check every nook and cranny of each piece that she was selling, in case there were any more hidden clues to family secrets. Apart from a few coins, an old pipe, and some seed packets, she found nothing of significance. Which was actually a blessing; she'd been deathly afraid of uncovering an ancient will that would require wrestling with her conscience.

After the last tag, Charlotte wandered over to the carport to check on the renovation progress. She found Joe inside, cutting shelves with a table saw.

"Morning!" Charlotte greeted him. "Want me to fetch you a cup of coffee?" she kindly asked.

"I'm good, but thank you, Miss Charlotte. I don't think that too much caffeine and an electric saw are a wise combination."

"Good point, Joe. This is coming along nicely." Charlotte scanned the four walls of her new shop. A wooden floor had been installed to correct for the uneven ground and give the place a more structured feel. "I have several rugs that I wanted to sell. We should lay them out to warm up the flooring."

"No problem. As soon as I finish sawing and the dust settles, we can move items in, and you can tell us how you want them displayed. Samuel's waiting for the water pump parts to come in, so your timing is perfect. I should be done here by end of day tomorrow."

She noted that Joe strove to always deliver good news to her. "That's exciting—I can't wait. I'll be sure to let Alice know that we'll be able to sell her jams by the weekend."

Charlotte walked around a bit and could visualize the place filled with fun things tucked into every corner; some old-time candy for the kids; a section for lamps of all shapes and sizes; racks of old, fancy clothes and hats; and a food mart filled with the season's best. She closed her eyes and smiled. And then she remembered Marcus and the murder—cold reality snapped her out of her reverie.

"Joe, can you take a break for a minute? There are some things that I want to fill you in on."

She watched him take in a deep breath as he wiped his hands on a rag.

"What can I do for you, Miss Charlotte?"

She explained about the possible relationship with the Avery family, Marcus Cordero's possible link to Tobias, and finally the claim by Wade that a will existed from their great-grandfather. When she finished, Joe took a bandana out of his pocket and wiped his brow.

"Wow, that's a lot for you to be carrying on your shoulders. Alice and I will do everything that we can to help you. I only knew your great-uncle for about eight years, but I can promise you that none of this ever came up. Wade and Clark may have yapped about an inheritance in town, but I certainly never saw or heard them make any claims directly to Tobias. So, they are either cowards or lying or both."

"I hope that you're right." Charlotte sighed.

"And as for the woman, Hera, all of that must have occurred before we moved into the caretaker's house. As best I recollect, your uncle had lots of lady admirers, but no one that special."

"Thank you, Joe, this has all been helpful. I just want to put all the bad parts of the farm behind me so that we can move forward, making this a success and a destination for families all over Southern California to visit."

"Does that mean that you intend to stay on and keep the farm?" Joe gave her a hopeful, raised-eyebrow look.

"It might, Joe, it just might." Charlotte pursed her lips and nodded at her own realization.

Joe seems so sincere and kind. I hope that's not a front to hide that he's a killer. But sometimes it's the person that you'd least suspect . . .

Charlotte next went to check on progress at the lake. Horse trotted along happily, and Charlotte was pleased to see that Mrs. Robinson was back on her perch beside his ear. She wondered if the ladybug flew to find Horse or if he came to her. The animals on this farm had their own special communication system that she might never be able to decipher. But Charlotte knew one thing for sure: if she could get them to talk, then she would probably know who killed Marcus Cordero.

When she arrived at the edge of the dug-out basin, she saw that one of farmer Javier Espinoza's assistants was managing a group of day laborers who were repairing places in the lake where the lining and concrete had been torn. She waved and approached him.

"Hi, miss, I remember you from the other day. My name's Hector."

"Hello, Hector. Thank you for helping out again, and please let Javier know how much I appreciate the assistance. I'll come back with pitchers of lemonade shortly. Is there a lot of work still to be completed?" she asked him, and he studied the basin. She guessed that he was about sixty, but it was so hard to gauge with people who have spent their lives doing manual labor out in the elements.

"No, this part is fairly easy. The test comes when we put the new pump in." Hector whistled to a couple of men who had stopped cutting vinyl and were engaged in animated conversation.

"We'll break in thirty minutes. For now, let's get this whole section done," he hollered to them, and they nodded back.

"I spent one summer here when I was a girl," Charlotte told him. "I remember my uncle explaining that the water reflected the bright blue of the sky. He loved to sit on that dock when it was in good condition and watch the kids swim. We always wanted to impress him, so we'd do flips and have chicken fights."

"I remember, your uncle was always so generous in letting everybody cool off in the lake. I'd bring my kids, and we'd make a day of it. Have a picnic lunch and everything."

"Oh, so you remember my uncle sitting in his Adirondack chair, being a lifeguard?"

Hector nodded and smiled.

This gave Charlotte an idea.

"Then you must remember his friend, Hera?"

"Who doesn't? She was the most beautiful lady in Little Acorn, and your great-uncle saw what an open mind she had and wanted to teach her everything. Whenever I saw them walking, I'd hear him telling her the names of the trees and plants and the history of the area." Hector hung his head recollecting.

Just like I remember him doing with me.

"She was always happy to learn from your great-uncle, but then unfortunately the people in town started to talk. Little Acorn is not short on gossip. She would never have wanted to hurt Tobias."

"Do you know what happened to her?" Charlotte asked.

"One day she was gone. Nobody knew where or why."

Hector looked at his watch and blew a different-sounding whistle, using two of his fingers. It was break time.

"I'll go get the lemonade," Charlotte said, suddenly flustered and overcome with sadness.

* * *

That afternoon Charlotte headed to the hardware store to get the supplies she needed to make the "you-pick-'em" road signs. She hoped that they'd have everything ready by the fundraiser so she could promote the concept of the barbecue to the crowd there.

On her way into town, the usually empty road up ahead was full of cars that were not moving. When she reached the last stopped car, Charlotte cut her engine and got out. She walked up to the woman in the minivan in front of her.

"What's going on? I hope that there hasn't been an accident." Charlotte stood on her tiptoes, trying to see up ahead.

"No, nothing so serious, although I sure wish that the cops would put a stop to these guys being allowed to ride in the road and show off."

"Who are they?" Charlotte asked.

"They are the poor man's version of the Rancheros Visitadores."

When Charlotte gave the woman a blank look, she explained further.

"Los Rancheros are a group of wealthy white men on horseback, basically. The tradition started in the 1930s with a ride to honor the ranching life. They do this once a year and trek through the Santa Ynez Valley. There have been all sorts of rumors about what goes on during these rides without their wives, if you get my drift. But the real rancheros have money, and they usually do something for a good cause."

Charlotte walked around to the side of the road so that she could see past the cars. She saw the men on their horses, marching along in a sloppy formation. They wore cowboy hats of all shapes and sizes, and the same went for their blue jeans. The only common and oddly incongruous part of their attire was that they were all sporting Hawaiian shirts.

There must have been a close-out at J.C. Penney's.

"In Little Acorn," the woman continued, "we don't have a lot of rich men. Believe me, I tried to find one, but we have guys who think that they are ranchers and horsemen. They do their own ride, parading through town for a few days like they're all that. You hear that howl?"

Charlotte nodded.

"That's got to be Wade Avery. He thinks that he and his horse can walk on water. He is the original 'big hat, no cattle' kind of loser. Sorry for being so blunt."

"You're just being honest. I've met Wade Avery."

"There you go then. It looks like they've cleared these horse's arses, and we're moving again. I've got to pick up my kids. Take care."

"You too—thanks for the history lesson. Little Acorn is certainly more than it seems to be if you are just driving through." Charlotte waved and walked back to her car.

"You don't know the half of it," the woman shouted back and drove off.

That's what Charlotte was afraid of.

When she reached the hardware store a few minutes later, she saw the Farm's truck parked in the lot.

I wish that I'd known that either Joe or Samuel planned to come here—they could have saved me a trip.

Little Acorn Hardware was nothing like the big box stores she remembered from the rare times that she'd frequented one. This was like something straight out of *The Wonder Years*. Aisles were narrow, with shelves on each side built all the way to the ceiling. A library ladder ran along the stacks, but access was denied by a sign strung across the handrails that read "Please ask for assistance."

There seemed to be a system for how the store was organized, if going by the local shoppers was any indication. They strode with purpose to the items they needed. Charlotte turned the corner and realized that she was in plumbing supplies and ran smack into Samuel.

"You know, if you're having an issue with one of the farmhouse's showers or toilets, you just need to let me know, and I'll fix it. I must be in this place at least twice a week." He smiled at her, and she tried to decide if he was joking. Samuel had a striking habit of turning from nice to somber in a split second.

"I'm actually looking for supplies to make a few signs to advertise the new You Pick 'Em." Charlotte tried to sound businesslike about this new venture. She wanted Samuel to take it seriously.

"I can make you the sign frames. Follow me and I'll lead you to the paint department." Samuel marched on without waiting for a response from Charlotte.

He sure has some odd social skills.

"Does this mean that you've finished 'processing'"—Samuel drew air quotes—"whatever you and the chief discovered? The farm can get back to life as usual?"

"Hardly, and I've been meaning to fill you in, but not in a public place. I keep discovering just how much this town is a breeding ground for gossip." Charlotte looked around her for listening ears and prying eyes.

"That makes you one step closer to being a respected resident of Little Acorn. Knowing when to talk and when to keep silent." Samuel watched Charlotte choose some small paint containers, a few spray cans, and a stencil. A set of eight brushes completed her errand.

"Let's settle this, and then we can talk in my truck. I'll even treat you to a root beer." Samuel reached into a standing cooler and pulled out two old-fashioned soda bottles.

"What a sport. How is it that you're still single, Samuel?" They both grinned to themselves.

When Samuel had finished loading the last of the supplies onto the flatbed, he hopped into the driver's seat of the cab where Charlotte was waiting.

"I wish I'd known that you were making a hardware run today. It would have spared me from being stuck in traffic while blowhard Ward Avery and his band of sycophants rode through town for their annual horse parade," Charlotte groused, remembering his hollering.

"It's that time of year again, isn't it?" Samuel shook his head and stared out the window in silence for a moment. "Just so you know, Wade's an equal opportunity a-hole. He's been a thorn in my side ever since I was a kid."

"I heard about what he did to you in that race in high school. The chief told me. What a rotten thing to do. He should have been arrested."

Samuel stared at her with a look of surprise.

"What? Weren't you just saying that the town gossip was practically a tourist attraction?"

"Yes, but that was so long ago, I'm surprised that people still talk about it. Is that why the chief came by to talk to you? Am I a suspect now?"

Here comes the sudden mood swing. Why would he think he's a suspect unless he's feeling guilty about something?

"Not that I know of. The chief and I were looking into my family, which led to a discussion about the Avery boys' claim that they were named as heirs in an earlier will."

"That's a total lie. Wade's been spouting that story since he was a kid."

"The chief feels the same way. We were talking about Wade's rotten character and anger, and she told me what he did to you. Charlotte was hoping that a window was opening into Samuel's life story.

"He was a bully as long as I've known him, always picking on the younger kids. He's one of those guys who always thought that he was smarter, funnier, stronger, and better looking than he really is."

"They had no mirrors at his house?" Charlotte was only half-joking. It was impossible to get past the nasty anger in Wade's eyes.

Samuel just stared into space for a moment. "After Wade won, he trotted back to me, putting on a big show of compassion for the crowd. He lifted me up and demanded that I walk off the track with his help. Wade didn't want the crowd to give me too much sympathy and forget about his victory. He ended up basically dragging me off. At the finish there were speeches, and by the time my ankle was looked at by a doctor, it was difficult to properly set it. Every morning I wake up to a dull pain that reminds me of that day and what Wade did."

"That's awful. I am so sorry, Samuel." Charlotte put her hand on his shoulder and looked into his eyes. She saw real pain. "I hope they get him for Marcus's murder and lock him up for good!"

"If anybody deserves it, it's Wade Avery," he sneered.

Hmm . . . Samuel was the first one to offer up Wade's name as a murder suspect . . .

"You sure have brought a hornet's nest into town with you, Miss Charlotte."

"Me? I had nothing to do with all this. A week ago I was in my apartment in Chicago, sipping a latte and looking out over Lake Michigan from my oversized living room window."

Samuel gave her a sarcastic laugh and shook his head.

"I wasn't happy, and it wasn't until I left the city that I came to realize that I never really belonged there."

With that Charlotte turned her body toward the door and jumped down from the truck. When she landed, she looked at Samuel and was about to deliver a few final carefully chosen words to him. That was, until her eyes caught something stuck under the seat that looked out of place. She pulled it out a bit and immediately recognized that it was a rag with dried blood on it. She quickly shoved it back under the seat and walked away, hoping that Samuel hadn't seen.

Why does Samuel have a bloody rag stuffed under the seat of his truck?

Chapter Twelve

Charlotte arrived home fuming and thoroughly confused. *It was unpleasant to witness how easily Samuel could switch moods, but could he really be capable of the rage to kill? He can be sullen and broody, but I've never felt afraid around him.* Then there was that rag. Charlotte knew what dried blood looked like.

Charlotte needed Diane's wisdom. She looked at the time and hoped to catch her before her shift began. It would be close.

"You answered!" Charlotte brightened immediately.

"I've literally got four minutes, but they are all yours, Char."

"Mostly I just want to hear a friendly voice tell me that I'm the sane one in this field of hard-to-read townspeople. And they say big-city people are aloof."

Charlotte gave Diane a much-abridged version of the latest news and events. "It is unsettling to think that Samuel could be setting up Wade as the murderer, because he does carry a vendetta against him. And if I recall correctly, Samuel was the first person to tell me about Wade's claims to inheriting the farm. Or was it Joe? Could Samuel have it in him to frame a possibly innocent man? And then there's the rag with dried blood that

I found in Samuel's truck. It could be like that for a million reasons."

"Right. He's around animals and machines and wire and thorny plants all day, Charlotte. You have to remember that you are living in an environment where people cling to predictability. They know their planting cycles, their irrigation systems, their crops, and what they will yield. Even the weather—that's how they make their living as farmers. Oh sure, droughts, fires, and floods can impact them greatly, but those for the most part are nature driven. Now you come along, find a man murdered in your field, have the police looking at locals as suspects, and every day it seems that a new revelation surfaces. No wonder they see you as a kind of pariah."

"How did you get so smart, Diane?" Charlotte asked. "We both brushed our teeth with the same water, breathed in the same Midwest air. And how do I fix this? I'll never be able to make a go of this farm if everyone is against me."

"You need to start over and make friends. Treat everyone like they are your closest pals. Give them a reason to trust you enough to confide their thoughts. Because ultimately this will only go away once they've found the murderer. Separate the wheat from the chaff. Pun intended! Which reminds me that I spoke to someone at the Olive and Whistle Inn about Hera, and there is still one old waiter there who they thought would remember her last name. I'll call again and see if I can get him on the phone. Oops—I've got to go, honey. Call me later tonight if you need to talk more."

"I'll be fine, and we'll be together Friday in person." Charlotte waited for confirmation that Diane was coming up to the farm for the weekend.

"I'm afraid not. Since I missed some shifts, I've got to make up the time Saturday and Sunday so other chefs can get a break. But we'll talk over the phone, and I'm pretty sure that Beau is driving up to Little Acorn. I'll make sure that he confirms. I've got pots boiling over so bye for now!"

Diane rang off, and Charlotte felt lonelier than she'd ever felt. As if sensing her distress, Horse trotted over to the sofa she was perched on in front of a fire in her uncle's bedroom.

"Hello, my dear pink friend. You'll help me solve this murder so that we can get on with our summer, won't you? You'd tell me if it was Samuel . . . wouldn't you?"

He looked at her for a long time, studying her face before responding. It almost looked as though Horse was going through the steps in his mind for how to lead Charlotte to the killer. Finally, he hopped up on the sofa and shoved his snout under her hand. He bobbed it up and down, looking at her, and then jumped down and headed to the doors to the patio.

"Tomorrow, Horse. I get it. You want to show me something. We'll go—after all, tomorrow is another day."

*   *   *

"Good morning, Alice. How are you today?" Charlotte asked in a rosy, friendly tone that was going to be her mien from now on.

"Good, thank you. Miss Diane emailed me some recipes for next weekend's barbecue, so I'm going to be testing them today. I know that you're going out to lunch, but I can serve you a tasting menu for dinner. This is so exciting!"

"I'm going out to lunch?" Charlotte's mind was a blank.

"That's what Annabel Andersen said. She's really looking forward to it." Alice nodded to Charlotte and then disappeared into the kitchen.

I never agreed to go. They really don't take no for an answer. And isn't it interesting that Annabel and Alice are in constant contact . . .

Charlotte was about to ask Alice for Annabel's phone number to call and cancel, but then she remembered Diane's words from last night. This would be a perfect opportunity to pump her for information. Charlotte decided to show Annabel the proper respect for a lunch date with such a "sophisticated lady" and picked out the fancy Neiman Marcus ensemble that she'd bought for the advertising awards luncheon. The navy and light blue shell and matching flounce skirt were even a little loose on her, what with all the exercise that she got around the farm. She added dusty-rose medium high heels and a blue-gray clutch to complete the look. Right at noon she heard a car in the drive and looked out to see Annabel's BMW. The windows were darkly tinted, so Charlotte couldn't see what Annabel was wearing, but she hoped getting all dressed up would be seen as a sign of respect. Charlotte caught one last glimpse of herself in the mirror and almost changed into the more casual, comfortable attire that she was getting very used to. But then she reminded herself that it was information that she was after from Annabel, and she'd use her fancy dress and perhaps a little attitude to get Annabel to want to impress her with her local knowledge.

"Alice, I'm off to lunch," Charlotte shouted as she opened the door. Call me if you need anything from town." Horse followed

Charlotte out onto the patio. "You need to stay here and guard the farm while I'm gone, okay?"

Horse wagged his tail and watched as Charlotte reached for the car door handle.

"Grrrrrr." Horse let out a menacing growl.

"Shh!" Charlotte patted her flat hand in the air and then raised it to her lips. "Quiet. I'll be back in a couple of hours."

Charlotte quickly got in and shut the door before Horse could make his disapproval felt again.

"This is so nice of you, Annabel. I've been looking forward to lunch with you all week." Charlotte settled into her seat after spreading out her skirt. Inside she cringed that right off the bat she was being disingenuous. She felt around for the seatbelt.

"You can tell her yourself when you see her," said a male voice that made her scream.

"Clark?" *The younger Avery brother.* "What are you doing here? You scared me half to death!"

"You sure did look surprised. My sister, Annabel, was running late and asked me to pick you up."

"I didn't know that you were on speaking terms." Charlotte tried to relax.

"Barely, but she couldn't find Serge anywhere, so I guess she was desperate. I help her out when I can." Clarke grinned.

"You are family after all. It would be nice if you could spend more time together. I bet under that rough cowboy exterior you're a real sweet guy."

Oh boy. I hope I'm not laying it on too thick, but Clark's my best bet for getting dirt on Wade.

"Maybe," he said, and Charlotte realized that he was actually quite shy.

This was Charlotte's first opportunity to get a good look at the youngest Avery. She had to look very closely to find the familial resemblance, but it was there in bone structure and complexion. Unlike Wade and Annabel, Clark had dark hair, almost jet black and wavy. His eyes didn't betray anger or envy or greed, but something even more upsetting to Charlotte: fear and skittishness. Like a dog that had been abused. Sure, he presented himself as a renegade without a conscience, but today Charlotte saw how much of a façade that actually was.

"Do you work on the farm behind mine with Wade?" Charlotte noticed him wince just slightly at Wade's name.

"Sometimes I do, but I have my own stuff too. Like helping Serge with distribution." Clark was gaining confidence with each word.

So Clark is literally playing both sides of the fence. He may be the smartest of the lot of them.

"That's great. So you'll be a master of at least two trades. That must double the opportunities. Is this the working life you've always wanted, Clark?"

He looked at Charlotte and thought for a second while they waited at a stop sign for a farmer and his sheep to cross the road.

"Kind of . . . except—" He caught himself before continuing.

"Except what? You can tell me, Clark. I promise that this will go no further."

"I like shooting things."

Charlotte audibly gasped.

"Oh, sorry—it's not what you think! I mean filming stuff like farmland, sunrises, and the animals. I'll see something when I'm out by myself and want to capture its beauty. I got my grandpa's old camcorder when he died, and I'm still using it today."

If this had been a cartoon, everyone would have seen Charlotte's ears perk up. "Did your grandpa live in Little Acorn? What was his name?" Charlotte tried her best to sound casual.

"Why are you so interested in me? Wade told me you'd be pesky."

"You sound like a very accomplished man with a vision of where he wants to go in life."

"I am!" Clark declared, puffing out his chest.

Whew—nice save, Charlotte. You don't want him clamming up now.

"You're the one who brought up your grandfather. I'm just trying to get to know the histories of the prominent families in Little Acorn," Charlotte said, hoping to settle Clark back down.

She noticed his shoulders relax. "Do you show your work anywhere that I can see it?"

"No. They're just for me right now. When I finally get something I'm okay with, I might send it in to one of those contests on the internet."

"You know who has connections with film and can always use fresh talent? Beau. He does special events for big time brands and artists. I bet that he'd love to see some of your work. He'll be back on Friday. Want me to arrange a meeting?"

Clark literally squirmed at the suggestion.

"No—like I said, I'm not ready."

The last little lamb had crossed the road to the field, due greatly to the leadership of a border collie.

"I understand, but if you change your mind or just want to bounce some of your clips off me, I'd love to see them."

Charlotte was pleased that she'd established a connection with Clark that was separate from Wade's bullying and suspicion. She definitely wanted Clark to be innocent of any crime. *I'll curry the relationship, and when the time is right . . . get him to talk about his grandfather.*

They rode in silence the rest of the way.

"That's the place," Clark said, indicating it with a nod of his head after he'd pulled the BMW to the curb and parked.

He got out, and for a moment Charlotte thought that he was coming around to open the door for her. But after about thirty seconds, she realized that she was on her own.

"Can you give Annabel her keys back?" Clark asked. "I'm meeting up with Wade in town," he said, dropping them into Charlotte's hand. This was a key fob with a brass ball the size of a marble, attached to a chain.

"Of course. Thank you for picking me up. And remember, anytime you want to show me your filming skills, just ask."

"Let's forget I ever mentioned it. I'm sorry that I told you."

"When you started talking about it, you got a whole new look in your eyes, Clark. There was a spark of passion in you just thinking about what you film. You can pretend that it's nothing, but inside I can see that it has a solid grip on you. Treasure that, Clark. Most people never find what they're really meant to do."

Charlotte left Clark at the curb with his mouth agape. She doubted that anyone had ever given him that amount of encouragement about anything he'd ever done or wanted to do.

* * *

Charlotte spotted Annabel holding court at the best table in the room. Two servers hovered over her and a lady in a floral dress who, Charlotte suspected, was the owner. Annabel's blonde hair was once again swept back into a neat French twist that she perhaps hoped would remind people of Grace Kelly.

While she had a moment, Charlotte discretely scanned the room to get a sense of the other luncheoners. This was the first chance that she'd had to take stock of the regular Little Acorn residents. What struck her was not so much the demographics of the group—they were almost equally Caucasian and Hispanic, and there were a few more women than men, their ages ranging from about twenty-five to fifty-five. No, what was so refreshing was how energetic and healthy they all looked. It was clear that these people enjoyed their lives. If there was a murderer among them, she'd have a hard time picking him or her out.

Annabel's booming voice drowned out her thoughts.

Charlotte had nothing against Annabel, yet her exaggerated sense of entitlement made Charlotte feel like a sneaker in a washing machine. It was time for Charlotte to stop second-guessing herself and take control.

"Ah, there she is," Annabel practically announced to the entire restaurant. "Don't you look lovely? I think that I have a similar ensemble. It's from a couple of seasons ago, no?"

Charlotte ignored her comment and accepted the seat from the woman in the dress.

"Charlotte, this is Karen Hubbard. She owns this lovely establishment."

"Pleased to meet you," Charlotte said, shaking her hand. "I can't believe that this is my first time actually dining in Little Acorn. It seems that I'm always running in and out for supplies while I get settled."

"Understandable, Miss Finn." Karen gave her a warm smile.

"Please, call me Charlotte. I am very much looking forward to getting to know you better, and perhaps you could introduce me around sometime. If one doesn't already exist, we could consider forming a 'women in business' group. I belonged to one with my last job, and I was so grateful for their support and friendship."

"That is a fabulous idea. Most of the men around here are farmers, while we ladies provide all the other essential services. I'm excited!"

"We'll need a minute to look at the menus, Karen," Annabel interrupted, clearly feeling that her plan to gain more admiration by bringing Charlotte into the fold had backfired. "I know what I would like, but I suspect that Miss Finn will need a bit more time to peruse a much simpler style of cuisine than what she was used to in Chicago."

"Nonsense. There is nothing better than dining farm to table, and I can already tell that you take great pride in your restaurant. I'll leave it to your recommendation, and I know it will be delightful." Charlotte nodded graciously to Karen and handed back the menu without opening it.

"It will be my pleasure," Karen said, backing away from the table. To her credit, Charlotte thought, she resisted giving Annabel anything but a very gentle smile.

That's the way to do it: swat them across the nose with a newspaper, but do it with grace.

"I hope that Clark didn't drive recklessly while bringing you here. He was a last resort. I was tied up on a conference call with a very well-known San Francisco art gallery. They have been trying to lure me up there to manage it for months now." Annabel gave Charlotte an overly wide smile.

"On the contrary, Clark drove like a gentleman, and before I forget, he asked me to give you your car keys. He said that you hadn't been able to locate Serge to pick me up. It would have been no trouble for me to drive myself, if I'd known."

Annabel tried to bury the sneer that was forming across her lips by taking a sip of iced tea.

"So, Charlotte, my dear, tell me about your plans. You can't possibly be considering staying on in this little peach pit of a town? You'd be bored to tears. Our friendship may have to become a long-distance one—we are this close to moving up north." She pinched her index finger and thumb almost together. "With Serge's business taking off the way it has, it's silly to waste our talents in a one-horse town, don't you think?"

"Actually, Annabel, I am seriously considering settling down here. In spite of all the obstacles, not the least of which was finding a dead boy on my property, I am enjoying the beauty and pure simplicity of this lifestyle. In Chicago, I was always trying to be more, to own more, and I rarely stopped to enjoy what I had. Here I am grateful for every day."

"That sounds like a motto to live by," Karen said, appearing with their lunch plates. "Your usual Crab Louie with fried goat cheese, Annabel, and for you, Charlotte, I present a butter-poached halibut on a bed of shaved Brussels sprouts, arugula, apricots, and California black walnuts. All our seafood is sustainably caught."

Charlotte used her hand to help waft the delicious aroma from her plate to her nose.

"I must admit that you had me at 'butter-poached halibut,' but the rest sounds just as spectacular."

"Is that on the menu? I didn't see it," Annabel complained. "And could you bring me a glass of Santa Ynez Cabernet?"

"We'll share, Annabel—isn't that what friends do?" Charlotte appeased her with that statement. "Now I want to know all about you—an art gallery manager? Your talents seem endless. You must be a very creative lady."

"I was quite the *artiste* before I got married and started a family. I painted, did a stint as an actress—lead roles in local theater and such. And of course my fitness regimen. In addition to yoga, I run, hike, do Pilates, and ride horses when I find the time."

"Very impressive, and do you have children? I don't think that I knew that." Charlotte was trying to artfully disguise her probing and also keep to herself the fact that the food was exceptional. She'd offered, but maybe out of spite Annabel had declined a taste of her fish.

"A boy and a girl both under the age of ten. Shoot me now," she half-joked. "And it being summer and no school . . . I can't find enough camps to send them to. Serge's off all day working, and I'm desperate for things to do with them. We even went to a farm so they could pet other people's goats. It is time to move to a city like San Francisco so that I can bring them up in the kind of sophisticated society that you and I are used to."

Is she trying to convince me that she grew up cosmopolitan? I've seen her birth certificate. Still, there's nothing wrong with having aspirations.

"Oh dear, that sounds like a lot for one person. Have you thought about a nanny?"

"We've gone that route, and let's just say that the Andersen kids have a reputation around Little Acorn of being hard to rein in. They're free spirits and all."

"I might be able to help in a few weeks—"

"Fantastic, I'll pay you whatever you ask. How many days a week can you take them? Would you consider overnights?"

"Er, I didn't mean in that way. You see we're starting a "you pick 'em" program aimed at kids. We're designating some fields for just that purpose, and we're planning on giving farm tours and having a petting area as well. So you could bring them as often as you like." Charlotte watched Annabel's face fall, not the reaction she was expecting.

"Serge hasn't mentioned this to me. Does he know about it?"

Ah, did her mind just go to the commission Serge will lose when we sell direct?

"I'm not sure. I've run into him at the garden center but have yet to see him at my farm. But he'll hear about it soon enough. We're working on signs now, and I plan to announce it at the Lake Finn fundraising barbecue. I do hope the Andersen family will be coming."

Charlotte noticed that Annabel seemed to have lost her appetite. She, on the other hand, had just joined the "clean plate league."

"We're still considering the offer. With there being a murderer on the loose who has already struck once on your property, we're not sure that we want to expose the kids to possible danger."

A moment ago, she was practically giving them away.

"We're hoping the case will be solved by then. I understand that the chief has some new leads and evidence that are bringing her closer to the killer as we speak."

Charlotte knew that statement was a stretch, but she needed to stir the pot.

"Is that so? Oh, we've been having such a lovely lunch that I lost track of the time. I have another call to hop on in twenty minutes, and they'll be calling my home number. Karen?" Annabel waved to her from across the room.

"Be a dear and drive Miss Finn home, will you? I have an important call to take and must scoot. It's been a pleasure, dear."

With that, Annabel disappeared almost in a cloud of smoke.

Just like the wicked witch. And how convenient that she left right after I hinted that the police were closing in on the killer.

"No worries, I'll give my caretaker a call. I'm sure that you have much more important things to do."

"Of course not. I'd be happy to run you up to your farm," Karen replied as her server cleared the plates.

That was when Charlotte noticed that Karen had come to their table with the check.

"If it's not a bother, that would be great. And let me take care of that." Charlotte reached for the check.

"Absolutely not! Your meal is my treat as a welcome to the community. And I'll get Annabel to take care of her share when I see her again."

Charlotte suspected that this wouldn't be the first time Annabel had booked without paying.

*   *   *

When Karen dropped Charlotte off in front of the farmhouse they promised to get together just the two of them as soon as things settled down. They exchanged cell phone numbers and Charlotte breathed a sigh of relief, knowing that she had made one new friend in town. As she climbed the steps to the porch, she noticed that Samuel had left her the frames he'd made for the signs, along with the art supplies from the hardware store that she'd left in his truck.

Time to make amends. If nothing else, he is true to his word.

Charlotte quickly changed into more suitable farm clothes and headed down to the paddock, hoping to catch Samuel before it got dark. She located him there, kicking around a soccer ball, and couldn't believe her eyes. Samuel was playing with the lean chestnut and white horse.

"What a beautiful roan. Am I to believe my eyes? Is he really playing soccer with you?" Charlotte said, approaching Samuel with a smile.

The farmer didn't respond.

Oops—the silent treatment. Time to try a new approach.

"I came by to thank you for the signs you made and to apologize for my outburst yesterday. There is no excuse for it, and I am sorry for the things I said."

Charlotte walked into the paddock, and the horse immediately kicked the ball to her. She passed it to Samuel, hoping that she'd put enough honey in her apology, but Samuel still didn't speak to her. They kicked the ball among the three of them for another minute or so.

"I'm hoping that you can forgive me or that I can find some way to make it up to you, Samuel. I recognize that I've stirred up a hornet's nest since I arrived, and—well, I'm going to make things right and stop anyone who has other ideas. For as long as I'm here, I'm going to run this farm, and that starts with me exposing the rotten apples!" Charlotte had really worked herself up into a lather.

"'Bout time," Samuel said, still not looking up from the game.

"I would have said that I'm sorry earlier, but I forgot that Annabel insisted I have lunch with her, and I had to rush to get dressed."

That made him look up at her.

"Annabel? And no, I'm not talking about your apology, nice as it was. I'm saying that it's about time you took the reins of this farm. Your uncle was a great man, but in his later years he no longer had the stamina to keep things in check, and people took advantage of his kindness."

Samuel stopped kicking the ball and led the horse toward the barn.

"I kind of suspected that from the little I know so far."

Charlotte followed him into the barn and watched him take off the horse's reins and hang them up. The horse then walked all by himself into his stall and pulled the door shut with his teeth before lowering the latch.

Charlotte's mouth dropped open, and Samuel grinned to himself, trying to hide his pride.

So deep down he's an animal nut too!

"When you arrived, we were all waiting to see whether you'd stay and take control or sell and run. I guess we still don't know for sure, but that murder put a stop to any immediate plans to sell." Samuel eyed her, waiting for a response. "For the longest time, we suspected you'd sell."

"I've decided for now to make a go of it, and I'm letting everybody know that I won't be pushed around. You should have seen how I showed Annabel her place today when she was so rude to the restaurant owner."

"I would have loved to have seen that." Samuel chuckled.

"I'd like to have a look at the accounting ledger that you keep for Serge's distribution of our produce. I don't trust him anymore than I could throw him, and that's saying something given his girth. Those two show off some major displays of wealth for a guy who sells strawberries."

"Sure—the accounting books are in the back here. Like I said, the financial side of things I leave to Serge and sometimes Joe, although I wouldn't be surprised if Serge has been cheating the farm for years."

He exited the stall and headed to the back of the barn. Charlotte gave the horse a pat on the head.

"If I find out that Serge has taken so much as one cent from us that he hasn't earned, he's going to wish that he'd stayed in Solvang cobbling wooden clogs!"

"Hah! I knew that red hair wasn't just for show." Samuel handed her the books.

"I'll need these for a few days, not that it matters. Is Serge ever going to show up for our haul?"

"He says he'll be here tomorrow morning. I'll call you when he shows. If he shows."

Samuel doesn't like Serge; Joe and the chief both told me that. But is the hate so deep that he'd throw suspicion for murder his way?

Horse came racing into the barn. He'd been so busy enjoying his supper that he hadn't come up for air, to greet Charlotte after she'd been gone most of the day.

"Pig sure does like you," Samuel said, smiling.

"His name is Horse."

"Of course, I meant to say that. And 'hello' to you Mrs. Robinson," Samuel said to the ladybug sitting beside Horse's ear.

"That's more like it. By the way, what's the roan's name?" she asked, giving him a pet on the nose on her way out.

"I guess we can't call him Horse now, can we? You'll think of something. Have a nice night, Miss Charlotte. You too, Horse, Mrs. Robinson."

"Pele. He'll be named after the world's greatest soccer player. Goodnight, Pele. Goodnight, Samuel."

When she looked back, Samuel tipped his hat to them just the way she remembered her uncle doing.

* * *

After such a spectacular lunch, Charlotte decided to forego dinner, but at the last minute brought a bowl of strawberries with cream into her uncle's suite. Her trusty sidekick, Horse, was amenable to the plan. She lounged on the sofa in front of the

171

fireplace, with her long legs curled up under her, and opened one of the farm's ledgers.

It took Charlotte a while to figure out the entries. The system had clearly been developed by her great-uncle and was a little cumbersome. But with a little help from some quick Web research on accounting, she eventually caught on. This side of the bookkeeping looked to have been done by Joe near the time of Tobias's death, but was soon after taken over by Serge. That was mistake number one.

On the farm side, Samuel kept track of the produce that went to market each week. It was only slightly more sophisticated than tally marks, but the quantities were crystal clear. It didn't take long for Charlotte to realize that Serge was consistently shorting the payments.

That explains Annabel's designer accessories. And it can't be cheap, keeping a mistress.

Charlotte felt the anger rise up in her cheeks. This was worse than simply stealing. This was taking advantage of a dying man who she was sure had treated Serge and his family with the utmost respect.

Just wait until he shows his face around here in the morning!

Charlotte swiped to the calculator app on her phone and got out a pad of paper. She'd decided to add up all the money that Serge had skimmed just for this year alone and present him with an invoice for the amount. She couldn't help but smile when she thought to include a twenty-five-dollar fee for the barn rental each time for yoga classes from now on. Payable a month in advance.

Getting the upper hand of her farm energized her, and she felt even stronger knowing that Samuel was behind her.

Just as she turned the ledger pages back to January, she heard the sound of glass breaking. She looked outside her French doors to the patio and noted that there was only a light breeze rustling the bougainvillea trees. She got up to investigate and wandered out of the bedroom and into the foyer.

Again she heard the sounds of glass breaking along with some thumping noises. To her ears, it seemed that the activity was coming from the kitchen. Suddenly she heard the loud clicking on the floor tiles of something approaching her from behind. When the frequency of the clicks increased, she quickly looked around in the dark for something she could use to defend herself.

That was when she heard a pleasant squeal.

"Horse! You nearly scared me to death, and I could have hurt you. From now on, only sneak up on bad guys."

His eyes glistened in the dappled light coming from the moon through the patio doors. She couldn't resist bending down to kiss his head.

Another sound of shattered glass told her that the noise was originating in the root cellar. Her first thought was that Alice was down there again and in danger from some trapped animal. She wondered if she should quickly call Joe. When she reached in her pocket for her phone, she realized that she'd left it with the ledgers, when she'd been using its calculator app.

Another series of thumps and pounding gave her no choice but to immediately investigate and help Alice. Charlotte had actually never descended the steps to the level below. She opened the door and felt the wall for a light switch. Two hanging work lamps came on, but almost immediately one blew out. She felt Horse peek from behind her legs at this new space to investigate.

"Oh no," she whispered. "This is no place for little legs and steep stairs, Horse. You are going to have to wait here until I get back."

When the pig kept inching toward the top riser, Charlotte slipped in and quickly shut the door behind her. She took several deep breaths, her anxiety level rising. It was impossible to see more than ten feet in front of her, with the only illumination coming from one bulb. Charlotte hoped that once she got down there, she'd find additional light sources.

The other thing that she immediately sensed was the drop in temperature. It was at least ten degrees cooler down there, and she was in shorts and a light T-shirt. The stairs had been carved out of the stone, and more than a few of the stepstones had broken loose from the aging concrete. She made a mental note to put the cellar on the list of items to be upgraded and made safe. When Charlotte reached the ground, she could tell that the space ran the length of the farmhouse.

This could be repurposed for so many things.

The ceiling and adjoining room entries were all made of stone barrel vaults, and Charlotte was beginning to think that this cellar was at one time part of a much older farmhouse. A rusted and misshapen arched gate sat partially open, leading to another chamber. Charlotte traced the noises as coming from inside that room. A little bit of moonlight spilled into the cellar from a narrow slit of a window, but it was only enough to guide her to the gate.

"Hello?" Charlotte asked into the dark but only heard the pitter-patter steps of something smaller running away.

Could one little animal be responsible for all that noise? And where's Alice?

Charlotte had to shimmy through the wrought iron gate to enter that next room, and once inside, she felt along the walls for a light switch. She wasn't finding one, but she remembered that Samuel had told her that the root cellar doors to the outside were always kept locked. Whatever was in here couldn't be bigger than a rat or a mouse, could it? She heard a loud thud of glass hitting stone and then smelled tomatoes. She remembered seeing a large mason jar of sauce in the kitchen pantry and knew that it was too big for a rodent to toss off a shelf. Charlotte felt a chill and searched more frantically along the walls of the chamber. When she moved to the center of the space, a piece of string glided across her face. She reached for it, made contact, and pulled it down. Another smaller work lamp came to life. When her eyes adjusted, Charlotte could see that the room's walls were lined with dilapidated wooden shelves that looked to be about the same age as the cellar itself. On them sat rows and rows of glass jars filled with what she guessed was strawberry jam on one side and, as she'd imagined, larger ones on the other side containing tomato sauce. The wood shelves bowed in places, succumbing to the weight of their occupants.

Charlotte then lowered her eyes to the floor and saw a pool of red liquid coming from the opposite wall and screamed. There was broken glass scattered all over the floor.

When she examined the liquid under the bottom shelf more closely, she could see and smell the ruins of spilt tomato sauce.

What or who is doing this?

Charlotte noticed that there was a wooden locker box sitting below the shelf.

What's that doing down here all by itself?

Charlotte bent down to try to open it, and heard a rustling from across the room. She looked in the direction of the noise and saw a jar of strawberry jam come flying toward her. She tried to stand quickly to get out of harm's way and slammed her head into the shelf above her. And that was the last thing that she saw.

Chapter Thirteen

Charlotte slowly woke to a throbbing pain that ran from the back of her head all the way through to her eyes. When she brought her lids to half-mast, she saw the shadow of what looked like a person through limited light. Something came forward toward her and lifted up her head. The next sensation was of a cool and soft material being placed at the back of her scalp.

"Don't try to talk," said a voice Charlotte recognized. "It's Alice, and Joe and Samuel are here as well."

"We've called for Doc Wilkins—he should be here any moment." That voice she knew was Samuel's.

"Where am I?" Charlotte whispered.

"You're in the cellar, Miss Charlotte. It would appear that you've been here all night." Joe reached for her hand.

Sweet man.

"We probably wouldn't have found you until much later if it weren't for Horse," Joe added.

"The pig went around trying to wake us all up—started with me, but I yelled so loudly that he finally gave up. I'll never ignore him again," Samuel said, and on cue they heard squealing coming from upstairs.

"He managed to get us to pay attention, but we couldn't understand what he wanted. I guess we need to learn how to speak Horse." Alice smiled.

Unless you were already in the cellar, trying to scare me away from finding something incriminating.

"When I got up to the farmhouse to wait for Serge, Horse wouldn't let me get past and go to the door. He grabbed my pant leg and pulled me to the cellar door. Joe and Alice had just come in, and we went down to see what the fuss was about. I thought that the raccoons had gotten in again," Samuel explained, and then spotted some droppings that confirmed his suspicion.

"Is Serge here?" Charlotte asked, trying to sit up, but a dizzy spell sent her right back down.

"Not yet," Joe said, examining one of the shelves.

Charlotte was lying out from under the danger of falling jars, on blankets that smelled to her like they came from a cedar chest. That stirred a memory, and she turned her head to one side to look for the locker box that had set this calamity in motion. When she spotted a rectangular form, she saw that the lid was open.

"An old blanket chest," Alice said, following her eyes. Remarkably, everything inside has stayed dry for who knows how many years. With all the time I spend down here, this morning was the first time that I noticed it."

It was then that Charlotte had an image of a strawberry jam jar soaring at her from across the room, and she tried to smell and look for its remnants.

"This wood's all rotted," Joe said breaking large pieces off the wall shelf.

Samuel also inspected the wood and then turned to study the ones all around the chamber. He walked over to the far wall. "These are still rock solid," he said rapping his knuckles with some force against the wood. "They're made of oak just like the columns and the beams are." Samuel pointed up to an example. "These look like pine and were probably added later."

"Anybody home?" They heard a shout coming from outside the chamber.

"In here, Doc," Joe replied.

"We didn't want to try to move her until you got here and gave the okay," Alice explained.

"Let's just take a look. Hello, Charlotte, we haven't met yet. I'm Doctor Wilkins."

* * *

"I know it doesn't seem like it, but you were lucky," Doc Wilkins explained to Charlotte once they'd brought her upstairs and laid her on a sofa in the living room. "That nasty shelf hit you on the hardest part of your cranium so I don't believe you've suffered a concussion."

"That's a relief," Alice said to the group surrounding Charlotte.

"However, I recommend that you take it easy for a day or so, just in case any small blood vessels were broken. And take at least two aspirins a day. Just to be on the safe side."

"Thanks, Doctor. Alice, could you fetch my checkbook from the bedroom please?"

"That won't be necessary," the doctor said. "This is really more of a social call to welcome you to Little Acorn."

"That's very kind, and I insist that you and your family come to our neighborhood barbecue a week from Saturday. There'll be lots to do, and we may even have the lake to admire again."

"Sounds like a can't-miss." The doctor checked Charlotte's forehead one more time before he was satisfied.

"I can't make any promises about the lake," Samuel said, entering the room. "But I can tell you that someone has opened and closed the outside cellar doors at the side of the house. I found the padlock open—not broken, so it was someone that had access to the key."

Hearing this, Charlotte sat up.

"Where is the key usually kept, Samuel?" she asked.

"I've got one on my key ring, and there's a spare on a hook at the bottom of the cellar stairs. I checked and it's gone."

Everyone let that news settle in their minds.

"Sounds like you've got a conundrum on your hands. I'll see myself out." Doctor Wilkins turned to leave.

"Thanks again, and don't forget about next Saturday," Charlotte said.

"Wouldn't think of it, and you'll get to meet my better half!"

"Samuel, are you sure that those cellar doors were opened? Maybe someone just forgot to close the lock or thought they had closed it?" Charlotte asked, hoping.

"They were used. I could tell by the way the grass growing around the sides of the doors had been patted down."

So, someone didn't want to be seen coming and going?

"We need to figure out who would want to steal the key and use it to sneak into the cellar." Charlotte tried to discretely look at everyone for telltale signs of guilt.

"It would seem that you surprised whoever it was, and they tossed jars at you, hoping to scare you off, and then you hit your head," Samuel summed up.

That's a very good assessment. Maybe too good?

"Helloooo! Daddy's home!"

"Beau? Is that you?" Charlotte asked, and he appeared in the living room.

"Are we posing for a family portrait, and nobody told me?" Beau asked, sauntering into the room and seeing Samuel, Joe, and Alice seated and standing around Charlotte on the sofa.

""What a nice surprise—I wasn't expecting you until Friday!" Charlotte reached for him, and he bent down to give her a kiss.

"It is Friday," Alice, Joe, and Beau said in unison.

"Having so much fun that you've lost track of time, my love?" Beau looked around the room for signs of a party.

"Not exactly. I'll explain over breakfast, or should I say brunch?" Charlotte asked. "Please tell me I haven't missed the entire day."

"It is the perfect time for brunch. Shall we repair to the kitchen?" Beau offered his arm.

"I can cook," Alice offered.

"I've got this. Finally, I don't have to fight my sister for chef rights." Beau smiled.

* * *

The table was a sea of empty plates and serving platters. Beau had gone all out, and Charlotte was surprised by how hungry she was. Which reminded her that she hadn't eaten dinner, and prior to that she'd had lunch with the most disagreeable Annabel. She brought Beau up to speed on everything that had happened.

"So, theories? You must have some," Beau said while dredging the last morsel of French toast through buttery syrup.

"I'm starting to, but the problem is that the suspect list is very long. Wade and Clark are still at the top. From what Samuel tells me, Wade was just born angry."

"You and Samuel seem a lot more chummy than the last time I saw you together . . ."

"We've reached a kind of truce, that's all."

"Are you sure?" Beau winked at her and raised his eyebrows.

"Positive. He understands that I want to get the farm back up and running well, and he wants to help. That's it. Period."

"Milady, that's a lot of protesting."

"And I haven't entirely taken him off the suspect list. So there." She told Beau about the bloody rag that she found under the truck's passenger seat.

"Okay." Beau put his hands up in surrender.

"Then there's Annabel and Serge. She's an unfulfilled person, and that seems to constantly trigger her hairpin nasty side. But given what we know about her brothers, she seems to come by it honestly. I know very little about Serge and his family—"

"Except that he likes his sugar on the side," Beau jumped in.

"Yes, faithful he's not, and who knows if he's seeing just one other woman?"

"Do you think that Annabel knows?"

"She's not one to miss a trick, pun intended."

"Hah! Charlotte—funny." Beau gave her some air applause.

"But she's not the type to go around saying 'poor me' either. She is much more likely to tuck that infidelity away and bring it out when she can strategically use it with maximum leverage."

"Agreed, from what you've told me about her. And she could be cheating on him as well. So that's the list?"

"There's one more, I'm afraid." Charlotte shook her head slowly.

"Alice?" Beau knew that this one was tough on Charlotte.

"I really want there to be solid alibis. She loves it here. You can see how possessive she gets about the kitchen and the fields. So where was she when we all met the realtor for a tour? And what does she do all day in that cellar? That's where I got this knot on my head. Maybe she's trying to thwart my future chances of selling the farm so her life can continue on as it was. Or—and this is far-fetched—maybe she thinks that there is something of value on the farm that she has yet to find. Like you said, Alice and Joe know where all the bodies are buried."

"Like something in the cellar? If you're suggesting going back down there tonight, count me out. I forbid you too." Beau got stern.

"I'm not—at least for the moment. But soon, Samuel noticed that the shelves on one wall were made of pine and must have been added later. The cheaper wood was rotting while the older oak was holding up just fine."

"Meaning?" Beau asked, taking plates to the dishwasher.

"Meaning that at some point someone might have opened up that part of the wall."

"To look for something?"

Charlotte thought about that.

"Or to put something in it." Suddenly, Charlotte had an urge to get right back down to the root cellar, her mind was racing. And she never did find that jam jar that surely should have broken on landing. "Oh my gosh, I can't believe I forgot this until just now!"

"What?"

"Before I went to see where the noise was coming from last night, I was going through the produce sales ledgers that Samuel had given me. Serge has been cheating us for months by skimming off the top. Selling the same quantity but saying that the market has dropped. Demand is strong!"

"Did I hear Samuel say something about Serge missing his appointment this morning?"

"Yes, you did, and he doesn't seem to be the type to turn down money." Charlotte started to gather up the platters to hand-wash. "I want to deliver my invoice for the money he skimmed from the farm produce in person."

Beau raised his eyebrows in a look of concern.

"And are you expecting him to open his checkbook and pay you on the spot?" Beau asked as Charlotte grabbed her car keys off the kitchen counter.

"Something like that."

Beau made a sign of the cross, checked his reflection in the stainless steel door of the refrigerator, and followed Charlotte outside.

Chapter Fourteen

Charlotte had found one of Serge's invoices that was printed with an office address in town, and that's where they were headed. After that big brunch and all the excitement, her adrenalin was suddenly plummeting, and it was hard to get her mind off curling up in bed with a certain porcine companion to snuggle with.

"What's your plan once we set eyes on slimy Serge?" Beau asked her.

"I printed out an invoice for him for the one year's skimming alone. I'll need time to see how far back his stealing goes to create another bill, but I want him to know that we are watching his every move. I also need to talk to Samuel and Joe about other methods of distribution. I really don't want Serge or Annabel to set foot on my farm again."

"That's poking the bear, my fiery redhead! You realize that he could drag his feet on paying—or deny everything. It'll come down to believing him or Samuel." Beau shook his head at that thought.

"I'm willing to bet that Serge isn't just cheating us. When we get to his office, your job is to look for and memorize the names of his other customers or farms. A handful should do to give Chief Goodacre enough evidence to make an arrest.

"Got it, Captain, my Captain." Beau saluted her.

When they reached the center of Little Acorn, Charlotte and Beau saw that the street lamps and businesses were all being festooned with red, white, and blue in anticipation of Independence Day. There were pull down flags, pennants, bunting and pleated fans, and stars-and-stripes windsocks fluttering from atop the town hall.

"I didn't think that it was possible for Little Acorn to get any quainter," Beau said after they'd parked and gotten out of the car.

"I love it!" Charlotte walked with purpose toward the small storefront that was their destination.

Just as she was about to open the door, her cell phone rang, and she looked at the caller ID.

"It's Theresa—I mean the chief," she told Beau. They shuffle-stepped to one side of the storefront, and Charlotte took the call.

"Hello, Chief—I'm here with Beau. We're just about to meet with my distributor and read him the riot act. It appears that he has been skimming off the top of our produce sales." She was holding the phone up to her ear and had motioned Beau to cock his head next to hers to listen in. Since learning over and over that this town was such a rumor mill, she didn't want to broadcast the conversation over audio speaker.

"Serge? He seems like such an honest man . . . I'd pay to see that, but unfortunately, I'm drowning in paperwork today. Hopefully you can settle this without the police having to get involved."

"But then I won't get to see you this trip," Beau said into Charlotte's phone.

"Sweet Beau, we shall meet up again soon. Charlotte, we're making some progress here, and I would like to see any correspondence that you received about the inheritance before you arrived here. The bank won't release anything to me without a warrant, and I'm trying to save some time."

"Sure, I even have digital files that I could send you. I don't see what would be confidential in those." Charlotte obliged, once again worried about her suspect status.

"I'm going to send you a different email address that we use for more secure communication. You should be safe," the chief replied.

"Okay, great. Can you give me any updates on the rest of the evidence that you're following? Charlotte hoped that she'd sounded curious rather than imposing.

"Did the coroner give any clues as to what might have been used?" Charlotte shook her head with frustration.

"Only that it was something smooth but powerful. The DNA results from all of you should be back in a couple of days.

"I've located a lab that can do the DNA paternity testing, but they warn that with your uncle's hair sample, even with the root, they can only promise at best sixty-percent accuracy. I'll keep you posted. Ta-ta."

Chief Goodacre hung up before Charlotte could say another word.

* * *

The small office for Andersen Distribution consisted of a reception and waiting area and a glass-enclosed space in the back that contained a desk, workstation, and a wall of old metal file cabinets. Photos lined virtually every space of wall, depicting Serge posing with local dignitaries and usually holding a cocktail or an award. Or both. Like in an art museum, there was a small description of the event posted under each photo. To Charlotte this all looked like a wall of shameless hubris. About a third of the photos included Annabel, usually at formal attire events, and Charlotte noted that she never wore the same gown twice. Or the same jewelry. Even in a photo of them accepting a trophy from a bowling league, her lavish makeup had been perfectly applied.

"May I help you?" asked the woman behind the reception desk.

"Yes, kind lady, we're here to pay a visit to Mr. Andersen. And may I say that that is a beautiful shade of red you are wearing. It brings out your captivating eyes." Beau flashed his one-hundred-watt smile at her. Charlotte gave him a gentle kick on the foot. Not everyone knew how to deal with Beau putting on the charm.

"Hi, miss, I'm a customer of Mr. Andersen's. Is he out of the office?" Charlotte asked, seeing that the back room was empty.

"It's Miss Reston, and I haven't seen or heard from him today." She shrugged as if to say, "Either way is fine with me."

"Change of plans since he's not here," Charlotte whispered to Beau after turning her back to the receptionist and pretending to look at the photos on the wall. "Follow my lead."

"Oh, what a shame, and you've come all this way to reconnect with your old friend," Charlotte said to Beau, and looked into his eyes to make sure that he had caught onto the ruse.

"Do you have any idea when he might return? I'm only in town for a few hours, you see," Beau explained to Miss Reston.

"Nope, he does this a lot."

"I see. My friend brought something to show Mr. Andersen, a trip down memory lane to the good old days. Would you mind if he left it on his desk with a little note?" Charlotte could see that Miss Reston wanted to get back to her social media account. She'd not closed it fast enough to hide her computer screen when they'd walked in.

"Suit yourself." She shrugged again and this time didn't make any effort to hide what she was interacting with on the computer.

Good for us.

"We'd better switch roles. You pretend to be writing a note to go with this invoice, and I'll snoop around for account names," Charlotte whispered to Beau as she handed him the envelope with the bill.

Beau sat down at Serge's desk and looked for notepaper and a pen. Charlotte double-checked that Miss Reston was busy posting, and opened one of the file drawers.

"Oh good, you found something to takes notes with—write down these names," Charlotte again whispered to Beau as she opened and closed file drawers in order to get a good cross section. "Rancho Hernandez, Goleta Valley Berry Farm, Mountainview Acres, Goodland Produce, Whitney Dairy, Avondale Avocados, Pico Goat's Milk and Cheese."

Charlotte was interrupted by the sound of a car door closing in the alley behind Serge's office. She then noticed that there was another door that led out there.

"Beau, I think Serge is here. Quick—we've got to go! Leave that invoice on his desk!" This time her whisper was louder and more urgent.

"You sure?" Beau asked, rising from the desk chair.

Charlotte nodded to him, saw that he'd taken the note, and then noticed a file folder with the word "Appraisal" on it. She was about to grab it when she heard the sound of keys jingling. They raced out of Serge's office.

"Goodbye, Miss Reston. Have a nice rest of the day. And he's cute. I hope he's your boyfriend," Charlotte said, pointing to her computer screen.

"Cheerio," Beau said speed-walking behind Charlotte.

They made it out just before they saw light come into the room from the back door.

* * *

"Whew! That was close," Beau said once they were back on the road heading to the farm. "What's the next plan, O mistress of all living and growing things?"

"I'm weighing whether we should bring Samuel and Joe up to speed on Serge's stealing and see if they know any of Serge's other customers personally. That might help persuade them to join our little crusade."

"As long as you believe you can trust them to keep this to themselves," Beau replied.

"I suspect that the rumor grapevine contributor on the farm is Alice, whether she is doing it innocently or not. I'll ask Joe to keep this knowledge to himself."

"Perfect—plus letting them in on Serge's dirty laundry might broker extra trust. So that's the plan?"

"Well, it's interesting that you called me a mistress of the farm, because I've been feeling that no one is really managing the evidence in this murder. Chief Goodacre may be doing things that we are not privy to, but I can't rely on that. There's too much at stake for the farm and myself."

"I feel safe with you at the helm. The more we know, the less chance that the chief can successfully point the finger at us without enough proof," Beau said.

Charlotte's cell rang, and she saw that it was Diane calling.

"Perfect timing. Beau and I were just having a confab about our progress on the case. I'm putting you on speaker."

"It is absolutely perfect timing. Hi, you two loves! I finally got a call back from that old waiter who works at the Olive and Whistle Inn. You remember—the place where Hera worked?"

"Of course. Did he remember her?" Charlotte quickly asked, excited.

"He sure did. She must have been quite a beauty. The guy's eighty-two but still asked me to pass along his love to her if we ever met up."

"Aw, I love the idea that he may not be able to find his teeth in the morning, but he still knows exactly where his romantic heart is," Beau declared. This was followed by a moment of silence from Charlotte and Diane, who were not quite sure how to take his statement.

"Did he have any news about Hera?" Charlotte asked.

"He sure did—he recalled her last name!"

"Don't keep us in suspense, Sis. What is it?" Beau was on the edge of his car seat.

"Cordero!"

"Bingo! Wow! Turn the car around, Charlotte—we should go tell the chief," Beau yelled.

"Not so fast, Detective Beau. Do you know how many people in this state have the last name Cordero? This is great intel, Diane, and now we need to qualify it," Charlotte said into the phone.

"I figured you would, Char, but I've got a perfect boil on my pasta water so will have to get back to it. We'll talk soon—love you both!" Diane disconnected from the call.

"Like I was saying, Beau, we need to be strategic about how we release any information on this case. We don't want to tip off the real killer before we have enough proof to nail him. I think that it will only benefit us by exposing Serge's stealing once we get corroboration from some other farm clients of his, as it will expose him as a crook. Even if they find that he's not a murderer, his crime will put a major spotlight of scrutiny on him.

But right now, it's important to keep the news about Marcus possibly being Uncle Tobias and Hera's son a secret. We still have so many dots to connect." Charlotte had reached the farm, but they remained in the car.

"You have my word. So how do we proceed?"

"If the motive for killing Marcus was to stop him from claiming a share of the farm, then someone had to believe that he was Tobias's son. And they would also have to able to prove that there was an earlier will stipulating that the farm be split three ways between my grandfather, Tobias, and this great-uncle Henry. Meaning that the Avery kids could launch a claim that they're owed a share of the farm."

"So, in order to get to the bottom of this, we play dumb, ask everyone what they know about Marcus, and hope that the killer reveals him or herself," Beau concluded.

"Exactly, and we do so by making it seem that we are taking each suspect into our confidence. In the process, we should also find out what they've heard about an older will."

Charlotte looked out of the car window at the farmhouse. They'd reached a turning point by establishing a connection between the murder victim and the woman that Uncle Tobias loved. They were close to establishing a motive and she wasn't sure she wanted to know whom that would lead to, but for the life of her she couldn't pinpoint what had brought it on.

Chapter Fifteen

The farm was buzzing with activity when they got out of the car. Joe and Samuel, assisted by Javier Espinoza and two of his men, were installing the new lake pump. Three others were working on mending the torn vinyl areas of the bottom sealer. Charlotte decided to head down there, and as she passed the cellar doors, she noticed that a new, larger padlock now secured them.

"Char, I'm going to go in and make some calls for work," Beau said, mounting the steps to the farmhouse's patio. "I take it that my bedroom from last time is still available?"

"Of course, and I think that you'll find a pitcher with fresh yellow freesia waiting to welcome you."

"I may never leave." Beau grinned back at her.

"How are you feeling, Charlotte?" Samuel asked after walking up the path to greet her.

"A little tired, but otherwise fine." She noticed that Samuel had stripped down to a white tank shirt that showed off his slim waist. His worn jeans looked comfortable for this sort of work, and she found the tan leather gloves that protected his hands to be somehow sexy. Then there was the shock of straight dark hair that had flopped down and was almost covering one of his eyes.

"We've almost got the pump connected, and then we can run a test to see if there's still a spring underground," Samuel said turning and walking toward the lake.

He must have noticed me staring. Charlotte, behave yourself!

She picked up her pace to meet up with the men.

"Hello, everyone. Javier, again your help is so appreciated. How will I ever repay you and your men?"

"Like I said before, Miss Charlotte, we farmers help each other. There will come a time when I will need to call on you for assistance, so don't worry about it. The lake will make us all happy, as it has for generations." Javier took off his hat and wiped the sweat from his brow.

Charlotte cast her glance to the men working at the bottom of the deepest part of the lake dugout. "Do any of you know how long this artificial lake has existed?"

Javier let out a breath. "All my lifetime, and I'm fifty-four. And I've heard my parents talking about parties and picnics that happened here. I've even seen a photo of them sitting in a canoe on the lake."

"How deep would you say the basin is at its lowest?" Charlotte asked.

"Generally, weeds can't grow in water over fifteen feet. This one's about double that, so we don't have to worry about plant takeover," Javier explained.

"Why do you ask Charlotte?" Joe was intrigued.

"Just curious. I'd like to walk down to the edge and get a closer look, maybe walk in a little bit. Humor me—I'm reliving some childhood memories.

Samuel and Joe looked at each other, and Charlotte took note of their uneasiness with her request.

"You're recovering from a bad hit on the head, Charlotte. The doc said you need to take it easy," Samuel reminded her.

"I have no intention of falling or even going very far down the slope, if that's your concern, Samuel. And I see that ropes and ladders have been set out to help the workers go up and down, so you're worrying over nothing." With that, Charlotte started walking toward the lake's crater, with Horse following at her heels.

"See? This is as far as I'm going, so you can stop being Samuel the killjoy."

Charlotte saw that he'd taken her comment personally and quickly changed the subject. "I saw that there was a new lock on the outside cellar doors. Did you and Joe manage to chase out the raccoons?"

"We didn't find any, strange enough. Despite signs of fresh scat, neither of us can figure it out."

"Strange indeed." *And not a good sign,* Charlotte thought. It seemed more and more likely that someone had orchestrated the cellar raid and caused the "accident."

"Since we're out here by ourselves, there is something that I wanted to talk to you about," Charlotte began.

"Yes?" Samuel stopped walking.

"Just before I went down to investigate the noises coming from the basement last night, I was going over some of the ledgers you gave me."

"I swear to you, Miss Charlotte, I may not be the best at the business side, but I made sure that each of my entries was correct. I always count twice!" Samuel was getting agitated.

"I have no doubt, Samuel. Your reporting was clear and easy to read. But Serge, on the other hand, adopted a convoluted system after taking over the sales side of the books, and it took me a while to decipher."

"So it wasn't just me. I couldn't tell what the hell I was looking at."

"Serge was counting on just that. He was underreporting our produce sales almost from the beginning."

Samuel kicked a piece of tree branch. "I never should have agreed with Joe and turned that job over to Serge."

"So it was Joe's idea?"

"He would never complain, but I could see that he had too many daily jobs. The guy was getting no sleep. Rats." Samuel seemed genuinely disgusted with himself.

It had gotten even quieter as Charlotte saw that the sun was beginning to wane. She looked down and also noticed that the men who had been repairing the vinyl had quit for the day and taken their ladders up with them. Leaving only the rope.

"So how are you going to handle this? Have you told the chief?" Samuel asked.

Charlotte shared the story of her and Beau's visit to Serge's office, the invoice she'd left, and the list of customers they'd acquired. Then she explained the plan.

"Great idea. I know pretty much every farmer around here, and by the time I'm done telling them what Serge has been doing, the guy won't be able to show his face within a fifty-mile radius." Samuel let out a guttural laugh.

"Don't do anything just yet. I want to make sure that the timing is just right."

Horse was happily exploring the basin's edge and watched with fascination as he kicked a stone hard enough for it to go rolling down the slope.

"Pig! You stay up here!" Samuel suddenly yelled, and Charlotte saw Horse grinning up at her.

"Horse, no!" Charlotte shouted, but it was no use. The pig was half-running and half-sliding down the hill.

"Aw, geez, I'm going to make sure that he's all right." Charlotte peered down to the lake's floor, ready to descend.

"The hell you are!" Samuel shouted, grabbing the rope and rappelling down the slope at top speed. He jumped the last six feet to the bottom and chased after Horse.

"Is my little man okay?" Charlotte yelled, and heard her voice echo in the empty space.

"He's on his feet, if that's what you're asking. And he's found some mud, so I'd say yes."

Charlotte watched Samuel pick up Horse, who was now half pink and half brown from the mud. He tried to squirm away, not yet ready to concede that playtime was over.

"Oh no, you don't." Samuel held the pig with one arm and with the other worked at taking off his tank top. Once he'd gotten it off, he tied it into a makeshift baby sling and secured Horse inside it.

Charlotte tried to be subtle in her staring while she inched a little further down the slope.

"Don't you dare!" Samuel hollered up at her, making fast work using the rope to ascend.

Suddenly the ground began to rumble.

"Was that an earthquake?" Charlotte shouted.

Samuel looked around. "Do you see anything swaying?"

It was then that Charlotte realized that the sun had almost set.

"No. I don't, but it's kind of dark to see," Charlotte shouted over a second wave of rumbling.

"That's not an earthquake—that's the pump starting up! I told Joe to wait until morning, and I know that he heard me. This is very unlike him." Samuel scratched his head as he watched water below start rushing into the basin. He quickened his pace, pulling himself and Horse up the hill.

"Could someone other than Joe have turned the pump on?"

"Yes, but who? It also could have been installed with the valve already open."

"How often does a new pump come out of the box that way, Samuel? You don't think that someone was trying to sabotage this operation do you?"

"I don't like where you're going with this . . ."

"Me neither, but given everything that has happened, it's not so far-fetched." Charlotte could now look Samuel in the eyes. He had only a few more feet to reach the top.

"Someone else could have opened the valve and not known I was down there. It's almost dark outside, and if they didn't know to look, they wouldn't have seen us."

"Like who, Samuel? Wade perhaps?"

"I don't know, Charlotte." He released Horse back down onto flat ground and headed in the direction of his cabin.

"Horse, I wish you could tell me what this is all about. But first let's warm up and get something to eat."

That was the buzzword that never failed to send Horse into euphoria.

Chapter Sixteen

Charlotte retired early to her room, begging off dinner with Beau by saying that she was dead tired from the accident the night before and the ordeal at the lake. He understood and seemed to take it in stride.

Horse ambled into her room not long after she'd taken a soothing shower and changed into jersey shorts and a nightshirt. Her damp hair was wrapped up in a towel.

"Have a nice dinner, little man?"

He inflated his rosy cheeks and gave her a big smile.

"Come up here and help me do a little sleuthing," Charlotte told him, firing up her laptop.

Horse hopped up onto the sofa and squealed when he saw the desktop image pop up. It was of him! Charlotte giggled too. She'd uploaded it a couple of days ago and wondered if it would register with him. She'd crossed her fingers, knowing how often Horse stopped in front of the full-length mirror to stare at himself

"Yes, that's you. Maybe tomorrow we can take a shot of two of us together."

Charlotte opened a search engine and typed in the words "Marcus Cordero."

"Oh, there are a lot of them in California. Time to narrow the search."

As Charlotte typed, Horse stayed glued to the computer screen, ignoring her dancing fingers.

"Now we're getting down to something manageable." Charlotte looked at the page of results after adding "San Francisco" to the query.

Charlotte heard a noise coming from outside her room and figured that Beau was sneaking into the kitchen for a bedtime snack. She paused to listen for a moment, and when she didn't hear anything else, she went back to her research.

"Seeing as Marcus was just a young man, I guess that I should check these social media accounts, don't you think, Horse?"

Charlotte swore that she saw him nod his head.

After a few dead ends, she finally located the deceased's account. A feeling of deep sympathy soon dissipated when she began reading his postings. Like Wade, he'd been an angry guy. He'd hated any kind of authority: cops, government, employers. And his rants had a tinge of violence to them that, thankfully, it seemed he'd never acted on. Charlotte shook from a sudden chill.

"Yipes!" she shouted after hearing a knock on her bedroom door.

"You okay, honey? Guess who got the weekend off after all?"

The door opened, and Charlotte saw Diane.

"Sorry if I frightened you—don't you two look cozy." Diane gave her bestie a hug.

"Oh Diane, you are a sight for sore eyes! I'm so happy you're here. And I was creeped out even before you knocked."

Charlotte explained what she had been doing and showed her Marcus's social media page.

"It seems odd that a guy with that much rage would want to or be good at working with animals. They can sense things," Diane said, giving Horse a kiss on the top of his head.

"Where's Mrs. Robinson, by the way?" Diane asked. "I thought that Horse and his ladybug friend were inseparable."

"She's out on assignment just now, leading the charge to control the aphid population."

"Interesting." Diane gave her friend a concerned look.

"I thought the same thing about Marcus, although maybe animals calmed him down." Charlotte thought for a moment. "Unless . . .

"Unless what?" Diane was curious.

"Unless his being in this area and working with animals was all by design."

"You think that he found out that his mother knew Tobias and came here to lay claim to the farm? Wow."

"It would sure explain a lot, like what he might have been doing in my tomato field. Maybe he'd come to spy on me . . . remember that we'd just arrived." Charlotte tried unsuccessfully to stifle a yawn.

"You look exhausted, hon. Go get some rest, and I'll make you a spectacular breakfast in the morning."

"Thanks, Diane. I'll fall asleep to dreams of fluffy scrambled eggs and biscuits."

Charlotte looked at Horse and saw that his eyelashes were now resting on his cheeks, and there was a content smile on his face. She turned off the computer, and the lights and carried him to bed.

Not more than a minute after Diane had left, Charlotte put her head down on the pillow and fell fast asleep. As did Horse.

* * *

The next morning after an indeed wonderful breakfast, the three childhood friends ventured outside to check on the progress of filling the lake.

"It already looks fantastic," Beau said, surveying the one-third-filled basin.

"Well, it didn't look so great last night when Samuel and Horse were stuck at the bottom."

Beau and Diane stopped mid-step and stared at Charlotte. She explained about the pump suddenly turning on and their risk of being trapped.

"Gee, that does seem like an awful lot of coincidences at once," Diane remarked.

"Exactly what I said to Samuel, but he refused to believe it."

"I don't suppose that the name 'Wade' popped into your mind did it?" Beau inquired.

Charlotte placed the end of her index finger to the tip of her nose, indicating to Beau that he was right.

A truck that was coming up the drive carrying day laborers interrupted Charlotte. Joe was waiting at the top to greet them.

"Let's go see what the plan is for today," Charlotte said, walking toward the farmhouse.

"Good morning," Joe called out, waving. "I see the gang's all here."

"And I see that you've got yourself a bunch of helpers. Is today special on the farm that you require extra hands?"

"We're ten days away from the July Fourth holiday, so we want to get as much produce to market as possible. Samuel told me last night that he wants to set up shop at tomorrow's farmers market and bypass Serge and his commission. So, I called for reinforcements."

"Sounds like a perfect plan, and count me in for picking duty," Charlotte replied, and Beau and Diane immediately volunteered as well.

"Great, why don't you head down and check in with Samuel while I get these fellows organized and signed in."

They nodded to Joe and started down the hillside.

"He still seems like such a nice guy," Diane remarked.

Charlotte shrugged her shoulders.

"What? Joe too? Next you're going to tell me that there's no such thing as Santa Claus." Diane looked at Charlotte.

"Understandable," Beau said. "Ah, Farmer Brown, top of the morning to you!"

Samuel nodded to the group.

"We've come to be put to work on the harvest; your other ten hands will be along in a moment." Charlotte tried to keep it light, they had not parted on the best of terms last night, and she wanted today to be as productive as possible.

"Good. How about you three work the strawberry field on the north side?" Samuel said, pointing. "You can take this electric cart with the trailer. It's charged and all set to go, with empty baskets. Make sure that the berries are plump and firm and completely red. Hold the stem of the berry about a half-inch from the fruit between your thumbnail and index finger. Use your thumbnail to sever the stem and make sure to leave some of it and the cap intact. I've got a bunch of hats on hooks in the barn. Help yourself—you'll need one against the sun," he told Beau and Diane. Charlotte was sporting her uncle's Stetson.

"Thanks, Samuel. We'll work all morning as fast as we can. After lunch we'll need to spend our time setting up the shop and antique mart," Charlotte told him.

"Is that when you'll need to move the furniture you want to sell out of the farmhouse?"

Charlotte nodded.

"Just let me know when, and I'll grab one of the guys and we'll do it." Samuel kicked the dirt on the paddock floor, something she noticed that he did when he was frustrated. "Listen, I'm sorry that I got so angry last evening. There's just been a lot of bad things happening lately, and I don't like it. At all."

"I understand, and it all started when I arrived on the scene," Charlotte said. "But I can assure you that I'm going to get to the bottom of this, and the murderer will pay."

"How do we look?" they heard Beau ask.

He had donned a pink visor with an extra long brim, and Diane was wearing an Australian Outback sun hat.

"You both look dashing. Hop in the cart—we're off to pick strawberries."

Charlotte started the motor and slowly pulled away from the paddock. She heard a loud squeal and slammed on the brakes.

She looked back and saw Horse racing toward the cart, still chomping on the last bites of breakfast.

"Chew it all up before you jump on, little man. I don't want you choking.

Horse stopped and did exactly that.

*   *   *

By one o'clock, the three had managed to pick fifty-two quarts of strawberries before cramping got the best of their fingers and hands. Samuel was ecstatic with their progress, and Charlotte told him that in an hour they'd be ready for help moving furniture.

She saw that one of the two open-bed farm trucks was almost full with boxes of tomatoes.

"We'll fill the other one with more tomatoes and the last of the strawberries. Season's almost over," Samuel explained.

"Charlotte, you look ravishing as usual," cooed Annabel, leading a trail of yoga students down to the barn.

"Hi, Annabel. Now is really not a good time for you to have a yoga class here. We're in the middle of harvesting for market tomorrow, and we need the space to sort the fruit into containers. I think that in the future you're going to have to schedule classes a week in advance so that we can avoid these conflicts. Also, we'll need to charge you rent to cover costs, Samuel's time, and the use of the goats."

It was like everyone, including the animals, froze in place. Annabel's mouth dropped to her chest, and her face was as red as a beefsteak tomato. Matching her lipstick perfectly. Charlotte remembered how much Annabel detested the word "no."

"Well, this is certainly an inconvenient surprise. We've been coming here for years," Annabel finally spat out.

"This is a working farm, and that comes first." Charlotte gave Annabel her brightest smile.

Samuel stifled a laugh.

"Back up, people—there'll be no class today," Annabel announced, flicking her hand at them as if she was shooing away a fly. Her water bottle dropped from under her arm onto the ground. She didn't even have the courtesy to retrieve it.

"But how am I going to find my flow?" asked one portly gentleman.

"I don't know—why don't you ask Siri?" Annabel snapped back at him.

Everyone watched them stomp off.

"Namaste," Beau said with a slight bow, pressing his hands together and pointing them upward with his thumbs close to his chest.

The goats wandered out of the barn and started a chorus of happy bleats. Horse joined in to provide the bass. Because that's what it's all about.

The afternoon seemed almost boring by comparison to the "showdown with Annabel," as it was being called. Alice and Diane slipped away early to prepare dinner, which was served family style and al fresco. Everyone had showered and cleaned up for the meal, and Samuel was even wearing a shirt with a collar. Joe brought some bottles of wine and proposed the first toast.

"Here's to the Finn Family Farm. May she continue to prosper and provide bountiful fruits and vegetables for the people of Santa Barbara County."

"Here, here," said Samuel.

Despite everyone being bone tired, it was a merry night. It was a "good tired" and oddly invigorating from a day well spent.

Supper was extra crispy and juicy fried chicken, creamy polenta, a huge garden salad, and Diane's signature garlic knots. Everyone was talking at once with excitement for tomorrow's farmers market—a nice boost in income for the farm was just what the doctor ordered.

Charlotte looked at the tanned, happy faces of the people seated around the table against a backdrop of verdant hills and a midnight-blue night sky. Its endless stars winked at her, and Charlotte thought that life was indeed good and that she could call the farm home.

"In addition to selling our produce tomorrow, let's pick up everything we need that will last for our barbecue a week from today," Charlotte suggested. "Alice, do you have a list?"

"Mostly, but I'll sit with Diane after supper and add anything I've missed."

"And I've got the napkins, plates, cups, and decorations covered, Char," Beau announced. "The theme is going to be Americana meets David Hockney!"

Charlotte couldn't exactly picture that, but she trusted Beau to create something festive.

"I'm in charge of the grilling and smokers. I'll set up barbecue barrel grills near the lake and your market. We've got enough wooden doors and saw horses for tables as well," Joe informed her.

"Wahoo!" shouted Diane. "This is going to be a humdinger of a hootenanny!"

Samuel started to giggle and then erupted into full-on laughter, to the point where tears were running down his cheeks. It was contagious, because everyone joined in, even though they weren't sure what they were laughing at.

"What's so funny, Samuel?" Joe finally asked.

"I'm just picturing Serge's face tomorrow when he struts around the market, trying to find more farmers to steal from, and sees that we've cut him out of his beloved money."

That started another round of snickering and guffawing.

"I bet that he already knows." Charlotte was finally able to get control to speak. "After my almighty upbraiding, I'm sure that Annabel went 'wee-wee-weeping' all the way home! And let's not forget the bill I left for him. They're probably plotting their revenge as we speak."

This time there was no controlling the roars of laughter. Charlotte watched Horse make an attempt to say "wee," and even Mrs. Robinson, who had returned from her duties and joined Horse for dinner, had a bemused look on her face. Or so Charlotte assumed.

Chapter Seventeen

Once dinner was cleaned up, everyone headed off for bed. They would have an early start in the morning.

"Goodnight, my BFF," Charlotte said, giving Diane a hug. "I can't tell you how special it is to have you by my side with all of this. I don't know what I'd do without you and Beau."

"Funny you say that, because my dear brother and I feel the same way about you. We talked about it the other day. Life would be so much easier for you if you got out from under this farm and moved in with me. I've got plenty of room, and then we could see you everyday!"

"Where is this coming from? I thought you loved it here. You said that it was so peaceful." Charlotte couldn't believe Diane.

"I did, but it sure isn't now. There's hostility around every corner of the place. Someone may have tried to kill you in the cellar, and when that didn't work, tried to drown you in the lake. There are people coming out of the woodwork plotting to take the farm away from you. And now that we suspect that Marcus was one of those people, it shows that someone wants it bad enough to kill for it. This is just not a safe place for you,

Charlotte, I know that it's hard to hear, but it's time for you to move to safer ground. Beau agrees."

"Wow—I don't know what to say. And after such a beautiful day and evening. I suggest that you go to bed unless you are too afraid to stay the night. And I've got some thinking of my own to do."

"Charlotte, don't be this way. We love you and we're worried about you."

"I can take care of myself, Diane. I always have. Come on, Horse, you're going to take the first watch."

Charlotte stormed off to her room, visibly shaking with anger and more than a little fear.

"Just when I'm getting control of this farm and getting close to solving the murder, Diane has to plant seeds of doubt and get negative," Charlotte said to Horse as she discarded her clothes and donned a nightshirt.

Horse listened intently and was the first to climb up the hope chest and then onto the bed.

He's had a long day too. Right now I just want to hug my sweet Horse and have sweet dreams.

She set her alarm and turned out the lights. Charlotte was asleep as her head hit the pillow.

* * *

She was startled awake by the sounds of clomping on the outside patio's Spanish paver tiles. She opened her eyes and waited for them to adjust to the dark. Charlotte looked over at Horse for his reaction, but he was sound asleep. Then she heard the sound of a snort. She could see the shadow of a large figure standing on the patio outside her French doors. Charlotte reached for the lamp switch, and just before she found it, she saw the unmistakable orange glow of someone smoking a cigarette. Charlotte let out a whimper and then heard sounds of horse hooves galloping away.

Wade.

She gripped the sheets and listened for what might come next. She fought exhaustion and considered getting up and going to investigate, but everyone had worked so hard today, and she didn't want to wake them. Wade was long gone. There was continued silence from outside, if you discounted the rhythmic showy love song of chirping male crickets. The first night Charlotte had gone to bed on the farm, she'd had trouble tuning them out.

Ah, my cricket friends, I'm not sure that I could fall asleep without you now.

Then Horse jumped up and began a loud squealing in the pitch-black room. Charlotte scrambled to find the switch for the bedside lamp. The lamp's dim bulb cast just enough light as she watched Horse slide another antique suitcase over to the ones he'd placed under the patio door handle.

"Horse, what are you doing?"

He gave her a wide-eyed look of pure terror and then climbed up the suitcases and attempted to turn the door handle. But Charlotte remembered locking it just before she went to sleep.

Wade.

The sounds and images of the horse and rider outside on the patio came rushing back to her, sending a fresh chill up her spine.

Horse jumped up and down angrily on the top case, in frustration at not being able to open the door.

It was then that Charlotte smelled the smoke.

She grabbed a sweatshirt, threw on some shorts, and dashed to the patio door.

Once she unlocked the French doors and stepped out back, she could see that the produce trucks were on fire. The Santa Ana winds were blowing the flames directly toward the barn.

"Oh dear God, no!" Charlotte yelled. "Diane and Beau, wake up!"

Before Charlotte could stop him, she saw Horse racing toward the livestock. Charlotte slipped on a pair of rubber boots that she spotted sitting outside the doors. They were too big but would have to do. Holding each boot by its top, she broke into a squatting run and followed Horse down to the paddock.

There was an acrid, vinegary smell to the air as tomatoes broiled and plastic baskets melted. Charlotte remembered from a briefing for an ad for a fire alarm company that fire requires three things to survive: heat, fuel, and oxygen. And as soon as all the produce burned, the fire would go searching for fuel and certainly find the barn.

When Charlotte reached the paddock, she saw Samuel battling the fire with a hose. He'd covered his nose and mouth with a red bandana to protect his lungs, and when he saw Charlotte, he moved toward her.

"Here—put this on to help with the smoke," he said, giving her his bandana. "And keep working the hose. I'm going to try to push these trucks away from the barn," he shouted over the roar of flames licking the wooden truck bed dry.

"But what if the fire hits the gas tank? The whole thing could explode!"

"Hopefully that won't happen," Samuel yelled, his voice getting hoarse. He got into the cab of the first truck and must have put it in neutral, because Charlotte saw it start to roll.

Joe rushed up and started pushing from the back as Charlotte continued dousing the flames around him. Out of the corner of her eye, she saw Alice grab another hose and go to work.

I wonder where Beau and Diane are. They must have woken up, with all this noise and smoke.

"The barn!" Alice shouted.

Charlotte watched embers float onto the barn roof just as she had predicted, and redirected the water.

The geese had woken up and were flying in formation—trying to shift the winds away from the barn, Charlotte guessed. She heard Horse let out loud, warning, growling oinks as he stood outside the barn doors.

"Don't you go in there, Horse!" Charlotte screamed as the little pig looked over his shoulder at her. She saw that he was torn between obeying her and running in to help save his friends. In the end, he resorted to more grunts and yelps, and, sure enough, the goats were the first to peek their heads out of the barn doors. The fire and the smell of whoever had set it must have scared them from coming out earlier.

Following close behind them was Pele. Charlotte assumed that he had let himself out of his stall.

"The fire's out on the trucks, but the produce is gone, and we'll have to rebuild the beds. We won't know about the motors until we try to turn the engines, but I don't want to do that until we're sure that there are no live embers floating around." Samuel looked tired and defeated; his eyes were red, and his face was streaked with smoke.

"We'd better check the barn and make sure that there's nothing in the rafters that could spark," Joe said, looking about the same as Samuel. "I see you two got the animals out to safety."

"We didn't do it—Horse got them to come out!" Alice declared.

"Well, I'll be darned." Joe smiled and shook his head, marveling at the pig.

"Any chance that this fire was due to the strong winds tonight?" Alice asked Samuel.

He shook his head. "The wind didn't help, but we could smell gasoline all over the trucks. This was deliberately set."

"I was afraid of that, and I have a suspicion that Wade had something to do with it." Charlotte felt a tear drop down her cheek. She coughed and pretended that it was from the smoke.

"Oh my good Lord, is everybody okay?" Beau shouted, racing toward them in lime-green pajamas.

"Charlotte!" Diane screamed. We called the fire department—they should be here in a couple of minutes. Are you hurt?"

"You'd better call Chief Goodacre," Samuel whispered to Charlotte before heading to the barn.

After telling Beau and Diane what happened, she sent them back up to the farmhouse to wait for the fire department. Apparently, Beau was in pain from the day's picking. He'd said it totally knocked him out. Diane was watching a cooking show on her tablet, and with her earphones in, she hadn't heard a thing.

Charlotte couldn't help but wonder if it was a coincidence that the fire had happened after Beau and Diane showed up. Just like the murder. Then there was Wade, showing up on horseback just before the fire. She remembered smelling a cigarette and wondered if he'd used it to ignite the fire.

Charlotte would need to check for horse hoof prints on the patio and in the dirt outside her bedroom window. And try to locate a cigarette butt. No one on the farm smoked, so it could hopefully be traced back to Wade. She walked up the hill with purpose, Horse at her heels.

Then, of course, there were Serge and Annabel. If they were grudge-holding types, which they surely were, then they certainly had motive for setting the produce on fire. This was savage even for them, but to keep their hands clean, they might have assigned Wade the task. Diane was right when she'd said earlier that the threat of danger had been brought to a whole new level. People and animals could have died.

Charlotte questioned whether this was the work of Marcus's killer. It showed the same kind of anger. She needed to refine the list of suspects and find proof. Suddenly, the need to find the murderer was critical, before someone else died.

Back in her room, Charlotte found her phone and dialed the chief's number.

Chapter Eighteen

There wasn't much for the firemen to do once they arrived, but they walked the area in a grid pattern, checking for hot spots and embers. They explained that one little hotspot could spark a fire that could destroy the barn and the farmhouse. A couple of them collected evidence from the burnt trucks but pretty much confirmed on the spot that the fire had been intentionally set with a gasoline accelerant.

Charlotte watched Theresa make her way down the hill. She almost didn't recognize the chief in plain clothes—it was the middle of the night after all.

"Arson, is it boys?" Goodacre asked the firefighters.

"Almost certainly," he answered her.

"Where's Samuel? He nearby?" This time she posed the question to Charlotte.

"Yes, I think he and Joe are in the barn."

"Let's go find them." The chief didn't wait for a reply and instead traversed the paddock with purpose. Charlotte and Horse quickly trailed behind her.

"There you are, Samuel. You keep gasoline around here for the tractors?"

"Hello, Chief, thanks for coming." The sadness in Samuel's eyes was palpable. "I moved all the gas cans away from the barn and the animals after last year's devastating fire. They're down by my cabin, and I even built a crate so that I can keep them locked up. Just in case someone needs a fill-up and gets careless."

"That's good to hear. Lead the way. We need to check to see if anyone broke into that crate. I'm desperate for some shred of evidence. Come with us, Charlotte. You said over the phone that you had several important discoveries to share with me." The chief was in charge.

Charlotte looked back at Diane and Beau talking to a firefighter. The fear in their faces seemed genuine. She would know: she'd watched their expressions nearly all her life, and often words were simply extraneous.

"They look to be all here, and the crate's intact," Samuel said when they'd arrived at the spot. He illuminated it with the flashlight that he still held from searching for embers. "Why don't we go in my cabin to talk? It's the middle of summer, but the mist from the sea air always seems to bless us with cool nights in Little Acorn."

Charlotte knew that to be true. She was about to see Samuel's inner sanctum for the first time, but she tried to hide her curiosity.

"There's a small living area. Seat yourselves on the sofa, and I can pull over a chair from the kitchen. I don't really have guests in here," Samuel told them, once inside.

The place had a pitched roof that made the small space seem airy. On one wall was a stone fireplace with a dark oak mantle, similar to the wood that she'd seen in the cellar and just as old. One of the first things to strike Charlotte was that the place was so tidy and clean that you could eat off the floor. Samuel was never unkempt, but given the nature of his work, she wasn't expecting this level of care.

The wall opposite the fireplace contained built-in, floor-to-ceiling wood bookcases, filled so that there wasn't even space for a field mouse to nap. Charlotte tried not to be nosy but couldn't resist scanning some of the book titles. Many were leather-bound classics.

"Your great-uncle gave most of these to me. You remember what a great teacher he was? I've read almost all of them by now. I think that Steinbeck is my favorite," Samuel explained, catching Charlotte examining the shelves. He turned the chair that he'd brought into the tiny living room backward, straddled it, and rested his arms on the ladder back.

"Okay, Charlotte, why don't you lay your cards out on the table?" the chief suggested.

Almost an hour later, Charlotte had told the chief about the run-in with Annabel, Serge's thievery, the doctored books, and the invoice she'd given him. She finished with the accident in the lake basin and the incident in the root cellar.

"It sounds like you've been through the mill, Charlotte." The chief shook her head. "I'll get my team out in the morning to inspect the trucks and see if they can pull any evidence, but I'm not optimistic. And I need to leave with the accounting books that you say Serge forged."

Charlotte nodded. "There's more. Maybe." Charlotte hung her head down, not knowing whether the next thing she was about to tell them was true or not.

"Go on, honey—it's just us here," the chief said, and gave Samuel a look that said this was to be between the two of them.

"With everything that has gone on the last two days and me being dead tired from the harvest today, I just can't be sure if this happened or it was a dream." Charlotte couched what she was about to say next, and then she told them about the horse and Wade. "I was going to check for hoof prints when I got back to my room, but after I called you, the fire trucks arrived, and I ran out to join them."

Samuel grabbed his flashlight off the side table and raced out of the cabin.

Charlotte stood, about to follow him, but the chief caught her wrist.

"Let him go. He and Wade have a long history, but I believe that Samuel is an honest man. If the prints are there, he'll preserve them. If they aren't, he won't try to create them." The chief patted the sofa, indicating for Charlotte to sit back down. "I'll check with the arson inspectors to see if they found any cigarette butts."

"Now, after I leave here, I'm going to go get in my uniform and surprise the Andersens with a visit. Find out just where they've been tonight and if anyone can corroborate their stories," the chief announced, looking at her watch.

"I have a list of some of Serge's other accounts. Samuel and Joe were going to check with them and see if they'd noticed anything odd with their books," Charlotte offered.

"How'd you get a hold—never mind; don't tell me. Just get me the list, and my department will follow up with everyone. Oh, and I got a call from the lab today, with a 'sort of' result on your uncle's paternity testing. I'm afraid it's not good news."

"A 'sort of' result?" Charlotte sighed.

"That's how he put it. Even though the root was attached to the hair sample we gave the lab, he said that it had deteriorated enough to compromise the test. Remember the sixty-percent accuracy rate they quoted us?"

Charlotte dropped her head and nodded slowly.

"Now the lab says any test results wouldn't be more than twenty-percent accurate."

"So that throws the whole 'piece-of-the-pie'-as-motive theory right out the window." Charlotte closed her eyes in an effort to dull the throbbing in her head.

"Not necessarily. Right now, only three parties know this: you, me, and the lab."

Charlotte looked at the chief and nodded.

Unless Marcus knew—or thought he knew—his heritage and told someone in Little Acorn . . .

"I wonder what's taking Samuel so long. He should be back by now," Charlotte worried aloud.

Yes he should, the chief thought.

Suddenly they both got up and raced out of the cabin as well. When they reached the portion of the patio outside Charlotte's bedroom Chief Goodacre turned on her penlight and pointed it down on the grass that edged up to the patio. The light revealed that the ground was indented in numerous places by the hooves of an animal.

"I stand corrected. My first order of business is going to be finding Wade Avery. Hopefully before Samuel does!"

The chief ran off to her car, leaving Charlotte and Horse staring at the prints that were becoming clearer with the sun peeking its head above the horizon.

* * *

After getting a couple of hours of sleep, Charlotte woke to an adrenaline rush from the events of last night surfacing in her mind. Her first thought was of Samuel, so she threw on a sundress and her sneakers and ran out to see if he'd returned.

"Charlotte," Diane shouted, hearing her in the foyer. "Come have some breakfast, and we'll talk about how we're going to attack this day and right the ship."

"Sounds good—I'll be right back!" Charlotte raced out and down to the paddock. Her heart was going a mile a minute. When she reached the split rail and saw that Horse was chowing down, she was relieved—it meant that Samuel was indeed back.

Samuel poked his head out of the barn; in his hands he held the reins of the horse's tackle as he polished the brass.

"Good morning," Charlotte greeted him. "I wasn't sure if I'd find you here or in jail, the way you took off last night." She paused. "I was worried."

Hearing her last few words, he put down the reins and joined her in the paddock.

"You were worried? Really?" Samuel studied Charlotte's face for the answer.

"Of course. You are a vital member of this team," Charlotte replied, looking away. She was uncomfortable with his inspection.

"Just so you know, I didn't do anything to Wade. I wanted to, but I didn't. I went to the stables where he and his Ranchero buddies keep the horses they ride. I found them all sitting outside around a fire, drinking from a whiskey bottle. They were all pretty incapacitated, so I kept my distance. When I saw Chief Goodacre drive up, I high-tailed it out of there."

"I'm glad that you didn't do any harm to Wade, and just so you know, I can fight my own battles."

"Damn it, woman—"

"You two ever do anything but hang out in the paddock and argue? This is pretty much where I left you last night." Chief Goodacre strode down to them with a couple of deputies in tow.

"Canvas all around here and then farther down the hill where the burnt-out trucks are sitting. Look for anything that is out of place. I would really love to find some fingerprints, preferably from a cigarette butt," Chief Goodacre instructed her officers.

"Good morning, Chief. I guess that you didn't find out who set fire to our produce?" Charlotte inquired.

"Wade admits that he rode up here, but he says it was just for fun. He and his boys were returning from a ride and were on their way to the stable. When they passed your farm, he told everyone to wait a couple of minutes, and he rode up the hill. His buddies claim that he wasn't gone more than fifteen minutes. Enough time to scare you, but not enough to set that kind of big fire."

"His buddies could be lying to protect him," Samuel suggested.

Or his buddies could have set the fire while Wade and his horse made sure that I'd be his alibi.

"They could, but I pressed pretty hard, and in their inebriated state, one of them would probably have slipped up. Also, I inspected the horses, and there was no smell of smoke. I did the same with Wade, but they had a campfire going, and that masked any other odors."

Samuel kicked up some dirt in frustration.

"What about Serge and Annabel? Did they have an alibi for last night?" Charlotte asked, hoping that they didn't.

"Yes and no. I woke up Annabel—I could have guessed that she'd wear one of those fancy lace negligees and robes—and she said that she'd been home all night. She told me that Serge had called around seven to say that he was taking customers out to dinner clear over in Los Cruces and was going to stay the night there so he wouldn't have to worry about drinking and driving. After I talk with the prosecutor, I'll pay old Serge a visit and see what he has to say for himself."

Charlotte watched the chief instruct the officers once more and then leave them to their inspecting. She admired how very focused the chief could be, and decided right then and there to do the same.

"Samuel, I'm going to paint those signs for the You Pick 'Em business, and I'd like to get them up today if possible. We're going to be open for business, starting tomorrow. And I want to include tomatoes in the deal. Maybe we should talk about diversifying our crops next season. I'm sure that folks would enjoy picking all kinds of fruits and veggies. One way or the other, we are going to sell what we grow!"

Charlotte stormed up the hill with the purpose of a woman on a mission.

* * *

The rest of the day was both busy and productive. Beau and Diane worked on fliers for You Pick 'Em that they promised to dispense around town on their drive to Los Angeles. Alice used brightly colored markers and ribbons to decorate strawberry and tomato baskets. And after Charlotte finished the signs, she went into the Farm Shop to put the finishing touches on the store. Horse happily followed along.

"You like all this activity, don't you, Horse?" Charlotte knelt down next to him and stared into his big bright eyes that were looking back at her through a wispy waterfall of light pink lashes.

"I'll tell you what, Horse: from now on I'm going to you, and you alone, with who I suspect murdered Marcus Cordero. You can tell me, in whatever way you like, if I'm on the right track or not."

He cocked his head to one side and studied her face as she was talking. His tail was spinning like a propeller beanie on a windy day.

"Do we have a deal, Horse?" Charlotte extended her hand to him. To her utter surprise he brought his upper right hoof up to meet it.

I think that Samuel has been secretly training this little guy.

"Hi, Miss Charlotte," Joe said, entering the farm shop with an armload of wooden boards. "Did I hear you say that you want You Pick 'Em guests to start in the store and then go out to pick?"

"That's right, Joe—will that be a problem?"

"Not at all, but I thought that we might need some directional signs to guide them, especially on days when it gets really busy."

"I like the way you think!" Charlotte smiled and looked at the boards.

"Should I just paint arrows on the signs?" Joe asked.

"I have a better idea." Charlotte took out a pad of paper and began to draw.

Charlotte finished the signs outside, where she could spread out her paints and brushes and not have to worry about being messy. When she handed the last one to Joe to post, she saw Diane and Beau approach. She knew that she'd been a little cool to them the previous night and wanted to make amends.

"Is it time already for you to drive back? I feel so bad that you came all this way and stupid people doing stupid things prevented us from having fun together." Charlotte gave them each a hug.

"Even though we all had a rough time of it, the farm is just so beautiful that I always return home feeling as rejuvenated as I do after a hydrating facial," Beau said patting his cheeks.

"I'm sorry—" both Diane and Charlotte said in unison.

"It is clear that you belong here, Charlotte, despite the mess that you found yourself in, and it isn't my place to tell you differently. If you are determined to make this farm successful, I'll support you, but you can't stop me from worrying. Remember, the last "F" in BFF stands for 'forever.'" Diane looked into Charlotte's eyes to show her sincerity.

"Thank you, Di, and I am and will continue to be ever vigilant. Somewhere out there is a rotten tomato on a vine, and I'm going to find it and pluck it out!"

"I have no doubt you will. Beau and I will be back on Thursday night to give you extra help preparing for the barbecue fundraiser. We made up our minds this morning, and we both got some time off. No arguments," Diane said, seeing Charlotte start to wind up.

"We've got the fliers, and we'll make sure that everyone in Little Acorn sees them, darling. Oh and I just love all your signs! Ta-ta." Beau waved.

Charlotte saw that Joe had nailed the signs on posts that lined the path down to the farm store. They really did look cute with the line drawing of Horse that she'd done and his hoof prints trailing behind him. In addition to the illustration, the arrow signs also had the words

"U Pick 'Em."

Things were turning around.

Chapter Nineteen

The next few days were so busy that Charlotte barely had time to do much else but lead U Pick 'Em groups. With school out for summer, moms and dads were desperate for things to keep their kids occupied—happy to pay for baskets of tomatoes in exchange for a couple hours of peace. And a few parents had even bought some of her antiques.

Chief Goodacre had called to say that the prosecutor wanted her to get statements from some of the other farmers that Serge may have bilked, and then he would consider an arrest warrant. Since the Finn Family Farm had a murder hanging over its head, he thought that the case would hold up better with a handful of grievances.

"What about Serge's alibi for the night of the fire. Did that check out?" Charlotte asked her.

"I'm afraid that it did. I would have loved to pin that on him. They had a room at a local Los Cruces Mexican restaurant, and the staff told me that the margaritas were flowing all night long."

Something was nagging at Charlotte about Serge and Annabel, but she couldn't quite put her finger on it.

They said their "goodbyes" just as two parents and six kids walked into the farm shop.

"Hi, welcome to the Finn Family Farm's You Pick 'Em adventure. You guys want strawberries or tomatoes?"

"Strawberries!" they all yelled.

"Okey-dokey, these are the last four wagons that aren't already out in the fields, so grab those. They're loaded with baskets and ready to go. I don't suppose that you all want to go to the paddock first and see the animals?" Charlotte gave them a mock shake of the head.

More shrieks and screams erupted from the excited bunch.

"You are a godsend," one of the mothers said to Charlotte as they walked.

Charlotte noticed that despite having her hands full with kids, she maintained a happy demeanor. She walked with her head held high and her home manicure, with kiwi green nail polish, said that she leaned toward the side of whimsy.

"I remember you. We were stuck behind the fake Rancheros led by Wade Avery about a week ago. You drive a blue minivan?"

"That's me. I'm Marcy, and this is my neighbor and partner in crime, Izzy."

"Pleased to meet you both, and thanks so much for coming. We've had some setbacks when I first arrived, but I think that now I'm finally getting the tiger by the tail," Charlotte told them.

"You got a tiger? Wow!" said a boy of about ten. His face was a roadmap of freckles, and his sunburnt nose told her that someone snuck out of the house without applying sunscreen first.

"No, that's just an expression, but we do have a horse that plays soccer."

"Cool." The boy ran on ahead.

"Have they solved the murder that happened in your field? Or at least, do they have any leads?" Marcy asked.

"Not yet, but I think I'm . . . ah, they're getting closer. Did you know the victim? His name was Marcus Cordero." Charlotte hoped that they did.

"We'd met him," Izzy said while holding a tissue to one of her kid's noses. "Blow!

"He tended the animals at that place . . . the Humble Petting Zoo. We've taken our kids there a couple of times, but by now it's old hat to them and they get bored." Her cargo shorts seemed to hold an endless supply of kid-related items, and almost before her daughter began to whine, Izzy produced a juice box from a lower-level side pocket.

"Oh wow, what was Marcus like? Did he talk about himself much?"

"You know, that's the funny thing," Marcy said, picking up the narrative. "At the farmhouse in front of the owners, he was very quiet, but when we got to the animal pens, he started yammering away, mostly to the kids."

They had arrived at the paddock, and Charlotte whistled the goats' favorite musical phrase. Moments later they came scampering out of the barn to greet their visitors.

"Was he telling them about the animals—what they eat and like to do for fun? That sort of thing?" Charlotte inquired. Charlotte had learned to have a pocket of food pellets on her at all times and was distributing handfuls to the kids for feeding the goats. This also helped disguise her questions about Marcus as nothing more than conversation.

"No, it was more like a fantasy story. He said that he was on an adventure in the quest to find a vast treasure. That came out of nowhere and was a bit odd," Marcy explained.

"I agree," Izzy said, quickly dispensing hand sanitizer after each child had fed a goat. "He kept saying that he needed to fight to get what was rightfully his. He'd challenge them to a duel if necessary. To the death. The older kids laughed at him or ignored him, and the younger ones were kind of creeped out."

"I can understand why." Charlotte tried to picture the scene. It might be time for her to visit the Humble Petting Zoo. She would find the time.

"Everyone, you're in luck. Pele the horse is entering the paddock. Now where has my little piggy gotten to?" Charlotte looked around, stopping first at the secret dugout he used to escape the paddock. When she saw that it was empty, her eyes went to the trough, which was devoid of both food and Horse. She then turned her head to the barn entrance and squinted her eyes.

"Your little piggy got his head stuck in a bucket that I was using to wash strawberries. I thought that I was going to have to cut through the metal pail, but some warm water finally did the trick." Samuel came out of the barn, cradling the animal, and set him down in the middle of the paddock. Seeing Charlotte, he squealed with delight and raced over to her.

"Everyone, this is my little pig. His name is Horse."

The kids stared at her, wide-eyed and silent, waiting for an explanation.

"I call him Horse because he eats like one!" She giggled and the kids joined in with laughter. Suddenly, Horse had become the star attraction.

Dead on the Vine

Everyone spread out along the split rail fence around the paddock as Samuel disappeared into the barn and returned with a soccer ball. Seeing this, Horse walked proudly to the center of the enclosure. He looked around and issued a report of grunts to the goats and to Pele. Like the call of the wild, a group of geese flew overhead and then landed to join the game. It was as if Horse were the captain, calling out the play in code grunts.

When Samuel thought that they were ready to start, he rolled the ball toward Horse.

"You guys are in for a treat. I've watched this several times and have tried to decipher the rules, which they definitely have, but then they do something to surprise me," Charlotte told the group.

Horse started the match with a kickoff to Pele, the actual horse. The goats then spread out as one accepted the pass from Pele and tapped it along to the next goat that, in a moment of glory, balanced atop the ball. When he hopped off, the geese took over and chest-pumped the ball around. Samuel noticed that the female goat hadn't had a chance to play yet, and grabbed the ball and tossed it to her for a spectacular header.

"The only things missing from this amazing show are peanuts and Cracker Jacks," Charlotte told the gaping audience.

*   *   *

A while later the two happy families left, laden with baskets of strawberries and tomatoes and a few of great-uncle Tobias's knickknacks from the shop. Charlotte went down to the barn to thank Samuel for his participation. It had been a good day.

"I'm going to have to get you a whistle and cleats, Samuel—that was some refereeing today!"

Horse had followed her and immediately went to his trough, hoping that the dinner hour was on us.

"Not yet, Horse," Samuel said, disappointing him. "That was fun. It's nice to have children on the farm again. Your great-uncle, always a kid himself, loved having them around." Samuel gave her a warm smile as he reminisced.

"It must have been sad and lonely for you after he passed, and I'm sure you were wondering if you would still have a job when the estate was settled," Charlotte said. "I can tell you right now that you do, and I am so very appreciative that you stayed."

"Thank you, Miss Charlotte."

"So may we close that chapter? You're not going to run away and join the circus?" Charlotte's heart sped up, hoping for the correct answer.

Samuel laughed. "Not any time soon."

"Thank goodness. So, Samuel, what's your theory on who set our produce on fire?"

He sighed and thought for a good long minute. "There's something that you should know about me Charlotte." Samuel turned his head to his right shoulder and looked out over the fields, avoiding eye contact. "This is a small town, and everybody knows everybody else and most of their business. That includes the kids."

Charlotte hopped up onto the paddock rail, sensing that this story was going to build to an arc.

"One summer—I guess I was probably eleven—me and my friends were hanging out by Whispering Palms Creek, digging out a section of rocks so that we could have a swimming hole. We had a system going, and by mid afternoon the water was already above our knees. So we took a break and sat in the water to cool off."

"Tell me about your friends—do you still see them?" Charlotte didn't want to interrupt, but she also didn't know when Samuel would open up again like he was doing now.

He might tell me something that either makes him look guiltier or exonerates him.

Samuel seemed surprised by her interest and inquiry. "Neighborhood kids around my age. There was Cade—his dad ran the gas station in town. I'd say he was my best friend at the time. He moved to Hawaii, and I think runs a sport fishing business. Then there were Tim and his younger brother, Paul. Poor little kid; he was born with this thing called Bell's palsy, where there's a weakness in muscle control on one side of your face."

Charlotte nodded, indicating that she'd heard of it.

"To us, Paul was just another kid, so we took him under our wing. So we're sitting in the water, trying to catch tadpoles, when Wade and four of his buddies showed up. They're all two or three years older than us. Bullies led by the biggest bully of all, Wade."

"I don't like where I think this is going." Charlotte wrapped her arms around her waist.

Samuel nodded and continued. "The minute Wade saw Paul, he started in on him, calling him 'palsy Paul' and 'Bassett hound.' Tim told Wade to shut up, but that only stirred the pot. Next the older boys decided to take over our swimming hole and yanked us out, one by one, except for Paul. They got in the water and crowded him."

Charlotte gasped. "Kids can be so cruel."

"Then Wade said that they should have drowned Paul at birth because he was a total misfit. I saw Wade swing his arm over Paul's shoulder and place his palm on the back of Paul's head." Samuel paused for a moment. "Then I heard footsteps behind me and turned to see Tim holding a boulder about the size the size of a bowling ball over his head, Tim's eyes were fixed on Wade."

Charlotte brought her fingers to her mouth in shock. Even Horse lay down and hugged the earth.

"'Get your grimy hand off my bother!' Tim shouted. I saw the look of surprise when Wade turned around. There was no way that he could stand up in time to avoid being hit. And a rock that size would surely have done some permanent damage.

"I calmly but sternly told Tim to put the rock down. I knew that he'd heard me, but he continued to hold the boulder over his head, staring at Wade. Paul, free of Wade's clutch, crawled out of the swimming hole. I explained to Tim that he could get jail time, and then Paul would be alone against these bullies.

"After some more pleading, Tim finally put the boulder down. Wade and his friends looked at me, stunned. Tim and Paul's family moved away that fall. They couldn't take the bullying any longer."

They sat in silence for a bit, and then Samuel let out a dry laugh from the back of his throat.

"Funniest thing: Wade never forgave me for saving his life."

"Wow, that was quite a story. So Wade is out to destroy anything good that comes your way?"

"Pretty much." Samuel nodded. "You asked me who I thought started the fire? Even though his friends gave him an alibi, I'd bet that Wade was involved. He'd have heard about our harvest and plans from one of the day laborers or someone else, and he decided to take a cheap shot."

"Then we're just going to have to get proof."

Samuel shook his head. "Best just to drop it Wade's got a lot of people in this town wrapped around his finger. All you'd do is expend negative energy."

Unless it leads to proving that he's a murderer as well as an arsonist.

"Why don't the goats have names?" Charlotte asked, trying to make things lighter.

"Who says that they don't have names?" Samuel grinned, and Charlotte studied his face.

"You've named them?"

Samuel nodded. "The boys are Cade and Tim, and the girl is called Pauline."

Chapter Twenty

The chief called the next morning and asked Charlotte to come down to the station. She told her that she had some news, as did Maria, who had driven back from Northern California the night before.

On her way to the car, Charlotte walked around the side of the farmhouse to examine the area around the cellar doors one more time. It continued to bother her that they had no explanation for the mess that was made the night she had hit her head and passed out. Both Joe and Samuel had told her that they didn't find any evidence of raccoons or other critters down there, so what or who had done the damage?

Charlotte was headed into Little Acorn when she saw a sign for the Humble Petting Zoo and turned around and drove along the dirt road to the farmhouse. When she pulled to a stop, she noticed that the farmer's wife was outside, sweeping the front porch.

"Hi, I'm Charlotte Finn," she said, approaching the woman.

"Oh my, you're the—I mean it was on your farm—" She stopped, too flustered to finish her sentence.

"There, there," Charlotte said, rushing to her. "Yes, it was a terrible thing, but the killer will be found and made to pay. And the Finn Family Farm will be back better than ever." Charlotte guided her to the front steps, and they both sat down.

After taking a deep breath the woman said, "I'm Marjorie Kincaid. I own this farm and zoo with my husband. He's gone to town for supplies."

"I'm on my way there myself, but I wanted to stop by, give you my condolences and hopefully ask a couple of questions."

"No need for condolences, Charlotte. May I call you Charlotte?"

"Of course, Marjorie."

"No one should die in such a horrible manner, but I wouldn't say that Marcus had established any sort of bond with us. He did his job, and we were grateful, but when he wasn't working, we never saw or heard a peep from him."

"That seems a bit odd, doesn't it? You never saw him bring groceries to his room? Have friends over to watch a game?"

Marjorie shook her head. "We invited him right from the beginning to have dinner with us, or at least let us make him a plate, but he declined. There's a small TV in his room, but I don't think he ever turned it on."

"Did he ever mention any relatives? His childhood or hometown?"

"No, nothing like that."

"Would it be too much to ask you to show me his room? Assuming that there isn't somebody new in there already."

"Oh no, it's as he left it. The police didn't want us to touch anything, but they came and did an inspection. I suppose we could clean it now and get it ready, but we just haven't gotten around to it."

Marjorie stood and motioned Charlotte to follow her around the side of the house to a garage. The inside was filled with small motorbikes and farm machinery, all in various stages of disrepair. At the back wall was a staircase that led up to a second-story loft. Marjorie motioned for Charlotte to ascend first.

The open space above the garage was dark and virtually barren. One small window had been cut into the front roof facing, and it let in only about a foot of diffused light. Marjorie clicked on a floor lamp, and Charlotte adjusted her eyes to take in the space and its contents.

"It doesn't even look like anyone was living here," Charlotte said, walking around the bed and bare nightstands to the lone dresser sitting against the wall. "Does he still have clothing here?"

"No, the police took virtually everything for evidence. Even his toiletries. There are still a few staples in the kitchen—a box of cereal, instant coffee. Stuff like that plus a bottle of local wine that had barely been drunk."

Charlotte turned her attention to the red wine sitting on the kitchen counter. "What did he do for glasses? Plastic disposable?"

Marjorie opened a kitchen cabinet. "We provide dishes, plates, cups, and glasses. Not many, but here they are."

Charlotte reached in and took out a stem-less wine glass. She examined it closer to the light before she asked, "Mind if I take this and show it to the chief?"

"Please, take anything that you think might help to solve this horrible crime." Marjorie opened the remaining cupboard doors for Charlotte.

*   *   *

Fifteen minutes later, Charlotte was seated in Chief Goodacre's office, waiting for the meeting to start. She'd passed along the wine glass to her for fingerprint comparison purposes.

"You arrived at the perfect time. I'm expecting Officer Maria at any moment. She returned from San Jose last night and has news about your great-uncle Henry."

"Oh, I hope it's good news, although I don't know what that would be any more," Charlotte replied.

"Ah, here's the woman of the hour," Chief Goodacre said, spotting Officer Maria enter the station. "I've got a fresh cup of coffee for you. Come in once you get settled."

Maria nodded to the chief and smiled at Charlotte.

"I'll be right in."

"We're getting close, Charlotte—I can feel it."

"I hope that you're right, Chief. I can't take much more of this. I want to get on with rebuilding and growing my farm." Charlotte nervously studied some fidget toys that the chief kept in a box on her desk. She pulled out a mini slinky-type spring and let it dangle from her hand.

"I don't suffer fools very well, and these help restore my patience," the chief explained, and Charlotte nodded.

"Sorry it took me so long, Chief. There were a pile of messages waiting for me, and I needed to make sure that there was nothing urgent," Maria said, taking the second guest chair, next to Charlotte.

"Was there anything?" the chief asked.

"Not really, but with my partner out searching for Serge Andersen to question him about the Finn Family Farm's books, I thought it important to check. Although the front desk has been told to reach me on my cell if anything needs immediate attention."

"Well done, Officer. Now show us what you've got."

Maria laid out some official-looking documents and a couple old photographs across the chief's desk. Charlotte moved around to her side so that she wasn't looking at them upside down.

The first stop I made was to the prison outside San Jose, where Henry Finn was incarcerated. The warden was only there for a handful of years, but she summoned a couple of longtime guards who worked in Henry's building and should remember him."

"What was the prison like? Was it austere like an Alcatraz, or more of a modern cell for less violent criminals?" Charlotte asked, hoping for the latter. Although she never knew her great-uncle Henry, he was family after all.

"Henry Finn was sent to the appropriate prison for his crime. This place will give me nightmares for a long while. It houses murderers and rapists, and reformation and redemption are in very short supply. But the good news is that the two guards remembered Henry very well, as he was nearly the only prisoner at the time who treated them civilly. And they returned the favor. They said he had a great sense of humor, and that ultimately led to his death."

"Oh, he's dead." Charlotte wasn't surprised, but sad all the same.

Maria nodded.

"Besides being humorous, he was a prankster and played one on the wrong inmate. He was found strangled in his cot on his birthday. He'd just turned sixty."

Everyone was silent and privately bowed their heads in a short prayer.

When it felt appropriate, the chief continued. "What about visitors, Maria? Did the prison have a record of who'd signed in to see Henry?"

Maria nodded. "In the beginning, the only name on the books was his attorney, but a few weeks into his sentence there were no more visits from him. Ever."

"Henry probably ran out of money to pay the attorney. Okay, who else?" the chief asked Maria.

"He had only one other visitation during his time, and that was by his wife and daughter. She signed in as 'Mrs. A. Finn' and the child was simply called 'daughter.' It was only about two months in, and the visit lasted less than thirty minutes."

"How sad." Charlotte tried to hold back tears.

"It *is* sad. So is that where the trail grew cold, Maria?" the chief asked.

"No." Maria sat up tall and brightened. "From there I went to the San Jose PD and spoke to their chief. He's no youngster, but not old enough to have worked on the Henry Finn case himself. But he had access to the files of the retired detective that had, and ordered them brought up from the archives. I spent the next five hours going through the boxes."

"I'm impressed. You'll make detective yet, Maria." The chief gave her a genuine smile.

"Documents confirmed that Henry Finn had married a woman named Annabel, and they had conceived one daughter, named Lucille."

Annabel? That can't be a coincidence . . .

"It sounds like you're about to close another loophole, Officer." The chief grabbed a toy from her fidget box.

Not a good sign.

"I did. It seems that Annabel legally changed her last name with the hope of erasing the stigma of her husband's crime."

"Let me guess. Annabel and her daughter Lucy Finn became Annabel and Lucy Ursin?" Charlotte nodded her head, already knowing the answer.

"How did you know?" The officer seemed genuinely shocked and looked to the chief who had just caught on.

"Because Lucy Ursin married Thomas Avery. Charlotte and I have seen the marriage certificate. She named her daughter Annabel after her grandmother." The chief leaned back in her chair, satisfied.

"And unfortunately this confirms a connection between the Averys and myself." Charlotte sighed.

* * *

Charlotte's head was spinning by the time she walked out of the police station. She now had proof that she was indeed related to Wade, which disgusted her.

Maybe he inherited the bad seed from his great-uncle Henry, and it skipped a generation? Maybe the other two were okay?

She saw Officer Maria come out and head to her squad car.

"Officer, great work. I owe you a lunch!" Charlotte thanked her again.

"Thanks, Charlotte—let's talk later. We've got a lead on Serge Andersen's whereabouts."

"Of course, but could you answer just one quick question? You said that you'd met Marcus Cordero the day that you and another mom took the kids to the Humble Petting Zoo. Can you tell me who that other mom was?"

Maria nodded, and Charlotte knew that she was about to get another piece to the puzzle.

Chapter
Twenty-One

As she drove back to the farm, Charlotte's curiosity got the better of her. The chief had given her copies of important family paperwork including birth certificates and other important records for her great-uncle Henry's side of the family. She pulled over before merging onto the road out of town and opened the file folder.

As she'd hoped, among the papers was the address for the Avery family home where Wade and Clark still resided. As it was the middle of the day, she was sure that both men would be out working on a farm. It was risky to go over there and snoop around, but she had an excuse prepared just in case someone questioned her.

Charlotte put the address into her phone for directions. She ended up on a fairly quiet street on the outskirts of town. This was family housing, she presumed by the tricycles and ride-on toys strewn around front lawns and driveways. She parked across the street and back a bit from the Avery house address and decided to just sit for a few minutes and watch. There were no cars or trucks in Wade and Clark's driveway, and the garage door was shut, but she could see ruts in the grass leading to the back of the house, so someone could still be home.

The house itself looked to be fairly well kept up: two stories, Cape Cod style, with sage green paint and white trim. Charlotte tried to visualize the three young Avery children playing in the yard in happier times while their parents looked on from the second-story balcony.

What happened in that house? The children turned into disillusioned and disimpassioned adults.

When almost ten minutes had passed and Charlotte hadn't see any activity from the house or the immediate neighbors' houses, she got out of her car and casually walked across the street to the Avery home. She was hoping to find anything to tie Wade to the fire. Empty gas cans out back, kindling—maybe even fire starters. She didn't think that she'd be lucky enough to find something linking him to Marcus's murder, but nevertheless she intended to be extra vigilant in her search of the perimeter of the property.

If Wade thinks he's entitled to part of the farm, he might rationalize all sorts of crimes.

She walked up to the front door and rang the bell and then quickly slipped to the side of the house. She wanted to double-check that no one answered the door; she didn't exactly want to test out her excuse for being there in the first place. When no one came, Charlotte was relieved.

Again moving like she belonged there, she went about her search along the exterior of the house. Leaning against the front side was a wooden pallet that had been painted into an American flag.

Patriotism is a good sign.

If they believed in country, then they couldn't be all bad. When she reached the back of the house, she was kept out by a six-foot, dog-eared, redwood fence that enclosed the backyard. She couldn't quite see over it, so Charlotte looked around for something that could act as a stepladder. Nothing really presented itself as an option.

Until she took another look at the flag-painted pallet. The gaps between the slats were exactly like steps . . . *Will I be able to lift and carry it over to the fence? If I drag the pallet, it will leave tracks.*

Charlotte walked back and tested the weight of the pallet. She found that she could lift it if she put one arm through the top slat and rested it on her shoulder. She quickly walked it to the back gate. No cover story would be able to explain away this particular act.

All she wanted was to do a quick survey. If she saw something suspicious, she'd take a picture and return another time with a better plan. The slat steps worked like a charm, and on the second one, she cleared the fence and had a full view of the backyard.

If you could call it that.

The area was a mishmash of dirt, stones, and errant pieces of cheap, Kelly-green Astroturf. The only cleared area was just off the house, where a cement patio held a grill and a few folding chairs.

I'm never going to be able to find any evidence, standing on the outside of the fence.

Against her better judgment, Charlotte climbed the remaining two steps of the pallet and hoisted herself over the fence.

Once she looked over the contents of the yard, she realized there was a reason for the way the junk was grouped. In one section she saw all sorts of items that belonged on a car or truck. The boys had probably picked them up along the way and used or sold them as needed. In addition to parts of motors, there were fenders, tires, roof racks, and even a windshield.

Anything and everything in this backyard could be the murder weapon!

In another area sat machine parts that Charlotte didn't immediately recognize, but guessed they belonged in farm equipment. Alongside those were a pile of garden tools including several pitchforks that looked identical to the one that had impaled Marcus. She took several photos. This could just be a coincidence, or perhaps that pitchfork was the only kind that the garden center sold. But just the same—it was a clue.

She walked around to another grouping of items that had caught her interest: sports equipment. There were balls of every shape and size, lacrosse sticks, weights, golf clubs, baseball bats, and bike parts. All stuff that you would normally keep out of the elements and in a garage. She looked carefully for any signs of blood on the equipment.

So if these are out here . . . then what's in the garage?

As if on cue Charlotte heard the motor for the garage door accompanied by the cranking sounds of the cables pulling the door up.

I better get out of here. Now!

Charlotte quickly looked around and found a cinderblock to use as a step. She dragged it to the fence figuring that it would give her just enough of a lift to be able to put her foot on the top horizontal rail of the fence so that she could climb up and over.

She had to hurry. She grabbed onto the tops of two dog-eared slats and used her muscle to raise her body and left leg up.

All of a sudden, she felt resistance. Her leg wouldn't budge, and her heart began to pound.

Charlotte looked over her shoulder and down to see if her foot was caught on something. And that's when she saw a big, meaty, dirty hand gripping her ankle.

Wade.

"What the hell are you doing in my backyard, missy?" he shouted into her face as he pulled her to the ground.

"I came to talk to you. Let go of me, you brute!"

"Is this how you usually talk to people? By breaking into their houses? I should call the cops."

"We both know that you're not going to do that, Wade. You're not exactly their most favored Little Acorn resident."

Charlotte noticed just a hint of agreement in his squinting, angry eyes.

"What the hell were you doing in my backyard?" He grabbed Charlotte's wrist and led her to one of the folding chairs by his outdoor grill and pushed her down into it.

"Ouch! That hurt. Touch me again, and I'll scream."

"Go right ahead. There's nobody home at this time of day," Wade spat out.

"So what are *you* doing home?" Charlotte quickly tried to turn the question tables.

"You want to know why I'm not working? I'll tell you why. Farmer Alou fired me, that's why!"

"You must have deserved it." Charlotte tried to sound defiant, but her heart was pounding.

With quick hands, Wade grabbed her shoulders and shook her.

"I didn't do nothin'! It's all your fault!"

"My fault?"

This is more than I bargained for. How do I get out of this mess?

"It is. You went squawking to the cops about Serge taking a little off the top, and they see the Alou's farm is on the list. So, they let him know, and on account of Serge being married to my sister, they think I'm in on it too. So they canned me. I had nothing to do with Serge's shenanigans!"

He's shouting again, and his face is an unhealthy cherry red. But for some reason Charlotte believed he was telling the truth.

"I'm sure if you went back and talked to him in a few days—"

"Shut up! I'm talking to *you*. What are you doing in my yard?" Wade sat down backward on the other folding chair. His anger was so close to the boiling point that she was afraid that if she said the wrong thing, he would pull the metal chair out from under him and swing it at her.

"I came here, Wade, to talk about family. Our family."

Charlotte could see signs of his ire beginning to deflate, but nevertheless she quickly continued.

"I have been looking into the Finn Family since I got here, wanting to know exactly who we all were and are. And while we're never, ever going to exchange Christmas gifts, it appears that the Averys and the Finns are, in fact, blood relatives."

She let that sink in for a moment and could almost hear the wheels turning as Wade rubbed his chin.

"I knew that. Why the heck do you think that I'm always claiming that the farm is ours? You got something to add? You find that will?"

"No, and I doubt anyone ever will." Charlotte shook her head.

"Annabel always talked about it when we were kids. She told Clark and me that she knew where it was. Now if I ask her about it, she just laughs. So, do I get part of the farm?" He said this more as a statement than a question.

"No, Wade, my great-uncle Tobias left a will and officially named me as the sole beneficiary to the farm." Charlotte tried to be gentle.

"But what if there was an earlier will that left at least part of the farm to my great-uncle Henry?" he asked, brightening.

"I'm no expert on the law regarding these things, but from the little I've read, it looks like there would have to be special circumstances for a prior will to be considered. Not that I think that one exists."

"I'm sure you don't . . . like what special circumstances?" He was persistent.

"I'm not exactly sure, but from the research that I've done, if one party can produce an earlier will, then they need to present it to the court." Charlotte wanted to nip this in the bud.

"Then what happens?"

"Each party hires a team of lawyers who file motions and arguments and drag the case on for years. By the time the issue is resolved, if ever, both parties owe so much money to their legal teams that they have to sell everything they own to pay them."

Wade looked to be weighing this information, and Charlotte could see the anger ramping back up.

Time to split.

"I've got to get going, Wade. As you know, we're throwing a big barbecue on Saturday. We're expecting most of the town to be there, so you and Clark must join us. We'll feed you real well, and there'll be lots of entertainment."

Charlotte got up and this time quickly made her way through the house toward the front door. As she passed through the kitchen, she saw two jars of tomato sauce on the counter that looked awfully familiar. She stopped to take a photo after turning the jar to the right angle.

"What the hell?" she heard Wade say as his heavy footsteps pounded into the house.

"I'll see you then, cuz," she said as she opened the door and quickly stepped out onto his driveway. By the time he made it to the front, Charlotte was about halfway to her car.

"Wait. You never told me what you were doing in my backyard!" This was a shout more of exasperation than anger.

"I thought that I smelled gas. I was concerned. Family takes care of family."

Charlotte gave him a wave just before getting into her car. As she drove away, she noticed that Wade's truck was parked on the lawn by the side of his house.

What the heck is in that garage?

Chapter
Twenty-Two

When Charlotte got back to the farm, she was in a state of shock but was determined to keep her news to herself until she could think through the implications.

"Hi, Alice. How'd everything go today? Sorry I got way-laid in town; I hadn't planned on it taking so long," Charlotte explained, getting out of her station wagon.

"It was great. We had three tours, and Horse did his thing with the soccer match each time." Alice shrugged her shoulders and grinned.

Charlotte and she had never talked about children, but she could see that Alice was thrilled with the pint-sized company.

"I even introduced them to Mrs. Robinson, and they couldn't believe that a ladybug and a pig could be best friends."

"Well done, Alice! Where are Joe and Samuel . . . and Horse for that matter?"

"There they are." Alice pointed. "The lake is almost filled, and they're building the dock. Samuel says that we should have a christening party before the barbecue."

"I one hundred percent agree! Beau and Diane will be back up on Thursday to help us get ready for the barbecue. What do you say we have our family party then?"

"Wonderful. I'm going into town in the morning to pick up the perishables for the barbecue. Shall I get some fresh shrimp as well, and we can have a boil Thursday night?"

"I love the way you think, Alice." Charlotte gave her a hug and meant it.

As she strolled down to the lake, she thought about how far the farm had come since she'd arrived. It seemed that harmony among the key players had been restored, and they were making money and had expanded their offerings. The beautiful lake was almost back to the way her dear Uncle Tobias had always loved it. Charlotte stopped walking and looked up into the sky. The sun was slowly making her way to her bed in the west, and birds of all sorts had already returned to the lake, including a snowy egret that Charlotte spotted near the shoreline.

The men had put in all the pylons for the dock and cemented them to the bottom before the starting to fill the lake. Joe and Samuel were attaching the floorboards and rails when she approached.

"I can't believe how much life the lake has already attracted. This is wonderful!"

On hearing Charlotte's voice, Horse, with Mrs. Robinson aboard, raced up to greet her, and she bent down to give them both some love.

"It is pretty great. Now we need to stock it to keep the ecosystem going," Samuel said with a big grin.

"Don't you mean so you can get some fishing in, Samuel?" Joe ribbed him.

"That too."

"You gentlemen have done a terrific job. Once we're past the barbecue and official lake opening—and have earned enough money—I'll take you wherever we need to go for freshwater fish, and you can pick out any species you wish."

"There's a place in Ventura—that's where we'll need to go." Samuel was like an excited schoolboy.

"I got a call that the trucks came in a little while ago," Joe told Charlotte and Samuel. I don't know how you managed to get that insurance check so quickly, but I'm sure grateful for it. I'm told that despite being used, they're in really good condition."

"Excellent! Sometimes all you need is a little sweet talk." Charlotte grinned.

"How are we going to work this?" Samuel asked Joe. We'll each need to drive a truck off the lot,"

"I thought that Alice could stay here and run the U Pick 'Em visitor tours, and you Miss Charlotte could drive us over to the used truck dealership. You only need to drop us off; you'd be back in less than an hour." Joe gave her a somewhat pleading smile.

"I love it when a plan comes together! Shall we rustle up some supper, boys?"

Joe looked at Samuel.

"She's started talking like a cowboy." Samuel grinned, shaking his head.

*　*　*

The truck lot was on the outskirts of town in an area that seemed to be designated for the buying and selling of every kind of motor vehicle. The only other places along this strip of road were fast-food joints and a couple of seedy bars.

Such a desolate and dark contrast from the beautiful hills and lush green fields just twenty minutes away.

"See you fellas back at the farm," Charlotte said out the window of her car. "Y'all come back now."

Joe was once again surprised by Charlotte's new lexicon.

When she arrived back at the farm, Charlotte saw that Horse was sitting outside, waiting for her.

Maybe he's becoming too dependent on me. He should be doing pig things and playing with the other animals . . .

He ran up to Charlotte as she got out of the car and let out a diatribe of squeals and grunts that seemed to ascend into a story arc. She listened intently and watched his animated eyes.

"Horse, slow down. If we want to really communicate, then we need to agree on a vocabulary. And since you seem to understand me better than I do you, I suggest that we use the English language."

Horse sat down, ready for his lesson.

"I can see that you know a lot of words so let's put them together with the things they describe. Come with me."

He dutifully followed her into the house and then the kitchen, where she found a box of sweet cereal.

"Just this once, for training purposes." She gave him a few frosted flakes, and his eyes lit up.

She walked out of the kitchen and pointed to a door in the hallway. "Cellar," she said, and watched to see if he understood. "Cellar."

Horse nodded, and Charlotte gave him more cereal.

"Let's go to the patio," she continued, and he happily followed along. He seemed to be thrilled with this new game.

An hour and a half later, they had covered all the important areas and people on the farm, and Horse looked to be in a sugar coma. Charlotte was also exhausted and suddenly realized that she hadn't eaten since breakfast. She also noticed that tricky Horse had led her back to the paddock, where his dinner was waiting in the trough.

"You're kidding me! You can't still be hungry after all that cereal?"

"You named him 'Horse' for a reason." Samuel chuckled. "Do you really think that he understood the words that you were teaching him?"

"Probably more than half. You yourself told me how smart pigs are," Charlotte replied, and her stomach grumbled audibly.

"Sounds like he's not the only one in need of supper. You have dinner plans?"

"Yes. I plan to eat it," Charlotte joked.

"It's time for you to experience authentic cowboy grub. And when you're hungry, it's the perfect place. We're going out, Miss Charlotte!"

Chapter
Twenty-Three

They met in front of the house fifteen minutes later and rode in Samuel's truck. It had four-wheel drive, which he told her might come in handy. It made her wonder if they were going to be eating off tin plates around a campfire somewhere in the middle of nowhere.

"Where exactly are we going, Samuel?" She looked at her sundress and sandals and wondered if she should have worn buckskin instead.

"We're headed to the San Marcos Pass. In the 1800s, it served as the stagecoach pass connecting Mission Santa Barbara to the Santa Ynez Valley."

"And there's a restaurant in there?" she asked as they exited a main road and began their incline up a mountain.

Samuel nodded. "The Cold Spring Tavern, said to have been built in 1868 as a stagecoach stop. You're going to feel like you've walked right into a Western movie."

"Wow, now I'm excited!"

"There are all kinds of stories about the place, involving both Hollywood stars and your basic bandits, thieves, and murderers.

I've heard that stagecoach robbers stole a bunch of gold and buried it in a river bed behind the tavern, but all that's ever been found is one nugget."

The scenery that was passing by Charlotte's window took her breath away. And not just because she was looking down into a steep valley. The eucalyptus trees and Canyon oak were strutting their impressive, majestic foliage. The sheer number of green tones that covered the canyon could never be reduced to a Pantone color wheel, and the birds, from finches to raptors, soared and swooped to gather their dinner. As it didn't get dark at this time of year until after eight, Charlotte had a front row seat to nature's splendor.

"Enjoying the view? Your eyes have gone so big it's like you've never seen views like this," Samuel said, smiling.

"I haven't! But keep your eyes on the road. This is as close as I wish to get to nature, thank you."

"Yes, ma'am."

Did he just tip his hat?

About ten minutes later, they pulled off the pass and onto a dirt lot in front of what looked like three wooden structures with thatched roofs. There were picnic tables with attached benches outside sitting aslant on uneven ground. Stone chimneys were emitting white smoke, and the air smelled of hickory and mesquite. There were lots of places to sit while you waited for a table or if you wanted to dine al fresco—all the seating was rustic. Stagecoach wheels and pine boards made an intimate settee. Whole tree sections with half-cut backs served as benches for three or more, and other stumps and oak barrels could accommodate any spillover.

Charlotte could easily picture a Wells Fargo coach making a pit stop for lunch before completing the journey to awaiting banks in Santa Ynez.

"Wow, this is amazing! Should we talk like cowboys the entire evening, pardner?"

Samuel laughed. "If you wish, pardner."

Someone's in a good mood.

The inside didn't disappoint. From the gingham red and white half drapes to the Dutch doors and the creaky wood plank floor, there was no mistaking the tavern's authenticity. Buck heads and other hunting trophies lined the walls in between laminated sepia photos of cowboy life in Cold Spring in the 1800s. Simple tables, covered in plain oilcloth, and wooden round back chairs filled almost every available space. They were seated at a small round table that was actually a piece of plywood resting atop a barrel in the far left corner. The dining area nestled up against the side of a stone fireplace. Charlotte took the bench and let Samuel and his long legs have the chair.

"I want one of everything," Charlotte said, glancing at the menu.

"I don't blame you. It's all good." Samuel looked around the room, and Charlotte wondered if he ever came here with friends . . . *He must have some.*

She ordered the buffalo burger, and he opted for a tri-tip sandwich. When the food arrived, they both dug in for a few minutes before speaking. Charlotte couldn't remember when something had tasted so delightful, even at all the fancy client dinners she'd attended in Chicago.

"I'm in heaven," she said, finally coming up for air.

"Um, you have a little something—" Samuel pointed to the side of his mouth. When she reached for it with her tongue rather than a napkin, he let out a chortle that even had the people at the neighboring tables smiling.

"You might not be laughing when I tell you who I'm related to."

That did stop Samuel, and Charlotte gave him the rundown on the Finn Family tree.

"If you look hard enough, there's probably a bad seed in every family, but that has nothing to do with you or the farm. Wade's a bitter man, Clark follows him blindly, and Annabel—well she's messed up in all kinds of other ways," Samuel said in response to her story.

"I'm still bothered by the fact that we never found any trace of evidence about who was in the cellar," Charlotte said. She wanted to tell him about the jars of tomato sauce she'd seen in Wade's kitchen, but she didn't want to admit to breaking into his property.

"Everything echoes down there. Someone would have to be very light on their feet not to be heard."

Charlotte's cell phone rang.

"Hi, Chief," Charlotte said after responding to the call.

"Oh no, that's horrible. Does his family know?" Charlotte looked at Samuel and slowly shook her head.

"Okay, and tell her that I'm here if she needs anything." Charlotte was about to end the call. "Chief? I've got a request, and I'll explain when I see you. Could you have your deputies search especially for any evidence of Wade in Serge's beating?"

Samuel motioned for the check and got out his wallet. Whatever had happened, it seemed pretty clear that they should get back to the farm.

* * *

"Serge has been taken to the main hospital in Santa Barbara. The chief said that he had been beaten so badly that he was barely recognizable," Charlotte explained as Samuel drove.

"Wow . . ." Samuel had his eyes vigilantly on the road. These curves at night had to be navigated with the utmost respect. "Someone must have been really angry."

"I was thinking the same thing, much like the ferocious way that Marcus was murdered." Charlotte watched the pass turns as well.

I also can't get it out of my mind that I stirred the pot with Wade today. Did that send him to Serge to get even for losing his job?

"We need to get back to the farm and warn the others."

Charlotte wished that she hadn't said that last sentence out loud. With threat of the family in mind, Samuel hit the gas. Charlotte could hardly hold on tight enough for the rest of the sharply curved drive home. When they were finally making their way up the hill to the farmhouse, Charlotte said, "Let's stop by Joe and Alice's house. I think that it's best we tell them in person."

Samuel nodded and veered the truck toward the Wong's house from the lower level. Joe was standing in the open doorway when they pulled up.

"Everything okay? I saw the lights and figured that it was you, Samuel. Someone been destroying our fields again?" Joe looked concerned.

"I think that we'd better come in to talk," Samuel responded, helping Charlotte down from the truck.

"Sure, come in. Alice was just putting on a pot for tea, Miss Charlotte." Joe nodded to her.

They sat down in the living room, and Alice came out of the kitchen, a deep look of worry on her face as well.

"I think you know that Serge Andersen hasn't been seen for several days now," Charlotte began. "The chief and myself assumed that he'd skipped town to avoid being arrested for cheating so many local farmers. And that may still be the case."

"That's odd," Alice said, shaking her head. "Annabel didn't mention a thing about him having disappeared when I saw her today."

Charlotte's head did a quick swivel. "Where did you run into her?"

Alice gave a dry laugh. "Funnily enough, in your root cellar."

"What the heck was she doing down there?" Samuel asked, his ire rising.

"She said that she'd come looking for me, and the cellar was a logical choice. She wanted to talk to me about her yoga classes and why she couldn't continue teaching in the barn."

"When you saw her, did she appear to be unsettled, Alice? A little bit taken off guard?" Charlotte probed.

"Maybe, but she has such a big personality that it's hard to say."

Now I know why Horse was grunting and squealing so much today when I came back from the station. He was trying to tell me that Annabel had been here. And now I know that she'd gone down in the cellar, supposedly looking for Alice. I still don't understand why those two are friends.

"What's this all about?" Joe rightly inquired.

"The police found Serge tonight. He was beaten almost to death. He's in the intensive care unit, and the chief says that chances are less than fifty percent that he'll survive. That kind of violence is consistent to what happened to Marcus, only hopefully with a better outcome. Something or someone has pushed the killer to act again, and it's highly likely that it could happen to one of us. I want to put extra precautions in place. Samuel and I spoke about this on the drive back."

"We still don't know what we're dealing with here because nobody's exposed a clear motive for wanting Marcus dead." Samuel turned to Charlotte, who nodded.

Samuel proceeded to lay out the latest facts and bring them up to speed on the evidence in the case. As he talked, Charlotte found her mind drifting and her thoughts swirling with all the seemingly unconnected things that had happened in the last few days. The more Samuel talked, the less any of this appeared to be tied to Marcus's murder.

When Samuel had finished, Charlotte said, "One last question and then I need to call it a night. Alice, how did Annabel know where the door to the root cellar was? And that you worked on your jams and sauces there almost daily? Did she often accompany you down there?"

"Oh, you didn't know?" Alice asked. "For a brief time she worked for your uncle, did some interior decorating and replaced all the window treatments and floor coverings."

I see.

Chapter
Twenty-Four

Although she was exhausted, Charlotte decided to make some notes and go over everything with her most revered sounding board, Horse. It was a warm night but Charlotte wasn't about to leave any of the French doors to the patio open . . . or unlocked.

She worked on her tablet because she didn't want anyone with the nerve to snoop around to find her written notes. To get into the data on the tablet, a password was required.

"Let's start by entering the latest event and work backward," Charlotte told Horse, who sat beside her on the sofa in front of her bedroom fireplace.

Using the note-taking function, Charlotte started a list.

1. *Serge was beaten to within an inch of his life. Who had motive?*
   - *Wade—he lost his job and blamed Serge*
   - *One or more of the farmers he cheated, including Alice, Joe, and Samuel*
   - *Annabel, if she found out that he was cheating*

"You got all that, Horse? Do you agree?" He puffed his cheeks out in a smile and nodded his head. "The farmers will be testifying to the police, so I doubt that one of them would risk taking justice into his own hands. But there could be others because we've only got a partial list. And I don't even know if the woman that Serge is having an affair with is married. She looked awfully young. So Wade's the obvious choice."

Charlotte made another entry onto her tablet.

2. *Who set fire to our trucks filled with produce for market?*
   - *Serge—revenge, because he knows that he was caught skimming the books. He may think that the fire will scare us out of reporting it to the police, but then, who hurt Serge?*
   - *Wade. Samuel is convinced that his friends would lie to give him an alibi. Plus I'd seen him on horseback outside my window smoking.*
   - *Annabel, who had just been told that day that she couldn't hold yoga classes in our barn without paying a fee. She hates the word "no."*

"I think that this one is a toss up between Serge and Wade. Serge for obvious reasons and Wade because he continues to harbor hatred and resentment toward Samuel since childhood. Plus, he wants a piece of this farm. It seems like a real stretch that Annabel would be so mad at not being allowed access to the barn that she'd turn to arson."

Horse did not react one way or the other to Charlotte's comments.

Things aren't looking so good for nasty Wade, are they Horse?" The pig's eyes got wider as he studied the screen of Charlotte's tablet.

Is he actually reading this?

3. *Who caused my accident in the root cellar?*
   - *Alice seems the obvious choice because she is always down there.*
   - *Joe could have been in on something Alice was doing and supplied her alibi.*
   - *What the heck was Annabel doing down there?*
   - *Wade is highly unlikely because he's too big of a guy to sneak around.*
   - *Clark is smaller and a possibility. Could Wade have sent him to scare me?*

Charlotte studied Horse's face and saw that he was getting agitated. He hopped off the sofa and went to the bedroom door leading out to the foyer.

"What is it, little man? Do you have to go out? I can open the patio door." Charlotte walked toward it, but Horse remained facing the door into the house and pawed at it. She went to him and knelt down.

"You're trying to tell me something, aren't you?"

This is the perfect time to test out Horse's new vocabulary.

"Do you want me to go to the kitchen?" Horse shook his head. "Is there something in the paddock?" Another shake. "The fields?" No response. "How about the root cellar?" Horse hopped up and down and squealed.

"Okay, but this time I'm going down there prepared. I'll finish the rest of my list in the morning."

Armed with both her cell phone and a powerful flashlight that could sub as a weapon, Charlotte picked up Horse and began her descent into the cellar. She'd also propped the door into the house open from the cellar side so no one could easily close it. When she reached the stone floor, she started to shiver, remembering the last time that she'd been down here.

This is déjà vu.

"Horse, I'm going to put you down, but I want you to stay by my side. Slowly lead me to what you think I should see. Is it Alice that you smell?"

Charlotte lowered him to the floor, and he started walking toward that iron gate at the back. After a few steps, he paused and looked back over his shoulder to make sure that Charlotte was following him.

"I'm coming—good boy!"

Horse had his nose to the floor and was following a specific scent. He totally ignored the field mouse that had frozen in its tracks as the pig trotted by. At points where there was nothing visible to deter him, Horse would stop and suddenly change directions. He finally ended up in the room with the shelves of tomato sauce and jam jars and began poking at the old wooden locker that had turned out to be a blanket chest.

"Oh Horse, I've already inspected that box, honey—it's just filled with old blankets." Charlotte tried to hide her disappointment as Horse kept pawing at the back of the locker.

"We should go to bed. We've got a long day tomorrow, and I want to be able to enjoy the family shrimp boil tomorrow night."

Thoroughly frustrated Horse turned around so that his backside was pressing on the side of the wooden box and with all his might he used his hooves to push it along the stone wall. Once clear he lifted his front hoof and brought down a loose stone. Charlotte bent down and shone a flashlight into the space. *The sewer line runs along this wall.*

Charlotte reached through with her arm holding the flashlight and stuck her head in to examine the line more closely.

"It looks like someone has taken a hacksaw to the pipe but, thankfully, didn't make it through. I can see shavings on the ground under it," she told Horse, and he tried to squeeze his head into the already-full space to have a look.

I hope this isn't what I think it is . . . more examples of sabotage.

"Good job, Horse, good boy. Now let's quickly get back to the bedroom."

Charlotte replaced the stone and slid the locker box back in front of it and picked up Horse. Very quietly she tiptoed up the stairs and headed back to her bedroom.

"This discovery is definitely something to sleep on, Horse. If someone can access the cellar without our knowing, that is more than a little scary."

She looked over and saw that Horse was already asleep. His head was resting on the pillow next to hers, and his face wore a peaceful smile.

Chapter
Twenty-Five

In the morning, Charlotte had decided to do nothing and say nothing about her discovery until after the Saturday barbecue.

Why turn everything on its ear and ruin a perfectly good party?

Charlotte spent a good part of the time before lunch working in the Farm Store, getting everything ready. Samuel had assured her that the goslings would be fine for several hours if they were brought up and placed in a pen in front of the store. He was hard at work filling it with straw and making a little house for them to waddle in and out of.

They'd suspended You Pick 'Em briefly for the rest of the week so that everybody could pitch in. The chief phoned Charlotte just before she was to take a break and let her know that Serge Andersen was awake but so far had no memory of the beating. She was going to try to talk to him again this afternoon.

Over a quick lunch of fresh bread, cheese, and apricots—Horse loved all three—Charlotte thought about her next move.

"We've got three days until the barbecue fundraiser, and so much needs to get done. When Beau and Diane arrive tomorrow, they'll take over the food and decorations, and I can then focus on solving this murder."

Horse sat on the patio, listening and watching as she compiled her three ingredients into another stack. His half smile made Charlotte think that he was keeping track of the "one for me, one for you" tally.

"We know so little about Marcus, and that's why we're having trouble figuring out why someone wanted him dead. It's always bothered me that a good-looking guy in his twenties would run a petting zoo all day and then just eat dinner and go to sleep. That would be a sorry existence for a man in his prime."

Horse looked to be pondering this, and Charlotte knew that she was confusing him with words he hadn't heard before.

"Where would a guy go if he wanted to have a drink and maybe meet some girls, but didn't want the whole town to see him?"

Horse climbed up onto an Adirondack chair and balanced on one of the arms. From that position he could look out over the lake and the valley in the distance.

"You're right! Why didn't I think of that before? It's one in the afternoon—I've got to get in the car and head toward town. Horse, I have a strong feeling that you saw or heard something the night that Marcus was killed. I want you to think back and try to remember, maybe retrace your steps. When I come back, we'll go out and do some recon, Lieutenant Horse."

Charlotte saluted him, and he hopped off the chair and trotted out.

Just a pig on a mission.

* * *

When Charlotte passed the last quaint shop in Little Acorn, the road widened and the scenery became characterless and barren. For whatever reason, this land must have been deemed unfarmable and, as a result, no man's land. A perfect escape from gossip-prone Little Acorn and the bars and eateries for people who cherished their privacy.

Just as she remembered, about ten minutes later she spotted the helium balloons in the air and the spout of the truck dealership's fountain. On the other side of the road, fast-food chains and casual dining restaurants had taken up residence. And beyond that her eye caught the neon sign advertising "Whiskey Pete's Outpost." Charlotte pulled into the adjacent parking lot and was surprised at the number of cars already occupying spaces.

It's happy hour somewhere, I guess.

Charlotte grabbed her file folder and headed to the entrance. Dressed in red capri pants and a white T-shirt, she perhaps should have considered a wardrobe change before going on this mission. She took off the bandana that had been holding back her rampaging scarlet curls. When she pulled open the door, she saw the squints of some of the patrons looking to see who had let a sliver of sunlight into their surreptitious sanctuary.

"If you're here about a waitress job, we're all staffed up right now, honey," said the woman behind the bar, who looked a little like the chief if the chief had been twenty years older and thirty pounds heavier. "You can leave your name and number with me, and I'll call you if things change. You worked a bar like this before?"

"Hi, I'm Charlotte," she said, extending her hand over the bar. "I'm afraid there's been a misunderstanding."

"Betty," she said, giving Charlotte a shake and a warm smile. "What'd I get wrong—you're not a short order cook, are you?"

"Hah, if my cooking skills were described in a book, it would be a one-pager. No, I was hoping that you'd be able to answer a couple of questions for me."

Betty took a step back from the bar. "We don't kiss and tell here. If you're lookin' to catch your fella in a lie, you'll have to do it yourself," she said loud enough for her drinkers to hear. "People come here for privacy and discretion, and that's what they get."

"And watered-down whiskey!" yelled the old geezer at the end of the bar.

"You seem to like it enough. You spend two-thirds of your day drinking it every day, Ed," Betty hollered back to him.

Ed chuckled and swatted his hand at her.

"It's not my guy—and besides this one's dead. I'm trying to find out who killed him."

"Whoa, that's heavy stuff. Sometimes fights can break out here after too many tequila shots, but the guys usually pass out before anyone gets seriously hurt. Plus we toss them out faster than a lit firecracker with a short fuse. You sure he's dead and not just missing?"

"I'm sure. I found him in my tomato field with a pitchfork driven through his neck."

Betty inhaled sharply before gathering her composure. "Floyd, take over for a couple of minutes, will you?" Betty shouted, and a moment later a rail-thin man in overalls appeared from the swinging kitchen door, with a white dishtowel over one shoulder.

"You really shouldn't have come here, toots, but I have a feeling that if I don't at least listen to your questions, then you'll start asking the fine folks in this establishment, and I can't have that."

"I would never cause any trouble," Charlotte explained.

Betty led her outside and around the back of the bar, where a couple of picnic tables served as a break room for the staff.

"We're going to need a couple of minutes, José."

The fry cook nodded, stamped out his cigarette on the dirt floor, and returned to the kitchen.

"Now what's this all about?" Betty straddled the bench and leaned a meaty elbow on the table. Charlotte sat down next to her, hugging her capri-covered knees tightly. She took a deep breath to try to relax. She had to play this just right.

"My cousin—his name was Marcus." This was a lie of course, but when practicing her story on the drive over, she'd figured that a grieving family member would seem the least threatening.

"I'm so sorry, honey, but I didn't know anybody named Marcus." Betty patted Charlotte's upper arm.

"Maybe a photo would help?" Charlotte reached into her file folder and pulled out the photo that she had printed from Marcus's social media page.

"He's Marcus? I guess I never knew his name. He and his girlfriend—if you can call her that—would hole up in a dark corner and talk for hours. He was always bragging about coming into a bunch of money any day now."

Charlotte felt her heart jump. She was finally onto something. "What do you mean about his girlfriend?" Charlotte tried to sound innocent.

"Well, for one she was twice his age, and for another, I happen to know that she's married. Like it or not, that's the kind of place this is. I've got one guy that comes in here at least once a week with his mistress, but his wife has never caught him. Even though she comes in every so often. So, like I told you in the bar, that's all you're going to get out of me."

"Wow, it must be like walking a tightrope in there sometimes. You're to be commended for keeping the peace, Betty."

"Done it for thirty years now and through two husbands. At this point it's second nature. Listen, I got to get back to work, and you've got to get going. I spend any more time with you, and the day drinkers will get restless and start needling me. You're a real nice girl, Charlotte, and I am sorry that you lost your cousin, but I can't help you."

Betty hoisted herself up from the bench, with the help of the table to hold onto, and walked back inside.

Charlotte got back in her car and called the chief, who was now on speed dial.

"Hi, I've got big news that's going to throw this case in a whole other direction. When can we meet?" Charlotte's mind was racing.

Chapter
Twenty-Six

When Charlotte returned home, she made a beeline for her bedroom.

"Horse? I'm home."

When she saw that he wasn't there, Charlotte went outside to look for Horse. She wandered down to the farm shop and saw that Samuel had finished with the gosling pen and was adding some finishing touches. He'd procured a sample of each of the eight vegetables the geese were named after and was hanging them on hooks attached to the outside of the pen.

"Perfect. Just perfect, Samuel."

He gave her his widest smile.

"Say, have you seen Horse?"

"Last I did, he was snuffling around the paddock and then the barn. Then he disappeared into the tomato field. Want me to go look for him?"

"No, but thank you. I sent him on a mission, so we must let him complete it."

That got Samuel's attention. He looked like he was about to ask Charlotte to explain, but then gave up and shrugged.

"Amazing what a beautiful stretch of water can do for the soul," said a woman's voice coming from behind them.

"Chief Goodacre, welcome," Joe said, coming up from the lake.

"Hi, Chief. Can you believe the incredible work these guys have done?" Charlotte asked.

"Your uncle would be so proud of all of you. Charlotte, could we go up to the house and chat about a couple of things?"

"Sure, Chief. Oh, Samuel and Joe and Alice and I talked, and we want to throw a christening party for the lake on Thursday, just for us family. We're doing a shrimp boil, Chief. You're welcome to join us."

"Thanks, but I'll wait until Saturday. I learned a long time ago not to intrude on family unless it's absolutely necessary."

From the men's faces, Charlotte could see that the idea of family suited them just fine.

* * *

"Let's go in my bedroom suite, where we're hopefully assured more privacy," Charlotte told the chief when they entered the house. "Can I get you something to drink, Theresa? Iced tea, lemonade, coffee?"

"I'm fine, hon, and I have some news. That wineglass that you gave me? The prints on it match some latents that we got off the pitchfork handle. It's not solid evidence—there were lots of prints on the stick—but it's something. "

"Wow, that's interesting." Charlotte processed the information for a moment

"By the look on your face, I'm guessing that there are some things that you're itching to tell me too." Theresa looked at Charlotte and cocked her head.

"There are, Theresa, but you go first." Charlotte guided her to the sofa in front of the fireplace, and she herself took the club chair. The French doors were open, and a salt air breeze occasionally tickled the sheer, light-filtering curtains into a dance.

"I really can't believe the wonderful change that has come over this place in the few weeks that you've been here, Charlotte. You are a goddess."

Charlotte laughed. "I wouldn't go that far, but I think that I'm getting closer to clearing the dark cloud that still hangs over my head."

"Wouldn't it be just peachy if we could solve this murder before Saturday's big barbecue?"

Charlotte looked at Theresa and realized that she was totally serious.

"Any words out of Serge? How's he doing?"

"He's doing better, I'm told—sitting up and walking a little bit. Still no recollection of the beating, but the docs say that will come. They just can't predict how soon."

"That's a relief. He's ripped people off, so he must have known that they'd want retribution. And Wade blames Serge for his firing. The farmer thinks that he was in on it. So that's already a list of suspects."

Theresa nodded. "I believe under all that gruff that Wade is actually a coward. He prefers threats and anonymous acts of destruction, but that doesn't rule him out. Plus, when Serge's memory does return, he'll certainly remember if it was Wade who did the beating."

"I agree. It would have to have been someone with an average build, with nothing out of the ordinary in terms of looks."

"Or several people: a couple to hold him and another to do the beating. In that scenario, they'd be done in half the time."

Charlotte shivered as she remembered Samuel's childhood story about how Wade and his friends bullied young Paul at the creek when they were kids.

"What does Annabel have to say about this?" Charlotte thought about her plans to raise her kids in a more sophisticated, city environment.

"She's beside herself, as you could expect, but more worried about herself than her husband. She's afraid that someone will be coming after her next."

She may be right.

"I didn't tell her why we needed to urgently talk to Serge, but she didn't ask either," Theresa continued, "which tells me that she probably knew what he was doing to Little Acorn's poor farmers."

"I wouldn't be surprised." Charlotte thought for a moment. "You know there's something that has been bothering me about the night of the fire, and I'm finally able to put my finger on it. You said that when you went to the Andersen's house that night, Annabel was wearing a fancy negligee and robe?"

"Yes, so typical of her." Theresa shook her head.

"But Annabel knew that Serge was going to be away overnight. That kind of garb can be uncomfortable and difficult to sleep in. Wouldn't you think that she'd just throw on an oversized T-shirt or something since her husband wasn't coming home?"

"Unless she was expecting someone else to come over that night?"

"Exactly." Charlotte proceeded to tell her about her field trip to Whiskey Pete's Outpost.

"Well, well, are you trying to make detective before Officer Maria does? So the bartender confirmed that she'd seen Marcus at her establishment, and it's probably a safe guess that Serge brings his mistress or mistresses there on a regular basis. What strange bedfellows."

"That's what it sounds like. I wonder if any one of them spotted the other and kept it to themselves. Have you ever had a reason to go in there, Theresa? For professional reasons of course." Charlotte wanted to be clear about that.

"No, but I know the owner and Betty runs a very tight ship. She makes it known, I'm told, that she has the right to refuse to serve anybody for any reason, and she only needs to enforce that every once in a while for patrons to behave themselves. Another bit of unsettling news," Theresa continued, biting one side of her bottom lip, "we were finally able to get in contact with Hera Cordero. She now lives in Petaluma, about an hour north of San Francisco. She works in guest services for a prominent winery."

"Wow, she must have been heartbroken to hear about her son's death."

Poor thing.

"Surprised, yes. Sad? Not so much. She explained that she and her son had been estranged since he left home when he turned sixteen. Apparently, while she was at work he took whatever cash was lying around and a keepsake box with the little bit of jewelry and mementos that she'd kept. She hasn't seen him since."

Charlotte felt a tear escape her left eye. "If there's any silver lining, I guess it's that my uncle didn't live long enough to see any of this. What a sad story."

Horse came bursting through the French doors and into the room.

"There you are! Say 'hello' to Theresa. Is it mission accomplished?"

Horse nodded his head and squealed.

"I'm not even going to ask. You said that you had a couple of things. What are they?"

Charlotte explained about the issue with the new pump at the lake and could see right away that the information was too thin for the chief to follow up on.

"I also can't be certain, but I think that someone has been sneaking into our root cellar, trying to do damage to the farmhouse. Either out of spite or to sabotage the place in order to chase me out and drag down the value for a quick buy," Charlotte explained.

"You mean that time when you hit your head? Are you sure that wasn't raccoons or some other varmint? There are plenty of those around here in addition to the two-legged variety."

"I'm not talking about that incident, although I can tell you that there was no evidence whatsoever of any animals having been in the cellar. Horse and I discovered the other day that in the same room where I had my accident, there's a stone in the wall that can be removed. Actually, Horse was the master sleuth, with his extraordinary pig sense of smell. The sewer line runs behind the wall, and I could see shavings where someone had tried to saw it open but was interrupted before he or she could finish the job."

"Curious. You're certain that Joe or Samuel or both aren't doing some sort of repair job?"

"Good question, Chief. But if they were, why go to so much trouble to hide the work from view? The loose stone was hidden behind a locker box. Plus they've been so busy getting the lake ready that I can't imagine when they would have time. And they certainly wouldn't just leave the job half-done.

"It was hidden behind a rock in the root cellar in the exact room where I got pummeled with tomato sauce and strawberry jam jars and hit my head."

"All good points, Charlotte. I'll send an officer over to inspect the scene. I'll call when he's on the way. It seems that we've got a lot of pieces to this puzzle. How do we put them all together to make a pretty picture?" Theresa scratched her head, perhaps hoping that an idea would fall out.

"I have a plan that I think could flush out our killer. Pun intended. Let's talk strategy, shall we?" Charlotte could see that the chief was intrigued.

An hour later they had hatched their plan.

"Okay, it's late." Theresa stood.

"One more thing." Charlotte squinted, hoping that Theresa wouldn't be too impatient.

"Make it fast."

"That keepsake box—did Hera tell you exactly what was in it?"

"No, but I can certainly ask."

Charlotte tried to come up with anything else she needed to tell the chief. Her eyes rested on another possible piece of evidence that she had in her room and she gave it to Theresa and suggested that she lift any prints to compare with the other evidence.

That's it?" Theresa asked.

"Isn't that enough?" Charlotte rested her chin in her hand.

Chapter Twenty-Seven

Charlotte walked Theresa out to her car and found Beau and Diane pulling up.

"Hello, my darlings!" Charlotte hugged each of them separately and for a good long time.

"Chief! Let me check your roots," Beau said, and did just that.

"I'm going to need a couple extra hands with this. I thought we could go ahead and walk it down to the Farm Shop and keep it safe until Saturday," Diane told the group standing over her open trunk.

Charlotte peered in and sucked in her breadth. "That is the biggest cake that I've ever seen! Oh Diane, it's so beautiful! Is that Horse?"

"It sure is, honey, and up here are the geese." Diane gestured toward a sheet cake that took up almost the entire trunk space. It rested on a base of plastic and had a matching raised lid that was clear. The words "Finn Family Farm" were written in bright green icing above a scene of strawberry fields. A pink pig was looking up at the words and the geese flying overhead.

"I thought that we could pass cake out to the kids first, and if there's any left, start on the adults. There's a layer of strawberry jam in the middle, and the icing is lemon and vanilla," Diane explained.

"If I have to get a subpoena, I will, but on Saturday a piece of that incredible cake is going home with me!" the chief said.

"I love her," Beau said, admiring the chief.

Alice and Joe arrived by golf cart and disembarked to greet Beau and Diane and the chief. They too marveled at the cake.

"I've got law to enforce, so I'm going to take off," the chief said. "I'll see you all on Saturday." She waved and gave Charlotte a slight nod of the head and a smile.

"Joe, why don't you help Diane and Beau carry the cake down to the shop?"

"Will do."

"And don't drop it!" Alice warned Joe.

"What can I do?" Charlotte asked.

"We've got a family feast to prepare!"

"I'm no cook, Alice." Charlotte cocked her head to one side.

"I know that. In the back of the barn we've stored boxes of solar-powered lights with stakes so that they can go into the ground. There's also a supply of batteries to replace the dead ones. If you're up for it, take the cart and plant them wherever you like for us tonight, around the table and dock."

"Great idea, Alice—consider it done," Charlotte said, saluting her. "Horse, want to go for a cart ride?"

He hopped up and onto the front passenger seat. Charlotte was warmed to see that Mrs. Robinson had returned and was riding shotgun on the pig's shoulder.

"It's uncanny how that pig understands you," Alice remarked. "I'm going in to peel shrimp."

When she reached the paddock and barn, Charlotte drove the cart around to the back door for easy loading of the lights. When she opened the door, she heard Samuel's voice. He was talking on his cell phone.

"Wow. That's great, but what do you think this means? Do they have the person or not?" Samuel said into his phone. "Okay, thanks."

Samuel put his phone down and noticed Charlotte.

"I guess you heard the news?" he asked shyly.

"What news?"

"That was Javier. He's at the feed store in town. Word is that the chief and her officers have evidence that links Marcus's killer to this farm and the farmhouse."

"What?" Charlotte slowly lowered herself down onto a sawhorse. "How do you know that this isn't just Little Acorn gossip that got out of control?"

"I asked Javier the same thing, but he said his friend heard it directly from a clerk who works with the chief."

"I don't know what to feel anymore. I went from being shocked that a poor man was killed so savagely on my farm, to thinking that he was family, to learning that he was not a very nice person, and now this. I can't be invested in this saga any longer, Samuel." Charlotte slumped and sighed.

I hope that I haven't laid it on too thick.

Then Samuel did something that she never expected, making her feel first relieved and then guilty.

He reached around and hugged her.

*   *   *

After an awkward moment, Charlotte told Samuel that she needed to put the lights in place for the evening and loaded up her cart. He retreated to his cabin.

"Okay, Horse, hop back into the cart. We're going to the lake."

The pig responded with several oinks and started walking toward the fields.

"Horse! It's getting dark, and I want to get these lights going. Are you coming?"

He continued walking toward the tomato vines.

"I get it: you have something to show me. Can it wait until morning? We're getting ready to have a fabulous dinner."

Horse's ears perked up, but he stayed in place.

"First thing tomorrow we'll go, I promise."

Horse looked out to the tomatoes and then back to Charlotte. He hung his head down and slowly trotted to the cart.

"Good boy, and I can't wait to see what you've found." She gave his snout a scratch and drove off.

On the drive up to the lake, Charlotte tried to get a grip on her feelings. She thought that her plan for catching the killer could work, but she hated lying to anyone.

Am I more bothered because it's Samuel? That hug was genuine. And nice.

She would explain it all to him as soon as she could. Charlotte also knew that she couldn't possibly lie to Diane and Beau, so she needed to carve out time tonight to tell them everything.

When Charlotte arrived at the Farm Shop, she saw that the long, wooden, rustic table outside had been set for dinner, and fresh flowers in enamel jugs acted as centerpieces. The entire scene took her breath away.

She created a pathway of lights that led from the table all the way down to the lake's dock. She still had about a half dozen lights left, so she spaced them out to the end of the dock, threading them through the gaps between the slats.

When Charlotte reached the end, she sat down and let her legs dangle over the water. Horse tried to do the same but had to be content with just sitting back on his rear haunches.

"You never knew my great-uncle Tobias, did you, Horse?"

He looked at her and smiled.

"His spirit is still very much here on this farm. Can't you feel it? There's a whimsy to the place, along with a sense that this farm has all the essentials for growth. And I don't mean produce like fruits and vegetables, but also animals like you—people too—and wonderful ideas and feelings. We must never take this for granted, and we must fight to keep the Finn Family Farm a nurturing, loving environment for all."

To punctuate Charlotte's statement, Horse stood up on all fours and pledged allegiance with a belly-born howl.

"Shrimp's been boiled, and butter's been melted," Beau announced. "Come on, Charlotte. Since this is a family dinner the fastest hands are going to get the most food!"

Horse understood enough of those words to hightail it toward the table.

When Charlotte sat down and surveyed the faces of the people seated around her, she broke into a deeply felt smile.

"I'd like to say a little prayer of thanks before we begin."

Everyone bowed their heads, and some put their hands together.

"Lord, we thank you for this incredible bounty and for bringing us together. We've been tested, and we've remained true to ourselves while overcoming adversity. Tonight we will celebrate the many magnificent gifts that nature endowed on us and count our blessings. Oh, and when you see Tobias, please tell him that the lake's full, the crops are brimmin', and we're having a big ole jamboree on Saturday!"

"Yeehaw!" shouted Diane.

As Charlotte sat back down, the table erupted in applause. As Beau had guessed, everyone dug in with gusto. In addition to a potful of shrimp, Diane had made cornbread, and Alice had skewered vegetables and roasted them on the grill. There were coleslaw and chips and all kinds of yummy dipping sauces. While Charlotte ate, she looked around the table and silently appreciated each person.

Lovely Beau—not a mean bone in his body.

Diane—wicked smart and in possession of a wonderful old soul.

She moved on.

Joe—always anxious to please and a spiritual man. I remember that he quoted the I Ching: "If we are sincere, we have success in our hearts, and we will succeed." I know that he loves his wife deeply. He is a compassionate lover, not a fighter. His boat tilts toward doing the right thing every time. He could not have killed Marcus.

Then there's Alice. She's a bit of a conundrum. She keeps secrets rather than tells lies. Alice will let me in when she's ready. And as with Joe, I also believe that Alice could never harm anyone.

Which leaves Samuel, looking handsome in the white dress shirt that he's put on for the occasion. He thinks of the farm as his home. Would he kill someone if he thought that the farm was in danger? He certainly has mood swings, but he loves animals, and they love him. Horse would've let me know if he distrusted Samuel.

Samuel caught her looking at him and smiled.

She sighed.

Chapter Twenty-Eight

E veryone was too full to go swimming, but they pledged to christen the lake on Friday afternoon. When the last bite of strawberry shortcake had been gobbled up and dinner cleared, Charlotte asked Beau and Diane to take a walk with her. She led them to the fields; she had the goslings' roost in mind for a destination, and along the way she would tell them everything.

"So, you and the chief have narrowed down the list to two suspects: Wade and Serge. What about Clark?" Diane asked.

"I pray that he wasn't involved. He seems like a good guy who's just been trampled by his siblings' bigger personalities. But I can't rule out that he helped the killer," Charlotte explained.

"Let me get this straight," Beau said when they stopped by a water station with barrels to sit on. "You think that Marcus, who'd run away from his mom and was probably barely making ends meet, learned that she'd been in a romance with Tobias from letters in the keepsake box. He decided to disclose that he was Tobias's son and heir, without proof, and came to Little Acorn to claim his inheritance?"

"Correct, but he needed to gather information or some sort of proof, and while he was doing that, my great-uncle passed," Charlotte explained. "He bided his time, associating with the shadiest people he could find, hoping to hear a secret or a nefarious deed that would help in his quest."

"Which means Wade could have killed Marcus, because Wade always claimed that the farm belonged to him. The barkeep told you that Marcus was always bragging in there that he was about to come into money. He could have been boasting all over town. Maybe Wade heard him and needed to get rid of another obstacle. And for sure, Wade was trying to drive you off with his scare tactics, like riding up to your bedroom window," Diane said to Charlotte, who nodded.

"Or Serge could actually have seen Marcus with Annabel at that bar on several occasions and chose to seek his revenge when there were no witnesses around." Beau filled in the gap.

"It would certainly explain the violence of the murder. Serge seems like the kind of man who would wear his double standard like a merit badge." Charlotte shook her head.

"All this makes sense except for one thing." Diane put an index finger to her lip. She had Beau and Charlotte's utter attention. "What was Marcus doing in your tomato vines, and how did the killer know where to find him?"

Charlotte smiled. "That's what this trap that the chief and I concocted is meant to expose. I can't tell you any details—not because I don't trust you, but because I promised the chief that I wouldn't breathe a word."

"Can you tell us when it will happen?" Beau asked. "I want to be dressed appropriately."

"Soon is all I can say. You may not even know when it happens." Charlotte and her friends had reached the geese.

"Better to let them sleep," Charlotte whispered. "We've all got a big couple of days ahead."

Agreeing, they all turned around and followed the path up to the farmhouse.

* * *

Just as the sun came up on Friday, everyone and everything seemed to hit the ground running. Charlotte opened her eyes to see Horse sitting beside her, watching her sleep. The moment she stirred, he hopped off the bed and went to the door.

"Okay, okay. Just let me brush my teeth, comb my hair, and get dressed," Charlotte told him. She could hear voices coming from the foyer and double-checked the time. It was still six thirty, but from the noise she assumed that everyone else was up and about. As Charlotte squeezed toothpaste onto her brush, she studied her face in the mirror.

This is the day, girlfriend, if everything goes right . . . by tonight a killer will have been arrested, and a pall will be lifted from my home. You can do this.

It was going to be a hot day, so Charlotte opted for denim shorts and a loose tank top. She wanted to be able to move easily and freely. When she opened the door to her bedroom, Horse bolted out, presumably heading to the paddock for a hearty breakfast. Charlotte heard the sounds of activity coming from the kitchen and went to investigate.

But instead of seeing preparations for breakfast in progress, she saw Alice and Diane working an assembly line that they'd devised for making large quantities of potato salad. Hard-boiled eggs were cooling in an ice-water bath; Alice was busy chopping and creating piles of chives and dill; and Diane was peeling more potatoes to boil.

"Wow. I feel like I've walked into the kitchen of a five-star restaurant."

"Morning, Charlotte," Alice said, looking up and briefly stopping her knife skills. "There's yogurt and fresh berries in the fridge, if you'd like."

"Perfect—thanks, Alice. I've got a couple of things to accomplish this morning, and then I'm all yours." This time Diane looked up and gave Charlotte a look.

She's wondering if these are "trap-related" chores.

Charlotte filled a bowl with delicious fruit and took it out to the porch. Just as she sat on the front steps, her cell phone rang.

"Good morning, Chief. You and everybody else have kick-started this day early, it appears."

"It's a big day—lots to do. I hear that they're releasing Serge from the hospital this morning. Either his injuries weren't as serious as originally thought, or he's just too obnoxious to keep around. Probably both. Everything hunky-dory on your side of town?"

"Everything here is hustling and bustling. The farm is in high gear to throw a most memorable party," Charlotte told her.

"Just as soon as we get this business taken care of, I'll be ready to pitch in. Talk soon." The chief hung up.

At the same time that Charlotte was enjoying her last spoonful of sweet berries, Horse came tearing around the corner of the house.

"Okay, I'm ready, Horse. Show me what you've found. And a heartfelt 'good morning' to you, Mrs. Robinson."

Charlotte had to speed-walk to keep up with the pig, who was trotting along at a healthy clip.

I know that this is probably a fool's errand, but he's learning language, and wherever he stops, I have to reward him generously.

Horse veered off toward the tomato vines, and when they passed a stack of crates, Charlotte saw that he was leading her directly to the murder site. Her pulse quickened. What on earth was he going to show her? When he stopped running, Charlotte watched Horse lower his head and snout down to the ground and use his nose as a kind of trowel. His ears flopped forward over his face as he pushed dirt away on two sides, leaving a narrow ditch in his wake. Mrs. Robinson, not happy with the bumpy ride, flew up and sat on Charlotte's shoulder. Horse went up and down in about a five-foot-square area, moving to the right after each search. At about the middle of his third attempt, Horse stopped and grunted with gusto.

"Is this the place, little man?" Charlotte asked, bending down to have a closer look. She looked at the spot where he'd stopped sniffing and saw that the dirt had been pushed aside to reveal more dirt. Horse's grunts now came in rapid succession. Charlotte felt like she was playing a game of "Hot and Cold," but there was nothing there. She reached down and pushed away some more of the mud and was about to give up when she saw something beige. When she did, Horse jumped up and down and grunted approvingly.

What on earth is this?

She'd thought ahead to bring a baggie . . . just in case. She turned it inside out and put her hand in to grab the object without getting her prints on it. When she had it completely in the bag, she pulled the bag right side out, over her hand, and stood to examine it. The object was about three inches long, made with some sort of wood or bamboo, and a fork shape was carved into one end. When she turned the bag over to examine the other side of the object, she saw everything that she needed to see.

Charlotte did two things next; she rewarded Horse with a hard-boiled egg that she'd swiped from the kitchen, and she called the chief.

Chapter Twenty-Nine

For the next four or five hours, everyone kept busy attending to the chores to complete their area of responsibility for Saturday's barbecue.

Beau had done a fantastic job creating the mood with accents and decorations from the artist David Hockney's palette of bright colors and bold strokes. In this case, Beau used found objects around the farm as his canvas. He'd found a rusty, old hand water pump and painted it red and white like a barber shop pole.

A conversation area was created near the lake with tree stumps and crates adorned with brightly designed throw pillows with different cow faces on them. Beau had even carved and painted a face into one particularly majestic Moreton Bay fig tree, using its naturally twisted and interwoven aerial roots as tresses of Samson-strength hair. The end result was both intriguing and a bit intimidating.

Red, white, and blue flags and other symbols of Americana were perfectly placed around the area where the barbecue would be held, and even everyday items like grill tongs and shovel handles were painted in the flag's colors. The decor in its entirety made you feel patriotic, whimsical, and comfortable.

"Beau, you've created a masterpiece!" Charlotte said, still letting her eyes dart hither and thither, discovering new decorative arts.

"Thank you, Charlotte. Want to dress like Dorothy and wear ruby slippers? It would totally complete the picture."

"I'll think it over." Charlotte laughed.

"What have you been up to?" Beau asked in full voice and then whispered, "Is Operation Jail Time afoot?"

"Shh. Just put that out of your mind for now. Where's the rest of the gang?" Charlotte asked.

"Diane's got a whole assembly line going, shucking corn, and Alice has others pulling out jars of all sorts of pickles, jams, and fruit from the root cellar."

Charlotte stopped in her tracks. "I'd better go see how I can help. I'm planning to treat everyone to a Mexican dinner in town, so dust off your sombrero, Beau."

"Olé," Beau said, striking a matador pose, holding one arm above his shoulder and the other akimbo at his waist. He even rose up on his toes.

I've got to make sure that everyone's done in the cellar as soon as possible.

When Charlotte arrived at the farmhouse, she saw Samuel and Joe shucking bushels of corn, much to the delight of the goslings that were grabbing the corn silk in their beaks and running around with it. Horse quickly joined in.

"Looks like you two didn't get the short straw. Sitting out here in the fresh air while watching geese frolic—that's not work-work, that's fun work."

"Until your hands start cramping," Samuel said, but he was smiling.

"Are the girls in the house?"

They nodded and Charlotte climbed the steps between them.

In the kitchen, Alice had stacked hotel pans on two tiers of a wheeled cart and covered them in plastic wrap and foil. She was now loading squeeze bottles with mustard and catsup.

"Hi, Alice—this is impressive. Why don't you take a break, and I'll finish up here?" Charlotte suggested.

"I'm almost done with the condiments, and then I need to run these bottles down to the Farm Shop to store overnight. But since we don't have nearly enough space in the kitchen fridge to store the burgers and dogs overnight, I figured that we could put them in the cellar with some ice packs around them. They should be fine there."

"I agree. Are they in these pans?" Charlotte asked while thinking.

"Yes. Each isn't overly heavy, but they are unwieldy. It might be easier to bring them in through the outside cellar doors. At least those steps are wider, and there are fewer of them to navigate." *Alice clearly thought this through. I thought she said she's never used the outside doors?*

"Perfect. Are these the lot of them?" Charlotte asked, and Alice nodded. "Great. I'll wheel the cart out onto the porch and get the new padlock key from Samuel so I can open the doors. The food will be down there in no time."

"Thank you, Charlotte. I have a feeling that people will be talking about this party for years to come." Alice beamed.

True, but probably not for the reason you think.

"One more thing, Alice. Do you have Annabel's phone number handy? I heard Serge is home, and I want to check in on her to see if I can do anything."

"Of course." Alice pulled a small notepad out of the drawer in the kitchen island and scribbled out the numbers. "This is her cell, and it's an easy one, so I know it by heart."

"Thank you. Now, I mean it: take a break and put your feet up."

Alice gave her a grin and a nod.

* * *

Charlotte wheeled the cart with the large pans through the foyer and out to the front porch.

"Samuel, I'm going to store the meat for the barbecue in the cellar overnight. We've got no more room in the refrigerators. Alice thought that it would be easier to bring them down from the outside doors. Do you have the key to the new padlock handy?

Samuel stood and pulled out his key ring. "Want me to help?"

"No, I'm fine, but there's still lots to do. If you guys are done with the corn, then I suggest that you check in with Alice and see what else she needs. I've been urging her to take a break, and besides, Diane is down in the cellar and she'll help."

Samuel took the key off his ring and handed it to her. "Don't forget to lock it back up when you're done. You remember what happened last time."

"Boy howdy, do I! And don't you all forget that we're going into town for a casual dinner on me."

Charlotte grabbed a couple pans and walked around the house to the cellar doors. When she arrived, she put down the pans and took her cell phone out of her pocket. She located the piece of paper that Alice had given her and punched in the numbers.

"Hello, Annabel—it's Charlotte Finn. I heard that Serge was home, and I wanted to check on you both to see if there was anything that you needed."

After a pause, Annabel finally replied, "How kind of you to think of us at our time of need. My dear Serge is home and on the mend. And I'm trying to cope with all the worry and trauma. I'm afraid that I've been tossing and turning at night and have really turned my muscles into painful knots. I'll have to go to the yoga studio in town on Monday as soon as they open."

Glad you remember that you can't use the farm, Annabel.

"I can only imagine how you feel, but he's safe now, so you can relax, Annabel. I do hope that you'll come to the barbecue tomorrow. The lake is open, and a swim will do you a world of good. And maybe sometime next week we can set up another lunch date?" Charlotte added.

"I'm not—"

"One other thing, Annabel: you'd mentioned a Mexican restaurant that you liked. I'm taking my entire crew out to dinner tonight as a thank-you for all their hard work. I was hoping that you could give me the name of the place so I can call ahead because there'll be so many of us."

"Oh, you mean you'll all be going into town for dinner tonight?"

"That's right."

Annabel proceeded to give Charlotte the information.

After Charlotte rang off, she used the key to open the padlock and the doors. She picked up the pans and, as she started down the steps, shouted, "Diane? It's me I'm coming down the back stairs with the food for tomorrow. And I'm going to need your help."

* * *

By six o'clock, everyone was well rested, washed up, and gathered in the foyer of the farmhouse.

"This is going to be an early night, but given all the hard work you've done over the past few days, I thought that it would be a nice break to relax and have someone else do the cooking tonight. My treat!" Charlotte told them as Horse stood beside her, listening intensely.

"And do the margarita mixing?" Beau asked.

"Silly not to." Charlotte smiled. "Beau, would you mind driving my station wagon? It will be able to accommodate you, Samuel, Joe, and Alice. Diane and I will be right behind you, but please go ahead and order anything you like—don't wait for us. I've called the restaurant, and they're expecting our party of six. I'm texting you the address," Charlotte concluded, gently ushering them out of the farmhouse.

Beau gave her a hug and whispered, "I hope I'm not going to miss all the fun."

"I wouldn't think of it!" Charlotte kissed his cheek.

Just as soon as the wagon had disappeared down the hill, Charlotte phoned the chief.

"Give it three minutes, and then you'll be clear to drive up," Charlotte told her. "As soon as you arrive, we'll leave."

"Roger that. We should have ample time to get in place. I can't imagine anyone trying anything before it gets dark, which won't be for another hour," the chief said.

"And so it begins," Diane said to Charlotte as they linked pinkies.

"Horse, I need you to do something for me, and I promise that when I get back, I'll bring you out to witness the conclusion of this murder nightmare. But for now, I want you and Mrs. Robinson to go wait in my bedroom. Come along."

Horse cocked his head at Charlotte. His corkscrew tail was wagging, but he had a wary look on his face.

"Shall we do a pinkie swear?" Charlotte asked, and extended her little finger toward his front right hoof.

That gesture produced a big smile on his face as he raised his leg up to her pinkie. Once that was done, Charlotte led him into her bedroom. After Horse entered, she closed the door and locked it from the outside.

"What's that for? Are you afraid that someone will go in and steal him?" Diane asked.

"No, I'm afraid that he will open the door and escape before we need him."

"But he's only—" Diane bent down and held her hand about a foot and a half from the floor.

"Trust me. I know my pig. He'd figure out a way." Charlotte heard dirt and gravel crunching outside. "Time to go."

They got outside just as the police van was pulling up. Charlotte watched the chief get out along with four officers.

She stuck her head back in the van and said, "Drive the vehicle back down, and park it where no one will see it, and then walk back up."

The chief nodded to Diane and Charlotte and gave them the "okay" sign. Moments later, they were driving down the hill just behind the police van.

*　　*　　*

As Charlotte had requested, Diane parked in the center of town, and they walked from there to the restaurant, making sure that they greeted and were seen by everyone in their path. Diane even handed out more of Beau's fliers, making sure that everyone knew that their party was the next day.

When they arrived at the restaurant, Charlotte saw the gang seated at a large round table at the back of the room. The decor was done in true Mexican tradition, with stone and cement walls, arched entries from one room to the next, and folk-art tiles cemented into designs along the walls. An elder woman was mixing dough and pressing tortillas at a station placed among the diners.

As they approached the table, Diane slipped Charlotte the car keys.

"I'm so glad that you didn't wait," Charlotte said, grabbing a tortilla chip and dredging it through a clay bowl of guacamole. "De-lish! I could see this place becoming a regular hangout. Along with the Cold Spring Tavern," Charlotte added, grinning at Samuel.

A server handed menus to the two new arrivals as he placed the first of the entrees in front of a guest. Another server delivered the other three.

Charlotte looked up and then pulled her phone out of her purse.

"Oops, it's the chief calling," she said to the table. And then to the server, "Is there a back door? I have a call I have to take, and I'd rather not traipse through the restaurant."

He nodded and motioned Charlotte to follow him.

"I'll be right back. Please eat your delicious-looking food while it's hot."

They all watched Charlotte disappear into the kitchen, and then Diane and Beau exchanged looks that could only be deciphered by siblings.

Charlotte heard Diane declare, "I'm ready for a margarita!"

Chapter Thirty

Charlotte parked Diane's car behind Joe and Alice's house, where it was out of sight from the main farmhouse. She quietly crept along the strawberry fields as the last remaining rays of sunlight disappeared like a warm blanket being slowly pulled over your eyes. As Charlotte approached the back porch of the house, she heard a twig snap and froze in place. She looked around but saw nothing until an officer partially revealed himself from behind a tree trunk. He gave her the "okay" sign. She nodded and continued on through the back French doors and into the house. When she reached the cellar door, she opened it and took out a penlight that she'd had in her pocket. She flashed it three times before descending the stairs.

Charlotte found the chief and Officer Maria staked out in the room where she'd found the loose rock and damaged sewer line hidden behind the stacks of hotel pans she'd brought down, with tomorrow's food cooling in them. From that vantage point, they could see anyone approaching from the outside cellar doors.

Charlotte took up a spot just outside the room and behind some wrought iron gates so that she could alert them if she saw someone entering the cellar via the house. It had been arranged in advance that all communication would be done via flashing lights.

As Charlotte sat on the cool stone floor, alone with her thoughts, she wondered who would be making an appearance in the cellar. *Am I right about this? It seems to make sense given all the clues and evidence that we've uncovered. But this is a crazy situation, involving money, family, and love, so isn't anything possible?*

Charlotte shivered and hoped that this would be over sooner rather than later. It didn't take long for her wish to come true. Or so she thought.

A dim bit of moonlight reached down into the cavern as Charlotte, the chief, and Officer Maria heard the outside cellar doors being pulled open. *Someone's fallen for the trap I set by leaving the padlock open and in plain sight.*

Charlotte knew who it was just by that sound. She remembered from earlier in the day that she didn't have a big enough arm span to reach and pull both doors at once. They were so wide that she had to open one door at a time. Only someone with long arms and a wide reach could accomplish this.

Someone like Wade.

Charlotte glimpsed a quick flash of light come from the chief and saw that the chief had her index finger up to her lips. Charlotte understood and remained silent.

Sure enough, the big lug came clomping into the room, shining a large flashlight at the place where the loose stone hid the compromised sewer pipe. The plan had been to catch the killer in the act of covering up any evidence of destruction. Charlotte watched Wade shine his light all over the space. He even had the nerve to grab a jam jar off a shelf and shove it into a pocket of his windbreaker. For that alone, Charlotte was ready to jump out and bop him over the head with a shovel.

But he walked right past the area behind the trunk where the destruction had been hidden. When he entered the main room and started poking around, the chief and Maria revealed themselves, with guns pointed, but motioned Charlotte to remain hidden.

"Wade Avery, you are under arrest. Put your hands behind your back and you'd best be quick about it. I'm tired of being in this damp dungeon!" the chief yelled at him.

"What am I being arrested for? I haven't done nothin'," Wade whined.

"Really?" the chief asked as Officer Maria grabbed his wrists and cuffed them.

"Really." He sniffled.

"What do you call this? Roaming around the Finn's root cellar? You going to tell me that Charlotte cordially invited you to visit at any time, day or night?"

"I saw that the doors were unlocked, and I got concerned. I came down to make sure that everyone was okay."

"Sweet Jesus, Wade, even you can do better than that. You saw that the lock was off while you were snooping around here again looking for your fantasy will. When you saw an opportunity to search the basement of the farmhouse, you jumped at it." The door up to the house opened, and a male officer descended into the cellar. "Ah, good. Officer Pindar, would you please escort this sorry gentleman into the living room and watch him."

"Yes, Chief," Pindar said, and shoved Wade toward the stairs. He matched Wade in size but came up short in weight, although every ounce on the officer was pure muscle.

As soon as they'd gone, the chief motioned everyone to get back into place.

They had to wait another agonizing hour before activity started up again in the cellar. This time the door from the house opened, and Charlotte could hear footsteps coming down the stairs. She sent a flashlight message to the chief, who acknowledged it by flashing back.

This time the person was moving with purpose, and the light beam was held steady on the back wall of the cellar. Charlotte could make out the shadow of a figure that appeared to be dressed in black from head to toe. Including some sort of hood over the head and part of the face. The person walked directly to the locker box and slid it out of the way. Two gloved hands reached around a large stone and pulled it away. *The stone.*

The figure peered into the space, held the flashlight up, and began rubbing the area all around it with a damp cloth. That light exposed the figure's identity, and Charlotte gave the chief the signal by dropping a couple pebbles onto the floor. The intruder looked up, sensing someone nearby but when silence followed, relaxed.

As the chief and her officer made their presence known, with guns raised, Charlotte appeared from behind the wrought iron gate.

"What is this—some sort of setup? You said that you were taking everybody out to dinner. Clark told me he saw you in town."

"Right on both counts. But then the chief called me for a little help."

"Clark didn't see you leave the restaurant."

"So, you were spying on me?"

"I have a harmless reason for that."

"A harmless reason for rubbing my cellar wall to get rid of your fingerprints? Do you also have a harmless reason for why your prints and DNA were all over a wineglass taken from Marcus Cordero's room?"

"You're making a fool of yourself, Charlotte. I have never given permission to anyone to take samples of either!"

"We didn't need to. You gave them yourself the day you threw down your water bottle in anger when I informed you that the barn was no longer available for your yoga class. I can't wait to hear your excuse now."

"This is ridiculous."

"Annabel Andersen, we have enough evidence to take you in for questioning," the chief calmly said while making swift work of cuffing her.

"Hah! You don't know what you're talking about, Chief. This is a serious mistake," she said, giving Charlotte an angry, squinting stare. "One that will probably cost you your farm, missy. My husband and I are respected citizens of Little Acorn." Annabel acted indignant.

"That's your best response to these accusations, Annabel? And here I thought that you were the creative type." Charlotte shook her head in disgust.

"We've spent the better part of two hours down here, and I need to sit down and drink a cup of strong coffee," the chief said, and nodded to Charlotte. "Shall we repair to the living room, everyone?" The chief motioned for Maria to herd Annabel toward the steps.

"This is all Wade's fault—he's the one you should be arresting," Annabel said in a vengeful voice.

"Funny you should mention that." The chief grinned at Annabel.

* * *

When they opened the doors and entered the living room, Annabel looked at Wade and said, "Ah good. Now, uncuff me immediately."

The chief ignored her and radioed the two officers who'd been stationed outside the farmhouse. "Boys, I need you to pick up Clark Avery and Serge Andersen and bring them over here as soon as possible. And be careful with Serge. I promised the hospital that I wouldn't do anything to cause him to return. They'd prefer to never see him again."

"Charlotte, you seemed like a decent person—a little dumb perhaps, but kind. Tell the chief to get her head on straight," Annabel ordered her.

"I'm sorry, were you talking to me?" Charlotte asked.

"While we wait for the usual suspects to be rounded up, I'd love a cup of joe, Charlotte."

"Coming right up, Chief."

Charlotte shut the doors to the living room before leaving for the kitchen, just in case anyone got any bright ideas. While the coffee was brewing, she unlocked the door to her bedroom and was greeted immediately by her beloved Horse.

"Hello, handsome, are you ready for the big show?" He squealed with delight. "And how about you, Mrs. Robinson?" She stood up on her tiny, reedy legs and stretched her wings.

"Fantastic. The show is about to start."

Charlotte went into the kitchen and loaded a wooden tray with the pot of coffee, mugs, and cream and sugar. When she stepped back into the foyer, she saw that Diane and the gang had returned.

"How'd it go?" Diane asked Charlotte, taking the tray from her.

"Pretty much as planned. Have you explained what's going on to everyone?" Charlotte asked Diane, looking at the worried faces in front of her.

"To the extent of what I know," she replied.

"Should I change for the occasion, or will this do?" Beau asked, clad in a tuxedo shirt and red pants resembling those of a flamenco dancer.

"You're perfect, Beau. After I've laid out the facts, you all are welcome to add anything that may help the case, but keep your statements brief. That request came from the chief. She doesn't want the defense to have anything that could backfire on us when the case goes to court."

"We're saddled up and ready for the rodeo, pardner," Samuel said to her, looking like a kid in a candy store.

"You are so brave, Charlotte, and I am proud to know you," Alice said, and Joe nodded deeply.

"Shall we?"

Charlotte opened the living room doors, and she and her entourage entered the room. Horse was among them and gave an angry grunt to Annabel as he trotted past her chair.

As coffee was dispensed and each person was adding the desired sweet and dairy accompaniments, the other officers returned with Serge and Clark in tow. They were not in cuffs, and Clark was taken aback, seeing that his brother and sister had been restrained.

"Okay, now that we have a heavy police presence in the living room, I'm going to ask that your cuffs be removed, but if anyone in here is stupid enough to try anything, they'll be put back on immediately, and you'll wait it out in the back of a squad car. Understood?" the chief asked to a room of reluctant nods from the opposition. When Annabel poured herself a mug of coffee, Charlotte thought that she saw her hands shaking a little.

"This is ridiculous. I demand that you let my wife and me leave immediately. Do you know that I've just been released from the hospital?" Serge shouted.

"Charlotte, how about you start us off. And so that you're all aware, I'm recording what is said here." The chief sat on a sofa and placed her cell phone on the coffee table, set to record.

Charlotte stood. "On the night that I arrived at the Finn Family Farm, sometime between midnight and four in the morning, Marcus Cordero was murdered in a field of tomato vines out back. The cause of death was the cowardly act of piercing his neck with a pitchfork. Some of my staff and I discovered the body the next morning. The chief was called in and a case was opened."

"We first had to identify the body and then go through the long process of determining a motive," the chief interrupted, picking up the story. "We finally got a break a few days ago when we located Marcus's mother, one Hera Cordero, a woman who once resided in Little Acorn when she was in her mid-twenties."

"You know I can't even watch TV for this long. Can you get to the point, Chief?" Wade grumbled.

Charlotte watched Annabel give Wade a half smile.

"You have somewhere to be, Wade? I suggest you forget about it because you've got a date with the jailhouse tonight for breaking and entering."

"Marcus and his mother were estranged. He was a bitter young man, and as soon as he could, he took what cash he could find and a box of mementos that Hera had kept, and left," Charlotte continued. "From letters and photos his mother had kept in the box, Marcus learned about my great-uncle Tobias and decided to return to Little Acorn and con him out of money, maybe by claiming to be his son. My uncle died before Marcus arrived."

"What does any of this have to do with us? I'm leaving!" Annabel stood, but the chief pushed her right back down in her seat.

"Perfect segue, Annabel," Charlotte continued. "You met Marcus Cordero when you took your kids to the Humble Petting Zoo, where he worked, and you were immediately smitten."

"Total lie. I've never been to that downtrodden, measly zoo in my life."

"Yes, you have Annabel," Officer Maria spoke up. "You went with me and my kids. I've got the pictures to prove it."

"It was that place? What a dump," Annabel retorted.

"You and Marcus started up a relationship after that first meeting, didn't you, Annabel?" Charlotte sat on the arm of the sofa, facing her.

"Now I know this is all a setup. My wife would never cheat on me!" Serge shouted.

Annabel let out a diabolical, throaty laugh.

"But you couldn't meet just anywhere, knowing how active the grapevine was in Little Acorn. So you'd rendezvous at a bar, way on the edge of town, called Whiskey Pete's Outpost. And that's where you and Marcus plotted to make the Finn Family Farm his." Charlotte glared at Annabel as she said this.

"You have no proof of any of this!" Annabel was shaking, and her face was turning red.

"Thanks for reminding me," Charlotte said as she was handed a plastic evidence bag from Chief Goodacre. She walked around the room, showing everyone the wooden swizzle stick inside.

"I don't even know what that is," Annabel proclaimed. "Never seen it before in my life."

"It's a cocktail stick. They hand them out at Whiskey Pete's," Serge blurted out.

"You can't fix stupid," Annabel said, glaring at him.

"May I, Charlotte?" the chief asked, and Charlotte nodded. "Let's talk about the story that has been circulating forever about there being an earlier will for this farm."

"That's all it ever was—a story." Clark spoke up for the first time. "Annabel told us about it when we were little and said that only she knew where it was hidden. She made us do whatever she asked and promised that when the time came, she'd go get it and we'd all be rich."

"That's what we suspected, Clark, and that's what Wade was looking for when we caught him tonight in Finn's cellar. Wasn't it, Wade? Did she whisper to you recently that she heard Tobias hid the will in the cellar? Hoping you'd get caught and assigned the blame for everything? That's why you were down there. In spite of knowing deep down that it was all just a story that a bossy older sister made up?" The chief nodded to him.

Wade sighed and looked totally defeated.

"Somebody's busted," Beau singsonged.

"Annabel, you stole the old key to the outside cellar doors one day after yoga class before I arrived so that you could sneak in later and sever our sewer line." Charlotte walked up close to Annabel as she said this. "A sewer leak like that would possibly lead to a loss in property value. Not to mention necessitating that we dig up and replace the entire pipe. During that time, we wouldn't be able to offer our You Pick 'Em tours either, essentially draining the farm of cash and forcing me to sell. It was all part of the plan that you and Serge had cooked up, wasn't it?"

"What's she talking about, lovey?" Serge asked his wife.

"Don't you 'lovey' me! You're the criminal here, Serge. I was just trying to protect myself from your mess," Annabel said to him, and then addressed the room. "He started skimming the farms he worked for to amass enough cash for us to buy a big place of our own. I thought that was going to be just outside San Francisco, but then I find out that he's working a scam to buy this place. Even bribed a real estate guy to come over and give a low-ball appraisal."

"The fabulous Mr. Lurvy," Beau said.

"Never heard of him." Serge crossed his chubby arms abruptly.

"So when the chief and her officers get a warrant and search your office, they won't find a written appraisal of the Finn Family Farm?" Charlotte already knew the answer.

"How'd you—" Serge caught himself.

"Here's where you ran into problems, Annabel." Charlotte sat down, and the chief took over again.

"When you went to lunch with Charlotte, you learned that our beloved redhead had no intention of selling her farm and was going to make a go of it," the chief told her. "With Marcus no longer an option for getaway money, you were concerned that Serge might fly the coop one day, so you let him know about your plan for sabotage. It was enough to keep him around to see it through. Serge, you wanted nothing more than to prance around town as a farm owner didn't you?"

"I don't know," he mumbled.

Charlotte filled in the pieces.

"When you snuck in one night, using the key that you'd stolen for the outside cellar doors, I heard you and decided to have a look around. After pelting me with some sauce jars, I hit my head on a shelf, and you must have quickly covered your tracks and raced away. Is that when you forgot to relock the padlock?"

"That's it! I'm out of here! Story time is over." Annabel turned to leave and was immediately restrained by two officers. "Let go of me!" She stomped her feet.

"At the time, none of us could figure out what had done the damage in the cellar. We found no trace of animals, but I wasn't going to let it go. I understand that you made a second attempt before tonight to continue your damage." Charlotte nodded to Alice, who stood and took in a deep breath.

"Remember the day when I found you in the cellar? You didn't know that I was in the back room, sorting jars. I heard your steps and came out into the main room, and you nearly screamed. You said that you'd been looking for me, but if you were, then why were you so startled to see me, Annabel? I thought that you were my friend." Alice grew teary, and Joe took her shoulders and walked her back to the sofa.

"It was Horse who actually found your little hidey hole. You must have drawn his attention to the cellar that day you snuck down there. I was out, but he was in the farmhouse." Charlotte motioned for the pig to come front and center.

"Ridiculous. Pigs are just dumb animals." Serge looked disgusted with this entire story.

Horse made his slow walk to the center of the room as applause started to grow. He nodded his head right and left to his adoring fans.

"I'm afraid that you're the dumb animal here, Serge." Charlotte walked over and stood in front of him seated and stared down. "Pigs outsmart dogs and are at an intellectual level comparable to a chimpanzee. I'd love to see how you would score on that test. Pigs also have an extraordinary sense of smell. Horse and all pigs have exceptional noses that let them root and sniff around the ground with the flexibility of a vacuum hose. Which is why, once in the cellar, Horse could follow Annabel's scent to the hole in the stone wall where she'd started sawing the sewer line." Charlotte gave Horse a kiss on the snout.

"Well done, Horse," Samuel said, and picked him up for a hug and scratch on the head.

"But Horse wasn't finished detecting. After following me around for a couple of weeks and listening to me talk, he was starting to understand some of my words." On cue, Horse nodded to Charlotte.

"Understand? They have whole conversations—it's remarkable." Joe grinned.

"For the past few days, Horse had been pestering me to follow him into the fields. Something kept coming up, but finally I obeyed his request. He led me to the exact spot in the tomato vines where Marcus was found. With his snout to the ground, he worked methodically until he uncovered this." Charlotte raised the bag with the swizzle stick once again. "It's a cocktail fork used in drinks to spear cherries or olives, that sort of thing. On one side of the stem, it's stamped with the words 'Whisky Pete's Outpost.' If you look at the fork end, you'll see red stains that appear to be lipstick. Pretty similar in color to what Annabel is currently wearing. Wouldn't you agree?" Charlotte held the stained fork beside Annabel's lips.

"You don't know what you're talking about. You think that I'm the only one to like red lipstick?" Annabel was defiant.

"Maybe that shade . . ." Beau muttered.

"So what? You call that evidence? Serge, do we have a lawyer that we can call?" Annabel asked.

"I'll take that mug of coffee from you now, Annabel." The chief picked it up, holding the outside of an evidence bag to safely preserve the evidence and lipstick print.

"Which brings us to the fire that was set on our trucks of produce ready for market," Charlotte said, picking up the story. "That was just pure spite on your part, wasn't it Annabel? I believe now that you can be that vengeful."

"What are you going to blame me for next? Global warming?"

Charlotte ignored her and continued. "Later that night the chief and a couple officers came to your house, hoping to talk to

Serge. But your husband was out of town for the night, entertaining clients."

"Oh yeah, I remember that," Serge piped up, and got a death stare from Annabel.

"Here's the thing, Annabel. Obviously you knew that you'd be home alone that night, yet you thought it necessary to put on a lacy peignoir set? You're vain, but still this makes no sense. Unless you knew about the fire because you set it and figured that people might be coming to your door to ask questions. Dressed the way you were would make you less of a suspect." Charlotte looked closely into Annabel's eyes and thought that she saw a crack.

"One of my officers later remembered smelling gasoline when you opened the door. He hadn't been at the fire, so he had a fresh nose, so to speak," the chief added.

Samuel quickly looked at Wade as Charlotte recalled how certain he'd been that Wade was the culprit.

"So it's time, Annabel. The evidence is insurmountable, which is why the chief spread the rumor that they were close to an arrest. We figured that would draw you back to my cellar to try to cover your tracks. Why don't you tell me what happened with Marcus that night after we arrived?" Charlotte was almost gentle in her request.

Annabel took on a look that made her almost unrecognizable. It was as if she'd turned into a zombie. She spoke in a staccato, emotionless voice.

"Marcus was growing impatient to get his hands on Finn money. He hadn't figured on Tobias dying, and he certainly hadn't expected you to show up and claim ownership." Annabel was still being held by the officers but had stopped struggling. "He was determined to confront you the night that you arrived, so he stormed out of Whiskey Pete's and drove off in his car. Yes, I've been there, Serge—you happy? Too bad I never caught you and your little honey on the side in that dump." She glared and him, and he slumped down into a chair, totally defeated.

"I followed in my BMW," Annabel continued, "and was able to pass him and arrive before he did. It was well after midnight, and the power was out. We pulled over and started to have at it. When we were almost to the farmhouse, I convinced Marcus to move down into the fields, where we could talk without being heard. I tried to convince him that we needed to be strategic about getting the money, and that's when he said it." Annabel was breathing heavily.

"Said what?" Charlotte asked.

Annabel gritted her teeth. "He said 'What's with this "we"? Who said anything about you getting a share? We're not a couple; you're not my girlfriend. I can have any girl I want. Why would I want to end up with a bitter, old woman?' I was so angry that I pushed him hard with every bit of strength I had. He stumbled backward, and as he was going down, he laughed and gave me a mean grin. That's when I saw the pitchfork."

"Annabel Anderson, you are under arrest for the murder of Marcus Cordero," the chief said, nodding to Maria to cuff her again. "You have the right to remain silent. Anything you say can and will be used against you in a court of law. You have the right to an attorney. If you cannot afford an attorney, one will be provided for you. If you decide to answer questions now, without a lawyer present, you have the right to stop answering at any time."

Epilogue

By late afternoon on Saturday, the fine people of Little Acorn had slowly made their way home with full bellies of the freshest food that the land provides. They'd quenched their thirst and then some with punch, squeezed lemonade, and—for some—ice-cold beer.

It turned out that with strategic portioning, everyone was able to sample Diane's divine cake. Once all the sugar was digested, the kids would go to sleep tonight with dreams of goslings, goats, and a magical pig named Horse.

Actually, the entire town was going to sleep happily and deeply that night, knowing that a murderer and a thief were behind bars.

The Finn Family Farm residents, along with Horse and Mrs. Robinson, had gathered at the edge of the dock, all exhausted, but in a way that makes it difficult not to smile.

"I think that everyone had a fabulicious time," Beau declared.

"Agreed," Joe said. "If 'fabulicious' means what I think it means."

Beau laughed. "It's all good, Joe."

"There are still some loose ends, though," Diane said, and everyone groaned.

"Like who beat up Serge?" Alice asked.

"I'm willing to bet that was Annabel's doing. She probably called up some of the more aggressive farmers and told them anonymously that Serge was skimming off them," Joe said.

"After she found out that they weren't taking the money and moving up north," Beau said, nodding.

"Actually I wasn't thinking about any of those things," Diane said.

"You were wondering what Wade and Clark kept in their garage?" Alice asked.

Charlotte looked at her.

"We're experimenting with growing leeks and new types of scallions," Alice continued. "When I was cleaning around the coop for the geese, I saw Wade on the other side of the fence, and we started talking about crops. He really does have a passion for it, when he's not being angry at the world. He told me that he was working on organically growing these vegetables, and I asked if I could help with the starter plants that he had growing in his garage. We've got a perfect spot to plant a field down by the geese."

"Good for you, Alice." Diane applauded her.

So that's why I found jars of sauce in Wade's kitchen. Alice must have given them to him.

"Thank you, Diane. Is that what you meant by 'loose ends'?" Alice turned to her.

"Not exactly, but it is related to my thoughts."

Everyone looked at Diane expectantly.

"We were having so much fun today, feeding people and enjoying their company and sharing our bounty, that I started to think again about a dream that I've had for as long as I can remember," Diane began.

Beau sat up. "You want to open your own restaurant! You used to always make me play the waiter while you were head chef when we were kids."

Charlotte looked at her best friend and smiled. A small tear ran down her cheek.

"With your permission, Charlotte, I'd like to dip a toe in and just explore what it would take to open a small farm eatery on the grounds." Diane was also getting teary-eyed.

"Nothing would make me happier." Charlotte hugged her.

"I thought that I knew just about everything that farming could throw at you until this bunch drove into town," Samuel joked. "When I realized that what you knew could fit in a thimble, Charlotte, I wasn't sure that I'd have the patience to teach you. Especially because you can be—well, sure of yourself."

Everyone laughed.

"But then you stood your ground and overcame every obstacle."

"Only those that I could control, Samuel."

"That's the biggest lesson of all, and you caught on so quickly." He gave her a warm smile. "That's what has made this land so bountiful for your family for generations. You can't control Mother Nature, but you must respect it. You have that in you, Charlotte. You'll see when we start the new season that you have to rely on your instincts and your experience because you are spending all your money on crops that you haven't grown yet. You have to hope that you'll be successful."

Charlotte nodded. "When I was in college for a brief time, I thought of becoming an architect. Eventually, all of the numbers and calculations pointed me in other directions, but I do remember reading about Buckminster Fuller, the famous architect, inventor, and overall incredible thinker. In spite of all that he accomplished, it was one simple quote of his that struck me most. He said, 'There is nothing in a caterpillar that tells you it's going to be a butterfly.' To me, that meant that I could do anything as long as I believed that I could."

Charlotte noticed that Horse had rested his head on her lap and was listening to her with half-lidded, dreamy eyes.

"You understand what I mean, don't you, Horse?"

He got up, gave her a chorus of grunts, and then took a running leap off the dock. Everyone got to their feet in time to see him swimming happily to shore, using his tail as a tiny rudder.

As the sun once again rested over the Finn Family Farm, all its occupants went to their rooms to do the same.

Except for Mrs. Robinson and her troop of ladybugs, who were about to launch a midnight raid on a band of unsuspecting aphids . . .

The End

Acknowledgments

Many thanks to my agents Sharon Belcastro and Ella Marie Shupe for recognizing that there was a book in my social media anthropomorphisms of the strawberries in my garden. Thanks to everyone at Crooked Lane it has been an entirely enjoyable experience. I'd like to especially express my gratitude to Jenny Chen for her publishing wisdom and gentle editing. You've made this book better.

Lastly I want to thank mother nature for your beauty and majesty. We share a beautiful planet and it should go without saying that we must treat it with respect and awe.